TRAITORS AMONG US

Volume Two in the Just Call Me Angel
Suspense Series

S.R.Claridge

TRAITORS AMONG US .... S.R.CLARIDGE
JUST CALL ME ANGEL SERIES   VOLUME TWO

Global Publishing Group

Printed in the United States of America

First trade edition: JULY 2011

ISBN 978-0-9898467-1-4

This book is dedicated to my husband and children with special thanks to my brilliant editing team, namely, Cash, Jerrye, Gary, Matt and Beth; to my Publicist and Publisher for their promotional efforts in bringing the Just Call Me Angel series to life. Thanks be to God for blessing me with life, love and ultimate joy.

~

Traitors Among Us is the second book in the Just Call Me Angel series. A complete list of books by S.R.Claridge is at the back of this book.

TRAITORS AMONG US .... S.R.CLARIDGE
JUST CALL ME ANGEL SERIES   VOLUME TWO

CHAPTER ONE

When he pulled the pillowcase from her head Sophia narrowed her eyes, trying to adjust to the change in light. The duct tape was pressed firmly against her lips, making it impossible to breathe through her mouth; and her wrists throbbed from the tightly taped restraints. Her eyes darted wildly around the room, trying to determine where she was and remember what had happened. She felt disoriented, probably from slamming her head against the side of the car when her kidnappers shoved her in the trunk. Sophia was overcome with shock, as this type of thing was known to happen in the big city, but not in small town Iowa, home to farmers and family values.

Beating frantically against her chest, her heart raced with fear as her kidnapper approached with a large, serrated hunting knife. The sweat of adrenaline covered her rigid body and she screamed a muffled cry into the tape.

"Don't move," he ordered, and she stared with wide-eyed horror at the demented grin forming on his thin lips. There was no escaping the crazy behind his dark eyes. He brought the knife toward her and Sophia went ballistic. She kicked her legs as best she could, but the duct tape held them taut to the chair. She bucked her whole body up and down, screaming and arching and begging for life, until the chair tipped over backwards, and her head slammed against the concrete floor. The wooden rungs of the chair dug into her back and she winced from the pain.

He shook his head as if disgusted and made a clicking sound with his tongue. "Now see what you've done? You've gone and hurt yourself for no reason."

Sophia sobbed, still trying to kick her feet, which were now sticking up in the air, as he grabbed her left leg. Shut up and hold still," he ordered, "or I won't wait until later to kill you." With the hunting knife, he sliced through the leg of her jeans as if they were made of butter; all the way from her ankle to her mid-thigh. She fought hard to swallow the nauseating lump that crept into her throat.

"This might sting a little," he grinned, and then dug the knife into her thigh, making a jagged hole. She screamed, arching her neck upward and clenching her fingers into tight fists. Excruciating pain shot up and down her leg and he bellowed out a sickening chuckle. "That's to make sure you don't try to escape. I can stab the other leg too if needed." Seeing the blood run down her thigh she could no longer cling to consciousness. A lightheaded feeling overtook her and she slipped into darkness.

When Sophia awoke she was still upside down in the chair, but her feet were no longer taped to it and there was a bandage covering the wound in her leg. She stared at the ceiling and for the first time noticed she was in what looked like a basement. The ceiling consisted of support beams and plywood, with one bulb hanging in the center of the room. The walls were rough concrete painted white and the floor was gray smoothed concrete. There was one tiny window at the very top of the back wall, but it was too small for a grown woman to climb through.

Rolling off the chair in a half backwards summersault, Sophia got up and quietly lifted the chair to a sitting position. Though her wrists were still taped together, she had free range of motion with her fingers, so she could grip the back of the chair and slowly drag it over by the window. She figured if she could stand on the chair, she might be tall enough to see out the window and determine where she was being held.

Just as she was about to step atop the chair, the basement door swung open and two men descended the stairs. Sophia's stomach twisted into jittery knots as she whirled around and plunked her bottom down on the chair, facing the staircase.

The first man down the steps was the insane kidnapper who had gouged a hole in her leg. He was so large that he filled the entire stairway, blocking her view of the second man until he had reached the last step. When Sophia saw him, terror consumed her. His face was a reflection of a painful past she had tried desperately to leave behind. She swallowed hard as the realization overtook her. It was Frank Vilachi. He was one of the mafia's meanest and she knew now, there would be no escape.

Frank pulled his black leather gloves from each hand and held them tightly in his grip, then slid off his black trench coat; all the while drinking her in with his eyes. His appearance held a sinister authority and his stare penetrated her with icy hatred. He snapped his fingers and the large man, obviously Frank's goon, grabbed Sophia by the hair with one hand and the chair with the other, and dragged them back into the center of the room.

"Take care of that window," Frank said to him, but kept his eyes on Sophia; and the goon nodded and ascended the staircase, shutting the door behind him.

Frank circled around her slowly, like a great white calculating precisely how to devour his prey. "It has been a long time," he said, "too long I think." He took the back of his hand and stroked it tenderly up the side of her cheek. She blinked slowly and angled her face away. Time had certainly aged him but hadn't changed him. Behind those hazel eyes lurked the monster she remembered.

"You are as beautiful as ever." She turned her gaze away from him, in a portrayal of disgust. "The years have been good to you, Sophia," he said, licking his lips. "How long has it been? Ten years? Eleven?" His tone mocked her. "Tell me, has it been eleven years since you turned me down and then came out here and married that countrified piece of rat crap?" His voice elevated to a yell and shot chills up her back.

She sat statue still, unsure of what she would say even if her mouth wasn't taped shut. She studied his face, his stature, his body language, all of it dripping hate. His hair was the same as she remembered, thick black waves, but now shown streaks of gray at the temples.

Wrinkles wrapped around his eyes and dark circles indicated sleep wasn't a frequent friend. It was hard to believe there had ever been a day when she found him attractive.

He leaned down in her face. "I have a proposal for you," he half-whispered. Then reaching over, he ripped the duct tape from her mouth. She winced and gasped in a deep breath of air. "Do you want to hear my proposal?" She stared at him, feeling anger well up inside and stifle her ability to answer. Wrapping his hand around her left thigh, he squeezed her knife wound until she cried out in pain. "I asked you a question," he hissed. "Do you want to hear my proposal?"

"No," she sobbed, "I'm already married." Her answer obviously amused him because he burst into a deep, sinister chuckle, releasing her leg and backing away. Sophia covered the wound with her hand, as blood seeped through the bandage.

"Do you honestly think I would propose marriage to you again?" He shook his head, condescendingly glaring downward. "You had your chance to be Mrs. Frank Vilachi and you blew it. Did you really think you could leave your roots behind? Did you think those skeletons you shoved in the closet would never come out and haunt you?" He walked behind her, placing his hands on her shoulders and rubbing his thumbs up the back of her neck. "Did you honestly think I'd never find you?" He gripped her shoulders tighter and Sophia's pulse quickened. "Didn't I promise that no matter where you went, I'd always find you?"

Sophia nodded her head.

"And don't I always keep my promises?" His grip loosened momentarily and he massaged her shoulders. "You see Sophia," he cleared his throat, "if you had chosen wisely eleven years ago, none of this would be happening."

"What do you want with me?" Her words came out quick and breathless.

He walked around to face her. "I want you to choose wisely this time." The eerie sarcasm in his tone sent chills up Sophia's spine.

"I chose wisely when I left," she spat and before she could block him, he backhanded her out of the chair. Her elbows crashed to the concrete floor and she cried out from the pain. Bending over, he grabbed her by the back of the hair and yanked her neck back so she was forced to stare up at him. Glaring down in her face, he seethed, "you will help me restore order."

"Restore order to what?" Sophia yelled. "I don't know what you're talking about."

He released her hair and stood up, straightening his black slacks, smoothing his hair and adjusting his gray tie. "It would appear I was right all those years ago."

"Right about what?"

"About you being a liar." He leaned down in her face and grinned. "And about you having a daughter."

A nauseating lump lodged in her throat and Sophia's mind whirled with questions. *How did he find out? Was he bluffing?* She tightened her jaw and lied. "I don't know what you're talking about."

He erupted into cynical laughter. "Sure you do. She's the reason you wouldn't marry me. She's the reason you left Chicago and went into hiding in this piss of a town." He circled around her. "She's the reason you've never returned to Chicago."

"You're insane."

He squatted down in front of her and held her face in his hands. "She's the reason you've been living a lie, but you don't have to live that lie anymore." He smiled and the evil leaked from his eyes. "Your Angel," he emphasized the word Angel with raised eyebrows and Sophia felt her stomach hollow out, "needs to pay the price for her family sticking their nose into other people's business." His face hardened and Sophia's Italian blood boiled. She spit in his face and cursed in Italian.

Frank slammed his forehead into hers, knocking her backwards. Then he rocked back and pushed himself up, pulling the leather belt from his pants in one fluid motion. "I see you're still feisty," he said, wrapping one end of the belt around his wrist, "let's see if I can't beat that out of you." He lashed at her with the belt, each slap stinging against her skin. She held her arms up to protect her face, and curled herself into a ball on the floor, but the lashes kept coming. He swung the belt with a grunt of ferocity, spewing obscenities at her. Each lash came harder and harder. Sophia lost count at eighteen slaps. When he finally stopped, he was out of breath and ascended the stairs without a word; leaving her in a trembling heap on the floor. When she heard the basement door slam shut, she broke down and wept.

CHAPTER TWO

Sophia wasn't sure how much time had passed, but the room was growing dark. By now her husband, Denny, had certainly noticed she was missing and notified the police. At least she hoped he had. She leaned against the concrete wall and pulled her knees up to her chin, looping her taped wrists around her legs and holding them tight. She tried to ignore the throbbing in her leg and replace emotion with rational thought.

How did Frank know about Angel? What did he mean when he said Angel would pay for her family sticking their nose into other people's business? Assuming Frank was referring to Mafia business, how would Angel know anything unless she had discovered her real identity? More frightening than the pain Frank could inflict on her, was the prospect that Angel's identity had been leaked to the bogatas. She hadn't seen her daughter in eleven years and she couldn't stand the thought that she might never see her again. Tears ran down her cheeks and dripped from her chin as Sophia buried her face in her knees and prayed, "Lord, please protect my Angel, wherever she is."

In the darkness of the room, her thoughts drifted back to everything that had happened to bring her to this point. Sophia was blessed with natural beauty. She was a slender woman, with dark brown hair, Italian olive skin and light brown eyes. At the age of eighteen she modeled in Sicily and eventually in Rome, which was where she met Joseph Maratinzano, fell in love and, against her father's wishes, moved to New York City.

She gave birth to Angel two years after coming to the States and then she and Joseph moved to Chicago. When Angel was five years old, Joseph, who was then head of the most prominent crime family in Chicago, was killed in a car bomb. Sophia wanted to take Angel out of the city and planned to escape bogata life altogether, but Joseph's Compare convinced her they would be safer under his watchful eye. For many years he arranged protection for them and they lived in secrecy with Joseph's aunt, Olga. Sophia had a small apartment under a separate identity, but she never felt safe taking Angel there. She lived as a recluse for the first several years after Joseph's death, having no contact with friends and pursuing no relationships with men. Her entire focus was the protection of her daughter and ensuring that Angel grew up unaware of her Mafia roots.

Over time, Sophia began to let down her guard and venture to her own apartment for an occasional date. She never brought friends or boyfriends to Olga's house and never told anyone she had a daughter. The mere mention of Angel's existence could have compromised her safety. Though it was a source of contention between them, Joseph had never officially married Sophia, which allowed her to keep her maiden name of Buscetta. This proved to be a wise decision on Joseph's part, because not bearing the Maratinzano name was the only reason Sophia lived through the massacre that took Joseph's life. She was left with the reputation of being Joseph's comare, or mistress.

This reputation marked her as a woman interested in bogata men; and having been the comare of the most powerful boss in Chicago, Sophia became a sought-after conquest. Her beauty alone drew men, but her reputation drew powerful, dangerous men like Frank Vilachi. The older Angel grew, the more Sophia relaxed and that's when Frank Vilachi came prowling around. At first, Frank seemed harmless, following Sophia like a lovesick puppy; but his romantic interest quickly became an obsession. He pretended to have mob affiliation but no bogata would claim him, deeming him untrustworthy. "Crazy Frankie" was his nickname on the street and it fit. When Sophia tried to end their relationship, he lived up to his nickname, slashing her tires, breaking into her apartment and threatening to kill her if she didn't marry him.

One night when he refused to leave her apartment and she threatened to call the police, Frank beat her within inches of her life. He claimed to possess proof that she and Joseph had a child; and threatened to go public with the information if she didn't marry him. Sophia denied Angel's existence despite the beating. Later, under the guidance of Olga and the Compare, Sophia accepted Frank's proposal and strung him along for several months, waiting for the day Angel would leave Chicago to attend college. Once Angel was out of the city and safe, Sophia made her escape. She left in the middle of the night, taking only what she could fit in her car and drove west until she came to the tiny town of Clearfield, Iowa. It was a quiet town and she was able to rent a small house and start a new life. She recreated herself, taking on a new identity and making up a past that would seem believable and make her acceptable to the people in town. It took time but eventually Sophia stopped looking over her shoulder and started living. Her new life included a sweet farmer named Denny, whom she married in a one room chapel on the outskirts of town. She couldn't imagine, after all this time, how Frank managed to find her.

The basement door opened, startling her from her thoughts; and Frank paraded down the steps with his goon in tow.

"Are you feeling more willing to help me?" he sneered.

Sophia set her jaw and didn't answer.

Frank motioned for the goon, who grabbed her by her hair and dragged her to the middle of the room, dropping her at Frank's feet.

Frank looked down. "I asked if you were willing to help me," he repeated.

"No," she blurted. "I will never help you find Angel."

Frank broke into a sinister laugh that echoed through the basement. "Sophia, Sophia, Sophia," he mocked, "I don't need you to help me find her. I know exactly where she is."

She trembled inside, looking up at him with a terror she knew shown in her eyes. "Then what do you want?"

He grabbed her face in his palms and stroked her head like a dog. "I want you to make wise choices."

"I won't help you," Sophia cried. "I will die before I'll help you."

Frank motioned for his goon who pulled a picture from his pocket and handed it to Frank. "Oh, someone will die alright, but you won't be first."

He threw the picture at her and it bounced off her chin and landed on the floor next to her knees. Sophia's heart stalled as she picked it up and beheld the image of her sweet Denny. His face was beaten, both eyes swollen black and blue, blood from his nose and mouth had dried on his face, and his wrists and ankles were taped. He was lying on his left side on a concrete floor, staring at the camera. Sophia's fingers shook and her mouth grew suddenly dry.

"Cooperate with me or I will bury him on that little farm of yours."

She looked up at Frank. "He doesn't know anything," she pleaded. "He doesn't even know who I am."

"I'll be sure and tell him before I kill him." Frank turned and started for the steps. "His blood is on your head."

The lump that had been stationed in her throat gave way to desperation and Sophia cried out, "Frank!" She dove for his leg, coming only close enough to grip the top of his shoe before the goon kicked her hands away. "Please!" She screamed and her voice gave way to sobbing.

"Not so strong and feisty now are you So-phi-a." Frank emphasized each syllable of her name with dripping disdain.

"What do you want me to do?" Her voice quivered, "I'll do whatever you want me to do."

The corner of Frank's mouth curled on either side, into a snake like grin. "I knew my Sophia would come around," he said to the goon. "I told you, all you have to do is put a woman in her proper place and she'll play nice."

He squatted down in front of Sophia, plucking the picture from her hand and lifting her chin to look into her eyes. He wiped tears from her cheeks with the back of his hand. "I always told you we'd be together. Didn't I always promise to find you? Didn't I?"

Sophia nodded yes.

"You were a bad girl hiding from me all these years, weren't you?" Frank's jaw tightened. "Weren't you Sophia?"

She nodded again.

"Bad girls get punished don't they? Don't they!" His voice escalated to a yell.

Sophia trembled as she nodded her head quickly up and down.

He stroked her hair and tilted his head to the side, staring at her. "I don't want to punish you, but I have to, don't I? I have to." He pulled her forward so her head rested on his chest and he continued to stroke her head. "You've given me no choice but to punish you. It's your fault Sophia." He rubbed his hands down her back, then pushed her back and took her face between his palms. He raised his eyebrows and nodded his head, speaking to her like she was a child. "But I forgive you. Frank forgives you."

Sophia stared at him, swallowing the sinking revelation that he wasn't just a little crazy, he was undeniably, certifiably insane.

Suddenly Frank stood and straightened his tie. "I will punish you later," he announced, "but now we need to get you cleaned up for dinner."

Sophia's mind was numb with panic. Experience taught her that Frank Vilachi would stop at nothing to get what he wanted. So, how could she save Denny and warn Angel at the same time? By cooperating with Frank she could at least buy time on Denny's life and maybe improve his chance of escape. Her heart ached for Denny. He knew nothing of her past. Frank was right about one thing, what was happening to Denny was all her fault.

Frank ascended the stairs humming Dean Martin's *That's Amore*, while his goon pulled her up by the tape around her wrists and lifted her like a sack of potatoes over his shoulder.

"Let's get you prettied up," the goon said, smacking his hand on her butt. "Frank's got something real special planned."

Sophia dangled limp over his shoulder as he bounced her up the staircase; her leg leaving a trail of blood.

CHAPTER THREE

Angel paced back and forth across the penthouse family room with a cup of coffee in her hand. She was anxiously awaiting Andrew's arrival. It had been over an hour since he called and told her he found something in Venito Barone's secret office above Capilino's restaurant. She shuddered at the very mention of Venito, the snake who killed her father and his Compare and then posed as the reclusive Compare for years, robbing her family of Rush Street pizzo. Not to mention, Venito single-handedly caused the darkest mafia war in Chicago's history, kidnapped Olga and attempted to kill Angel. Needless to say, his death was one few mourned.

Olga waddled in from the kitchen and sat down at the dining room table with a cup of coffee and slice of strudel. "Merciful Heavens child, you're gonna wear right through the carpet if you keep up at that pace," she said.

Angel grunted frustration, "What's taking him so long?"

"Who dear?" Olga asked, taking a bite of strudel.

"Andrew," Angel exhaled forcefully. "He's bringing over something he found in Venito's office. I bet it's something about my dad."

"Come sit with me." Olga patted the chair next to her. "He'll be here when he gets here."

"That's profound," Angel teased, rolling her eyes.

"How can you be full of sass already? It's only 8:30 in the morning." Olga shook her finger. "You better watch yourself missy. It isn't wise to mess with an old lady before she's had her morning strudel."

"When is it ever wise to mess with you?"

"Don't you forget it," Olga replied with a wink.

Angel grinned. Despite Olga's seventy-year-old orneriness, matchmaker meddling and feisty sarcasm, she was just plain cute sitting there in her sunflower yellow fleece robe with matching slippers.

"What are you grinning at?" Olga asked, glancing up from her strudel. "You look like the Cheshire cat grinning ear to ear like that."

"And you look like big bird in that robe," Angel teased. She stood and kissed Olga on the forehead, then returned to pacing around the family room.

"Pacing won't make him arrive any quicker."

"I know, but it helps me think."

Angel opened the long drapes and let the sunshine penetrate the room through the giant windows. She stepped onto the balcony and looked out. There was a definite advantage to living in the penthouse suite at Heavenly Towers. Aside from one building across the street which stood equal height, there was an unobstructed view of the city. Though the fact that her grandfather, Giovanni, owned Heavenly Towers and gave her the penthouse still felt surreal, she knew she could get used to living like this. Her two cats, Midnight and

Mo, had no trouble adjusting to their new home either. In her old apartment they were forced to be inside cats, but now they enjoyed lounging on the warm balcony and scratching their backs against the rough texture of the concrete.

Angel sat down in a wrought iron chair and held her coffee close to keep warm. Fall was approaching and the morning breeze grew brisk, especially so high off the ground. It had been two weeks since Giovanni left Chicago for New York, promising to return soon and begin Angel's schooling on mafia life. She replayed their conversation in her mind.

"There are things only I can teach you," he told her before leaving. "Assets and information you will need in order to be successful here in Chicago."

"Why can't you tell me everything now?" she asked, anxious to have her questions answered.

"You need time to rest and build up your strength," he said, squeezing her hand,."You make me a list of questions and I will answer them when I return."

She'd made a mental list but hadn't put her thoughts on paper yet. There was too much bouncing around in her mind and tripping up her heart. There were answers she needed but they weren't the answers Giovanni, even though he was the Capo di tutti Capi, could give. They weren't about the family business, but about people she wanted to find. Paying respect to Mable Tetterbaum for everything she and Mr. Tetterbaum had done was top on Angel's list. After all, it was his tapes that cleared her father's name and inevitably brought Venito down. Finding Dr. Manzini and better understanding his connection to Grayson was another item on her list, as was locating where Grayson was buried and paying proper respect. She dreaded the thought of visiting his grave, but knew it was the only way she'd ever gain closure on his death. Whether or not that closure would help her reconcile her feelings toward him was another issue altogether.

Most of all, she wanted to contact her mother, who had left shortly after Angel turned eighteen. For eleven years, Angel had grown bitter and angry toward her mom, never understanding why she left. Now things were different. The new perspective Angel had gained these past few weeks shed light on her mother's actions and Angel wanted her mom to know she understood.

Andrew arrived wearing black jeans, black boots and a black leather jacket. A manila envelope was tucked under his left arm and the smell of musk scented aftershave filled the foyer, as he slipped in the door.

"Merciful Heavens, don't you smell nice," Olga gasped, turning around to see him. "And you don't look so bad either," she added.

Andrew gave Olga a wink, slipped out of his jacket and hung it on the back of a chair. "Where is she?" he asked, glancing around the room.

"On the balcony with Midnight and Mo," Olga answered and then took a bite of strudel.

"Oh." Andrew pursed his lips together. "I should stay in here then."

"Still afraid of the cats, huh?" Olga chuckled.

"Not afraid, as much as cautious," he replied. Olga giggled and Andrew cleared his throat. "I'm careful."

"Uh-huh."

"Those cats don't like me. The one cat moans real low and looks at me like he's ready to attack and the other one just plain hisses and growls at me." Andrew pulled out a chair next to Olga and sat down. "I didn't even know cats could growl until I met these two."

Olga shook her head, "Merciful Heavens, look at you, a big strong man afraid of two little kitties."

"Not afraid." Andrew lifted his finger into the air. "Vigilant, watchful, and alert."

Olga laughed out loud. "You want some strudel Mr. Vigilant?"

"No thanks, I already ate."

"What's that got to do with strudel?" Olga asked wide-eyed and Andrew grinned. She was right. He'd forgotten his Italian upbringing. Whether a person had eaten breakfast or not had little to do with the indulgence of pastries.

"I guess one piece of strudel won't kill me," he appeased.

"Won't kill you!" Olga exclaimed, "Why, strudel has been known to improve a person's outlook on life." Olga waddled to the kitchen and returned seconds later with a plate and fork. She sliced a thick piece of strudel and passed the plate to Andrew. "Now, strudel won't improve your mood like my homemade Cannoli, but we can't expect miracles from a German dessert."

"We certainly can't." Andrew smirked.

"No sir," Olga added, shaking her finger, "it takes authentic Italian cooking to lift spirits around these parts." Olga plunked down in her chair and adjusted herself until she was comfortable. Once settled, she exhaled. "You should see the power of my cannoli over Angel."

"Really?" Andrew was intrigued.

Olga nodded and lowered her voice to a loud whisper. "She can be in her sassiest, pissy-est mood…" Olga stopped and lowered her eyebrows, "…you know how she gets that way."

"Yes, I've seen it."

"One bite of my homemade Cannoli and it's like a halo sprouts from her head and there is peace and harmony in the world again."

"It's that powerful, huh?" Andrew grinned and Olga nodded.

"You mark my words," she said, patting the top of his hand, "my cannoli can work miracles."

Angel stormed in from the balcony. "What took you so long?"

"Nice to see you too," Andrew answered.

"Angel May, where are you manners?" Olga shook her head, "you don't talk to a handsome man with that sass."

Angel rolled her eyes and grunted, then turned her attention to Andrew. "What did you find?"

Andrew slid the envelope across the table with one hand and shoveled in a bite of strudel with the other. Angel followed his hand from the

plate to his mouth. She frowned, realizing he had
been there for a while; at least long enough for
Olga to talk him into a piece of strudel. "I see you
took your time in getting this to me," she
sarcastically quipped.

Andrew looked at Olga. "You got any of
that mood-enhancing cannoli?" he asked and
Olga burst out laughing.

Angel didn't get the joke and rolled her eyes
in disgust. She slid into the chair across from
Andrew and opened the envelop flap. It was filled
with small white, letter-sized envelopes. Flipping
the manila envelope upside down, she dumped its
contents onto the table. There must have been
fifty letters inside. Her breath caught in her chest
as she picked up an envelope and instantly
recognized the handwriting on the outside. It was
unmistakably her mother's penmanship. Angel
was certain because her mother double crossed
her cursive "t." It was a quirk Angel used to tease
her about.

"These are all from my mother," Angel
uttered quietly, as if she was half speaking to Olga
and Andrew and half to herself. She picked up
envelope after envelope, glancing at the
handwriting. "All of them are addressed to me,
care of dad's Compare." She stood up and leaned
over the table, rapidly flipping over each envelope,
displaying the address line. "Why didn't I get
them?" The question no sooner left her lips when
the answer struck her brain and anger welled up
inside. "These went to Venito!" she seethed. Her
blood began to boil as she noticed every letter had
been sliced open and read. Her mother obviously

didn't know Venito had killed her dad's Compare and taken over his reclusive identity. How would she have known? They had all just discovered it.

She sank back down in her chair. "My mother thinks I've received these and never bothered to respond." She sighed. "She must think I hate her for leaving."

Olga reached over and patted the top of Angel's hand. "Now, now, Missy, don't you go putting thoughts in your momma's head."

"Do you know where she is?" Hope lit Angel's eyes as she stared at Olga.

Olga shook her head, "No, dear." Compassion filled her face as she explained, "All communication was to go through the Compare for safety reasons."

Angel started pulling the letters from their envelopes. "Surely she put a return address in one of these."

Olga shot Andrew a glance of fear. "Merciful Heavens, I hope not," she said.

Angel looked up. "Why not?"

A quiet tension filled the room as Angel's mind answered her own question. If her mother had put a return address, Venito could have found her and done unthinkable things. Angel knew what he was capable of and her skin crawled at the thought. She fought back the lump rising in her throat and met eyes with Andrew. "We've got to find my mom."

He reached over and grabbed a handful of envelopes. "Mind if I look at these?"

Angel shook her head.

"Well, hand me some too," Olga said. "No sense in me sitting her stuffing my face when I could be helping."

They spent the next twenty minutes in complete silence, each reading the letters from the pile in front of them. There was no return address in any of the letters. Angel slammed her hands on the table. "How was I supposed to ever write her back if she left no address?"

Andrew leaned back in the chair and crossed his arms over his chest. "Maybe you weren't supposed to write back."

Angel narrowed her eyes. "Why not?"

"Because she knew it was too risky," he explained.

"Why would it be more risky for me to write to her than it would be for her to write to me?"

Olga piped in. "Because you had the protective covering of the Compare but she didn't."

Angel shrugged to indicate she wasn't following. Andrew leaned in over the table, nodding at Olga. "That makes sense." He tapped his fingers against the table and pursed his lips. "Your mother could send her letters to the Compare, who, if it was safe, would deliver them to you. This wouldn't jeopardize your safety because there were no outside sources involved."

"What outside sources?"

"Postal workers, for one," he replied.

"You think some random mailman is going to identify me or my mom?" Angel quipped.

"Humph," Olga burst out. "Merciful Heavens child, you just don't understand it yet do you?"

"Sweetheart," Andrew began and reached across the table and took her hand, "people are paid off in every industry. Mailmen. Policemen. Doctors. Lawyers. Even grocers and hairdressers."

Angel slid her hand out from under Andrew's and leaned back in her chair. "So, if I wrote back to my mom, it could have jeopardized her safety because the mailman would have been involved." It seemed far fetched and her tone displayed doubt.

"All I'm saying is if one of the bogatas was actively seeking you or your mother, they would most certainly employ what you call random people to keep their ears and eyes open." Andrew leaned back, obviously frustrated by Angel's stubbornness.

"Well, we KNOW they were actively seeking," Olga said, gawking at Angel. "For Heaven's sake, how many times did they try to kill you?"

Angel forcefully scooted her chair back and shot up. She felt helpless. "So, you're telling me that no one knows where my mother is?"

Andrew picked up an envelope and pointed, "These are all postmarked Iowa. If you want to find your mom, I say we start our search there."

CHAPTER FOUR

Once Andrew was gone, Angel left Olga sitting at the dining room table reading the letters, while she got ready to head into the Pub to open. Olga glanced up as Angel walked back into the dining room, adorned in her usual blue jeans and black Tetterbaum Pub t-shirt. She had her dark brown hair pulled back into a ponytail and silver hoops in each ear lobe.

"You should dress better when you go to work," Olga said, as Angel plunked down in the chair next to her and slipped on her black Converse tennis shoes.

"This is my work uniform," Angel pointed at her t-shirt that read, *Tetterbaum's Pub*. "What else would I wear?"

Olga shrugged. "Something a bit nicer perhaps. Something that says you're the owner and not the hired help."

"Everyone knows I'm the owner."

"Well, you certainly don't look the part." Olga took a sip of her coffee. "And why do you always wear your hair in a ponytail? You have such lovely hair, Angel May, you should leave it down."

"If I leave it down I might get hair in people's food and beer, and I don't know about you, but most people frown on that."

"Humph," Olga grunted and Angel looked up from tying her shoes and stared at her.

"What's the matter with you? Why are you so crabby?" she asked.

"Are you pot or kettle?" Olga snapped.

"I'll be pot today," Angel joked.

Olga set down the paper. "I don't know what's bothering me, child. These letters make me feel all edgy inside."

"You're acting all edgy on the outside too," Angel teased and Olga grinned. "You want to come over to the pub for lunch today?" she asked Olga.

"And eat food cooked by THAT chef? No thank you." Olga shook her head.

"He's a great chef," Angel said, feeling the need to defend her hiring decision.

"He's pasty white," Olga complained, "and good heavens, what happened to his hair?" She shook her head in disgust. "How's a woman supposed to run her fingers through that spiky, military doo?"

Angel rolled her eyes. lga, whose libido thought she was still in her mid-thirties instead of seventy, liked the previous chef, Antonio, because he was all Italian and all hot. The problem was Antonio got his head blown off, leaving Angel desperate for another chef. She interviewed a handful of men and women, but felt Chase was the best fit. True, he wasn't anything special to gawk at, but his references were good and as far as Angel could tell, he wasn't mafia.

"I didn't hire him to run my fingers through his hair," Angel replied.

"What about eye-candy for your patrons?"

"He's in the kitchen!" Angel raised her eyebrows, "I don't have patrons hanging out in the kitchen."

"Humph," Olga smacked her lips and crossed her arms. "I liked Antonio."

"So, you're never going to eat at the pub because the chef isn't hot?" Angel couldn't believe how ridiculous it sounded.

"He's not even Italian," Olga blurted.

Aw, thought Angel, *the heart of the issue now exposed.* "I hate to point out the obvious," Angel said and then cleared her throat to add drama, "but Tetterbaum's is an Irish pub."

"Merciful Heavens, what's that got to do with it?" Olga threw her hands in the air.

"We don't specialize in Italian food so why does my chef have to be Italian?"

Olga crossed her arms again and narrowed her brow. "Because everyone knows Italians are the best cooks!"

"Oh." Angel laughed. "Well, then, I think we should let Wolfgang and Emeril know their food sucks because they're not Italian!"

"I didn't say their food sucks..." she paused, "and you know I hate that word." She shook her finger at Angel. "I said it just isn't as good as, say, Giada's food or that Lidia Maticchio Bastianich."

Angel put her hands on her hips, "Well, how about I fire my chef and just serve everyone Chef Boyardee? He's Italian!"

"Now, now, dear, you're just being ridiculous."

"I'M being ridiculous?" Angel could feel her eyes bulging and she thought she'd better end the conversation before she developed a permanent facial tick.

Arriving at the pub, Angel peered into the kitchen, said good morning to Chase, and headed to the bar to get things ready to open. She still loved owning Tetterbaum's Pub, but working at it felt different now. Sadness shrouded her heart and she knew it stemmed from the memories of Grayson and the nights they shared. She was still mourning his death in ways even she didn't understand. She also felt lonely and she knew that was because she missed Andrew's presence behind the bar. Now that the Tetterbaum tapes had been located and secured there was no longer a reason for him to work undercover at the pub. She never found out whether Andrew was originally placed undercover as a policeman or as a Venturini; not that it mattered now.

Today her mind danced with thoughts of her mother, hoping she could find her after all these years. Locating someone who didn't want to be found and was probably living under an alias somewhere in the state of Iowa felt like a long shot; but it was something she had to try. Angel needed her mom to know she understood why she left and that she loved her.

By three o'clock the lunch rush died down and Angel began restocking the bar for happy hour. When she saw Andrew come through the back door she felt a sudden excitement. She rushed toward him with a big smile. "What are you doing here?"

He shrugged. "Just miss the place I guess. I spent a lot of time here the past couple years."

He walked to the bar and leaned against the back of it, folding his arms over his chest.

"Are you hungry? she asked. "Despite what Olga says, Chase makes a mean meatball."

"Yeah," he smiled, "I am hungry."

It was something in his smile or a spark in his eyes that made her mind leap into a momentary flashback of standing in the pub kitchen, kissing Andrew. It had only happened once, a couple weeks ago, and she hadn't thought about it since. Well, she had thought about it, but they hadn't talked about it. Now, she felt her face flush as the picture filled her head. She quickly turned her back toward him and started to wipe down the top of the bar. He must have felt her sudden awkwardness because he grabbed the knot on the back of her apron and gently tugged until her back pressed against him.

She could smell his musky aftershave as he leaned down and whispered in her ear, "Are YOU hungry?"

The emphasis on the word YOU made her body temperature rise. Was he flirting with her or was she just so desperate for a man's touch that she imagined it? Her hands felt clammy and she was afraid to turn around. *What are you afraid of?* Her mind taunted. *Just turn around, you know you want to!* Her breathing quickened. *If I turn around I'll want to kiss him,* she admitted to herself and then wondered if he wanted to kiss her too. She was driving herself crazy. With her heart pounding nervously in her chest, Angel decided she would turn slowly, giving Andrew the opportunity to let go of her apron and back away if he wanted. If he didn't back away, and she secretly hoped he wouldn't, then she would remain close enough to be kissed.

Swallowing hard and mustering up courage, Angel twist her body to face Andrew, when the front door of the pub flew open and Tony strutted in. "There you are man," he hollered to Andrew, "I've been looking all over for you."

Andrew released Angel's apron strings and stepped away. "What's up?"

Tony gave Angel a nod, "Hey babe."

She gave a quick wave and excused herself to the bathroom, exhaling a sigh of both relief and disappointment. There was no denying her attraction to Andrew, but kissing him now would certainly complicate their relationship; as if it wasn't complicated enough already. With the return of Tony, her ex-fiancée, and the knowledge that he left to protect her, not because he had stopped loving her, Angel's heart was in a constant state of flux. Andrew held a unique place in her heart, somewhere between friend and potential boyfriend; but Tony shared an intimacy only years of love can create.

While Tony and Andrew talked, Angel joined Chase in the kitchen. She ordered up three plates of spaghetti and meatballs and some warm bread, then carried them to the booth in the back, commonly referred to as "Capone's Corner." Andrew and Tony instinctively followed the plates of food and slipped into the booth, Tony beside her and Andrew across the table.

The chatting ceased momentarily while all three shoveled in forkfuls of pasta. "This is really good," Andrew said.

"I was gonna say the same thing," Tony replied. "Excellent."

Angel grinned, "I told you, he's not bad for a non-Italian chef."

Andrew fetched a bottle of red wine from behind the bar and poured three glasses. "I don't normally drink on duty," he said, "but this sauce is so good it needs the compliment of wine."

"I think you just need wine," Tony joked.

"I notice you're downing it pretty quickly," Andrew rebutted, filling Tony's glass for the second time.

"It compliments the pasta," Tony teased.

As they finished up, Tony angled his body to face Angel. "Babe, we need to talk."

Uh-oh, she thought, *nothing good ever starts with "babe, we need to talk"*. In fact, if she remembered correctly, that was exactly how he began when he announced their engagement was off and left. She narrowed her brows. "What's wrong?"

Andrew interjected, "There's nothing wrong, sweetheart, we just need to discuss a few things."

"We?" Angel looked from Andrew to Tony and back to Andrew. "So, you two have already discussed whatever this is and now you've decided to let me in on it?" Angel rolled her eyes and crossed her arms, "Why am I always the last to know about everything?" This had been an ongoing frustration from the moment she found out she was Joseph Maratinzano's daughter and granddaughter to the Capo di tutti Capi. She knew it was Andrew and Tony's way of protecting her, but it was infuriating to not be trusted with pertinent information.

Tony grabbed the wine bottle and filled Angel's glass, handing it to her. "Why don't you have a drink, babe." That was Tony's way of telling her to chill out and it wasn't appreciated.

Angel set her glass down. "Just tell me."

"Giovanni isn't going to be able to come back to Chicago for a while." Andrew said.

"And so he wants us to look after you. No big deal, " Tony added.

Angel studied their faces. She could tell there was more to this story. "Why can't he come to Chicago for a while?"

"We don't have all the information yet," Andrew explained, "but there was a substantial mob bust in New York early this morning."

"I didn't see anything in the paper," Angel said.

"It won't hit the media 'til tomorrow," said Tony.

"Then how do you know about it?"

"Giovanni," Tony and Andrew said in unison.

Angel's mouth fell open. "You've talked to Giovanni?"

"He called to give us instructions," Andrew started to explain but Angel cut him off.

"Why didn't he call me?" She felt her face flush with anger. "I'm his granddaughter."

"Babe," Tony shook his head, "this isn't about favorites."

"So, he called both of you to tell you to babysit me?" Angel spewed sarcastically.

Tony grinned, "Well, sort of."

Andrew threw his hands up at Tony. "What are you doing? You're making this worse."

"I don't need a babysitter, thank you very much," Angel said and scowled at Tony.

Andrew put his face in his hands and moaned. "I knew I should have told her alone."

"What?" Tony defended, "I'm just trying to lighten a heavy moment."

"Don't," Angel and Andrew blurted in unison, which made Angel smile.

Tony threw his hands up and left the table. Andrew reached over and placed his hand on Angel's arm, which made it difficult to concentrate on his words and not his touch. "Listen, sweetheart, we don't have all the details yet. What we know is that the FBI made a huge mob bust in the middle of the night. All five families were hit, but your family, Giovanni's people, were hit the hardest."

"How?"

"That's what I'm working to find out. All we know is that the information received by the FBI had to come from a source within your own bogata."

"What makes you think that?" she asked.

"The detail of the information given wasn't your run of the mill stuff trusted to the average cugine." Andrew's eyes lit concern. "It wasn't even information that would have been trusted to most of the bogata buttons." He lifted his hand from her arm. "This was upper-level stuff."

"Is Giovanni okay?"

"He's going to have to stay in the city and answer questions, but he's got people to handle these things. He won't get pinned with anything."

"So, why did he ask you guys to babysit me?"

Tony came back and scooted into the booth, draping his left arm around Angel's neck. "Don't worry, babe," he said, "we won't let anyone get your blood."

Angel gasped, "My blood?"

Tony shot Andrew a look and Andrew slumped over. "I hadn't gotten to that part yet."

"Oh," Tony grimaced, "my bad."

"What about my blood?" Angel looked to Andrew, then to Tony and back to Andrew.

Andrew exhaled loudly. "Early this morning Giovanni received a note ..."

"A note about my blood?" Angel interrupted.

"No, there was a note threatening that the next blood shed would be yours," Andrew explained.

A hollow pit formed in Angel's stomach. Tony put his arm around her shoulder. "Don't be afraid, babe, we can handle this. Nobody's gonna touch you."

Angel looked at Andrew, who was either more concerned than Tony or was not as good at hiding his concern. She could see actual fear in Andrew's face and it scared her.

Tony picked up her glass. "You want that drink now?" Angel took it and emptied the glass in one long gulp.

Tony left his arm draped around her shoulder and Andrew took her hand from across the table. Being touched by both of them at the same time was almost more than her senses could handle. Andrew gave her fingers a gentle squeeze and Tony stroked up and down her shoulder with his thumb. "We're going to work in shifts and make sure you have protection 24/7," Andrew explained.

"Giovanni's going to send one of his men to help," added Tony. "It's the only guy he trusts and one of the only ones not lifted last night by the Feds."

"Do we know him?" Andrew asked.

"Shark."

Andrew's eyes widened. "The Shark?" Tony raised his eyebrows and smiled like an excited kid.

"Who's the shark?" Angel asked, obviously in the dark.

"He's more of a what than a who, at least that's what I've heard," Tony answered.

Andrew grinned, "When does he arrive?"

"Sometime tonight. He'll meet us at the Towers."

CHAPTER FIVE

Until they could meet up with the Shark and work out a 24/7 protective watch program for Angel, Andrew decided he would stay at the pub and help close up while Tony would head to the Towers and wait with Olga. It was almost midnight when Angel and Andrew arrived at the penthouse. Tony and Olga were sitting at the dining room table snacking on Olga's homemade cheesecake.

"No sign of him yet?" Andrew asked, taking off his leather jacket and slinging it over the back of one of the chairs.

"Nope," Tony answered, shoveling in a bite of cheesecake.

"Merciful Heavens," Olga threw up her hands. "I'm just a bundle of nerves."

Angel kissed Olga on the top of the head as she walked to the kitchen, returning with two plates, forks and cups of decaf coffee. She sliced cheesecake for Andrew and herself and joined them at the dining room table. "Don't worry," she said to Olga, "nothing's going to happen." Angel tried to hide her own fear. The truth was something didn't feel right but she couldn't put her finger on what it was. She could tell Andrew sensed it, too.

Olga sipped her coffee and set the cup back on the saucer. "I'm so excited to meet the Shark I can barely enjoy my cheesecake." That was saying a lot for Olga, whose round little body was proof she typically had no trouble enjoying cheesecake.

"Me too," Tony grinned, taking a big bite and talking with his mouth full, "but I can still enjoy the cheesecake."

"I'm amazed Giovanni is actually sending the Shark to work with us," Andrew said and Angel marveled at the disbelief on his face as he spoke.

"Well, Angel IS his granddaughter so he's obviously sending the best to protect the best," Olga replied and gave Angel a wink while patting the top of her hand.

"I don't get what's so special about this Shark guy," Angel said, leaning back in her chair and twisting her ponytail between her fingers. "Why is he called the Shark anyway?"

Andrew, Tony and Olga looked at each other, as if to see who wanted to offer an explanation first.

"I heard he's the largest dude alive," Tony blurted.

"But you've never actually seen him right?" Angel asked, with a tone that said she wasn't buying into all the hype.

"Babe," Tony raised his eyebrows, "few have actually seen the Shark."

"Then how do you know he's huge?" Angel threw her hands up and made a *duh* face.

Tony narrowed his eyes at her. "They say his shadow alone can crush a grown man."

Angel laughed out loud and Andrew covered his mouth, trying not to visibly mock Tony for his over-stated drama.

"You just wait and see, babe," Tony said, tightening his jaw, "just wait."

"I heard they call him the Shark because he just appears, like a great white in the depths of the sea appears from the darkness. People say you never hear or see him coming until he's right there and BAM!" Andrew slammed his hands on the table and everyone jumped. "He devours you." Angel's fork flipped out of her hand and landed on the floor and she exhaled an irritated sigh while Andrew grinned, pleased with his antics.

"You guys are ridiculous," Angel said, shaking her head and getting up from the table to retrieve her fork. She went to the kitchen, returning seconds later with a clean fork and the glass coffee pot. "Would anyone like more coffee before I sit back down?"

Olga lifted her cup and Angel tilted the pot to fill it. Suddenly, the sound of shattering glass thrust her into that surreal realm where everything appears to be happening in slow motion. She saw the glass door to the balcony shatter and felt the coffee pot explode in her hand, splattering hot coffee on her face, arm and all over Olga.

She heard Olga scream and Andrew holler, "Get down!"

She saw Tony flip the entire dining room table on its side and then he and Andrew dove behind it like a shield. Andrew drew his .45 and Tong gripped a .38.

Angel's eyes filled with terror as Tony grabbed her by the bottom of her t-shirt and pulled her to the floor.

"Get them out of here!" Andrew yelled to Tony, who quickly lifted Olga under her armpits and dragged her into the kitchen where there were no windows. Angel crawled after them.

"Stay on the floor," Tony instructed Olga, and then turned his attention to Angel. "Where's your gun?"

"In my purse," her voice quivered. "In the foyer."

"Stay here," Tony ordered, leaving the kitchen on his hands and knees and returning a few seconds later, sliding Angel's purse across the floor. She grabbed it and pulled out her 9mm.

She looked at Olga, who was wide-eyed, pale and breathing heavily. "Are you okay?"

Olga nodded.

Angel checked the clip and shoved it back into her gun until she heard it click. Safety off. She was ready.

Several shots fired, though she couldn't tell from the sound whether it was Tony or Andrew or both; and then silence.

"Where the hell's the Shark?" Tony griped.

Angel listened intently from the kitchen as Andrew and Tony bantered on possible motives, who the hitter could be and from where the shots were fired. "You think this is random or all connected?" Tony asked.

"I think it's too coincidental to be random," Andrew answered.

"I was afraid you were gonna say that." Tony exhaled several curse words. "You gonna call this into the precinct?"

Andrew didn't answer right away and Angel could imagine the wheels turning in his brain. "I can't," he sighed. "Not until I know what family we're dealing with. I can't have cops crawling around here until I know who ordered the hit."

"It's got to be the Galantes," Tony spewed.

"This doesn't feel like the Galantes or the Cullatos," Andrew said. Everyone knew the Galantes and Cullatos were by far the least sophisticated and least respected of the five Chicago bogatas. They had a lot of young cugines or thugs working for them, with a reputation for being violent and messy with their crimes.

"I agree," Tony said, "they'd have just gunned her down in the middle of the pub."

"During dinner," added Andrew.

"Well, we can figure it's not the Maratinzano's, because why would her own family try to take her out?"

Andrew shook his head. "I don't know."

"So that leaves your bogata and mine," said Tony.

"Something's not right about this." Andrew peered around the table. Though there had been years of power struggle between the top families, Andrew couldn't get his head around the idea that his family, the Venturini's, or Tony's family, the Andriachini's, would have ordered a hit on Angel.

"Nothing's right about this man," quipped Tony, "we're on the floor hiding behind a table."

"No, what I mean is, the shooter shouldn't have missed." Andrew and Tony locked eyes. It was a fact they had both overlooked in the confusion. The shooter was in the building across the street, probably using a rifle with a scope. "You were in that building a couple weeks ago, the night you brought Angel back to meet Giovanni, right?"

"Right," Tony answered.

"You had a clear shot through the window right?"

Tony nodded, "Crystal clear. Had I needed to take a shot I would have easily dropped my mark."

"Angel was standing in plain view, so why did the shooter miss?" Andrew shook his head. "Something's not right."

"Maybe he's a bad shot?" Tony said.

Andrew grimaced, "I don't buy it. If I'm a boss sending someone to take out the granddaughter of the Capo di Tutti Capi, I'm sending my best guy."

Angel hollered from the kitchen. "Can we come out now?"

"No," Andrew and Tony yelled in unison.

"But the shooting has stopped," Angel argued.

An eerie silence filled the room as Tony and Andrew eye's lit with knowing, the same thought hitting their brains at the same time. It was a set up. A decoy. The shooter was a distraction. Tony and Andrew simultaneously leapt to their feet, heading toward the kitchen, but before they could even get across the dining room, the front door blew apart with an explosive force that knocked them both backward. Tony hit the wall that separated the kitchen from the dining room and the hanging picture shattered against his back. Andrew flew backwards against the overturned dining room table and tried to scramble up, but his legs were like rubber from the bomb blast. Two canisters of tear gas hit the kitchen floor and billows of smoke filled the kitchen and seeped into the foyer.

Angel screamed with the blast and dove toward Olga, who was covering her head with her arms. She tried to open her eyes but the tear gas burned them to the point that she couldn't even force them open. Tears streamed down her face, though she wasn't crying and her nose ran like a faucet. She tried to wipe the mucus from her lips with the bottom of her black, Tetterbaum's Pub t-shirt, but the touch of the material against her skin hurt, as if she had been sunburned. She laid her face against the kitchen tiled floor and tried to breathe. Hearing footsteps but no voices, she tried to call out for Andrew and Tony but the tear gas stung and gripped her throat, allowing no sound. When she opened her mouth to speak all she could do was gag.

Two shots fired and Angel frantically searched the kitchen floor for her gun. She must have dropped it with the blast. Her hands ran across the top of a shoe and she became suddenly aware of their presence. She didn't know how many there were but they were in the kitchen with her, their legs brushing against her and pushing her out of the way. *Who were they? What were they doing?* She couldn't open her eyes and she couldn't speak. She could hear them shuffling about as if they were moving something. *What did they want?* Olga moaned and fear gripped Angel. She crawled back toward the corner where Olga had been sitting, crazily waving her arms, searching for Olga; but she was gone. Angel lowered her face to the floor, trying not to inhale the thick smoke as panic filled her. *Someone took Olga!*

The next sound she heard was the crunching of glass beneath feet and the unmistakable whirling of a helicopter blade.

Her heartbeat echoed loudly in her ears as she pressed her cheek to the floor and breathed in small breaths. It burned in the back of her throat. She slowly slid like a snake thru the kitchen and into the foyer where the smoke was less intense, wanting to get to the hallway where she hoped she'd be able to open her eyes. She made it to the foyer and stopped when she heard a man moaning. *Andrew? Tony?* She wanted to call out but her vocal chords weren't cooperating. Her eyes were tearing heavily and stinging and she reached her hands up to rub them.

"Don't touch your face!" His voice was deep and raspy and it startled Angel. She felt his hands grip her waist and then he lifted her as if she were weightless. He slung her over his shoulder and carried her out of the penthouse suite, through the emergency exit door to the right and down a flight of steps. She heard the distinct beep of a key card allowing entrance to one of the apartments and a door opened and then closed behind her. Wherever she was, she could now breathe without feeling like her throat was on fire. Angel gasped in breaths of air and winced from the deep burning sensation in her lungs.

He set her on what felt like a smooth countertop, which she ascertained it was when he started spraying her in the face with cold water from the sink nozzle. She squirmed at first, but the cold water felt so good against her skin that she finally sat still and let him spray her. Whoever he was, he was helping her and at this moment that was all that mattered.

"When you can see again," he rasped, "make yourself vomit, then take off all your clothes and shower. Don't touch your clothes again." She heard the door open. "Don't leave this place." The door closed.

CHAPTER SIX

Sophia lay on the concrete floor in the dark basement, unable to sleep. The tape had been removed from her wrists long enough for her to dine on Chicken Marsala and white wine with Frank Vilachi. The mere sight of him sickened her stomach, but she forced the food down to maintain her strength. She knew she needed to make Frank believe she would cooperate, if she had any hope of saving Denny.

The floor was cold against her skin and Sophia shivered. Her leg throbbed from the stab wound and she tried to take her mind off the fact that it was probably becoming infected. Thoughts of Angel and Denny drifted in and out of her mind and she quietly prayed.

The sound of creaking on the steps startled Sophia and she abruptly sat up, pressing her back firmly against the concrete wall and staring into the darkness. The small window had been boarded up so not even a hint of moonlight or streetlight shown through. Her wrists had been re-taped after dinner and this time they were behind her back. She leaned forward, sliding her hands under her bottom, down the back of her legs and under her feet, so her arms were now in front of her body. In case Frank was coming to issue another beating, she wanted to be able to use her arms to protect her face.

Another creaking sound made Sophia cry out, "Who's there?" There was no answer but she heard footsteps. Her heart raced as she spoke again, "Who is it?"

"Shhhh," he whispered from very close to her. "You don't want to wake the whole house now, do you?"

"Frank?" Sophia's hands began to tremble. "Is that you?"

He bent down in front of her and grabbed her face with both palms. "I thought you might be lonely," he whispered. Sophia could barely make out the outline of his face, but saw enough to know it wasn't Frank. It was the goon who stabbed her.

"Leave me alone," she spat, but as the words left her lips he forced his tongue into her mouth. Sophia squirmed and pushed at him, but she was no match for his girth. She bit down on his tongue with the force of desperation, feeling it pop beneath her teeth and spew blood in her mouth. She gagged and spit out the blood.

He grunted, "You bitch," and then grabbed her stab wound and squeezed hard, making pain shoot up her leg. She cried out, but he slapped his large palm over her mouth and muffled her scream. Sophia felt the wound in her leg reopen and blood trickle down her thigh. She kicked her feet, but he slid her away from the wall, onto her back, and climbed on top of her; fumbling with her jeans with one hand and clamping her mouth shut with the other. She tried to scream again, but he was pushing down on her mouth so hard she couldn't make a sound.

Suddenly, the basement light flashed on, momentarily blinding Sophia and causing the goon to lift and turn toward the steps. Frank didn't miss a beat. He shot him straight through the forehead. The back of his head splattered all over the concrete floor and wall and his body fell backwards off of Sophia. She rolled to her side, trembling and scurrying away from the goon.

Two men she hadn't seen before came barreling down the steps, with their guns drawn.

"What the hell happened?"

"Holy ..."

Frank cut him off mid-sentence. He touched what's mine. Now bring her upstairs and clean up this mess."

Frank ascended the steps and left his men obviously stunned. Sophia looked over at them, panic filling her eyes. Neither man moved toward her. "My leg is injured," she said, wanting to get out of there as fast as she could. "I'll need help up the steps."

The younger man, who looked to be about Angel's age, glanced at the older man. "I'm not touching her, Uncle Vince," he said, "Frank's crazy, man."

"This schmuck had it coming," Vince exhaled, walking over to Sophia and pulling her up by her wrists. "Just help her hobble up the steps and deliver her to Frank."

"For all we know that's all he was trying to do," the young man said, pointing to the goon's body.

"You want to clean up this mess instead?" The young man was visibly trembling and Vince grabbed him and pulled him toward the far wall. "You better pull yourself together and act like you belong here."

The young man's eyes grew wider and Sophia could see him swallow hard, as the color drained from his face and he shook his head. "I'll take her upstairs," he stuttered.

Sophia looped her taped wrists around his neck to support her weight as she hopped on her good leg up each step. The young man was visibly nervous by the physical contact and tried to hurry her along. Sophia could tell he was new to the business and she made mental note that he might be one she could manipulate into helping her.

Halfway up the steps she faked a sudden cramping in her leg and fell against him. He shifted to balance her weight, trying to touch her as little as possible. When she was seemingly re-balanced she looked deeply in his eyes. "Thank you for helping me," she said.

"I'm just doing my job," he blurted, quickly darting his eyes away.

"Please don't let Frank kill me," she whispered. "He's crazy."

He paused for a second and met her eyes. She could see fear in his youthful face and it was clear he was in way over his head. What's your name?" she whispered.

He answered without hesitation. "Stefano Carlachi." As the words left his mouth Sophia saw him wince as if he knew he shouldn't have told her.

"I'm Sophia," she said, trying to keep the communication going.

"I know who you are." He said it with a certain tone in his voice that made Sophia believe he must know more about her than she thought.

Stefano didn't speak again until they reached the top of the steps, and he delivered her to Frank. "Where do you want her," he asked Frank, who motioned down the hallway, toward a bedroom near the back of the house. Stefano led her to the bedroom, lifted her arms off his neck, and left the room without uttering a word or making eye contact.

Sophia lowered herself onto the bed and glanced around the room. There wasn't much to it, just a double bed with plain white sheets and two pillows. The windows to the left were painted black and covered by thick black curtains that were opened slightly in the middle. There was a dingy pale, yellow armchair in the far corner and a wooden door Sophia guessed led to a closet. The floors were wooden and old and the walls were painted pale yellow.

Frank walked in and stood facing her with both hands on his hips and anger on his face. "Were you unfaithful to me?" He demanded, with clenched teeth.

Sophia's mind felt numb. She knew she had to somehow gain his sympathy and even on some level, his trust; but the depth of his delusions amazed her. She slowly stood, limped toward him and knelt down at his feet. "No," feigning tenderness, "I would never be unfaithful to you."

She felt his hand stroke the back of her hair. "Good," he said, petting her like a well-behaved dog, "that's a good girl."

Sophia didn't have the energy to fight or try to rationalize with him. Frank was crazy and the only way to stay alive was to play along.

"I saved your life tonight," he stated matter-of-factly. "I believe you should thank me."

He held out his hand in front of her chin. Sophia was no stranger to the bogata custom of showing respect with a kiss on the hand of the boss. It was clear that Frank, in his insanity, was pretending to be the head of a family. She kissed the top of his hand and played into his warped fantasy, "Thank you for saving me," she whispered.

Winning good behavior points with Frank awarded her the luxury of a hot shower and a toothbrush. She washed the goon's blood off her lips and face and scrubbed her stab wound with soap, hoping to ward off infection. When she earned more behavior points she would ask Frank for medication.

After her shower, Frank taped her wrists again and escorted her back from the bathroom to the bedroom, which was only a few steps down the hall. "You will sleep in here," he said, opening the closet door and tossing a pillow and sheet onto the floor. "You'll be safe in here."

Sophia stepped into the dark closet and lowered herself to the floor. "Thank you," she said.

Frank leaned down in her face. "I won't let anyone touch what's mine." He ran his index finger over her lips. "And Sophia's lips are all mine."

Sophia forced a smile and fought the nausea rising from her stomach. When he closed the closet door, she laid down in the darkness, unable to fully extend her legs because the closet was too small. Wrapped only in a towel, Sophia rolled into fetal position, trying to stay warm, but it didn't work. Her hair was damp and her shoulders and back were cold. She tried to wrap herself in the sheet, but it provided little warmth. The temperature in the closet dropped as the night went on and Sophia shivered uncontrollably. The back wall and the wall to the right of the door were exterior walls, obviously lacking insulation. There was no heat vent inside the closet so with the door shut, the tiny room grew quickly colder.

She didn't want to draw Frank's attention to herself, but with her fingers and toes now numb and her teeth chattering, she cried out, "Frank?" Sophia put her ear to the door but heard nothing so she called out again, this time a little louder, "Frank?" She reached up and twisted the doorknob, but it was locked. "Frank, please open the door," she cried and knocked lightly against it. "I'm so cold."

Minutes slipped by with no answer and Sophia was beginning to lose hope. "Please Frank, I'm freezing," she wailed. Huddling in the corner where the interior walls met, she focused on wiggling her toes to increase circulation. Soon exhaustion gave way to emotion and warm tears streamed down her face. When a light shone through the bottom of the door, she was filled with both fear and hope; fearful of any encounter with Frank but hopeful that she could convince him to let her sleep outside the closet where it was warm.

She heard the key and saw the door inch open a crack. "Frank," she blurted.

"Shhhh," he cut her off. "Here." Through the crack came a man's flannel red and black plaid shirt and a light blue fuzzy cotton blanket. "You didn't get these from me," he whispered.

Sophia grabbed them and looked up in time to see Stefano push the door closed and lock it.

It was impossible to put on the shirt with her wrists taped together. She made several attempts at tearing through the duct tape with her teeth, but there were too many layers. Besides, she worried what type of punishment would ensue when Frank discovered she had torn through her restraints. She turned the shirt upside down and backwards and stuck her legs through the arm holes. The flannel felt good and the shirt covered her from her toes to her knees. She then wrapped her shoulders and chest as best she could in the fuzzy cotton blanket. Warmth soothed her and the uncontrollable shivering began to subside.

CHAPTER SEVEN

Angel stood in the shower for what seemed like an eternity, until her skin stopped burning. She found towels in the bathroom and wrapped herself in one, draping a second one around her shoulders. She was careful to step over her pile of contaminated clothes without touching them. Sticking her head outside the bathroom door, Angel peered down the hallway. To the left was the family room, kitchen, balcony and front door. To the right she could only assume was a bedroom. She crept down the hall and into the master bedroom, where there was a king size bed and a floor lamp. She slid open the mirrored closet doors that took up the entire wall to the right of the doorway, expecting to see a suitcase or some hanging clothes; but the closet was empty. She walked across the room and into the master bathroom, expecting to find a toothbrush or razor, anything to denote someone was staying here; but there was nothing.

She walked back down the hall and into the family room which consisted only of a white couch and a glass end table with a lamp. All the walls were bright white with no pictures or decorative touch at all. It looked like a vacant apartment with a couple pieces of furniture and plain white vertical blinds covering the glass sliding door. She wondered who brought her here and how it was that they had a key. *Could it have been the Shark?* That was the most logical assumption, as Giovanni could have easily given him a key. *But if he had traveled here from New York, he would have luggage or at least a change of clothes and a shaving kit.*

In the kitchen, Angel opened the stainless-steel fridge but there was nothing inside. Nothing in the freezer and nothing in any of the cabinets, with the exception of four white plates, four rectangular shaped water glasses and four red wine glasses. There was nothing in the drawers except four forks, butter knives and spoons. It seemed Giovanni had it furnished with basic essentials needed for someone to stay.

She sat down on the white couch and stared up at the ceiling. There was no television, no books and no magazines; nothing to distract her from her thoughts of Olga, Andrew and Tony. Her mind replayed the events of the night and all she wanted to do was get back to the penthouse and find out if they were okay. Her gut told her Olga was missing, but she tried to convince herself that in all the chaos she could have been wrong about Olga being taken. *Maybe it was Tony and Andrew that carried Olga out? Maybe the same person who rescued her, rescued Olga first? But then, wouldn't Olga be here in this apartment too?* Angel gnawed on her fingernails, trying not to imagine the worst.

As time passed, Angel's patience wore thin. How long was she expected to sit and wait? She didn't even know if whoever rescued her was coming back, nor if he would be bringing her some clothing to put on. It was the middle of the night and she couldn't go parading around the streets of

Chicago in a towel. Her head ached from sheer
exhaustion and worry. She checked the bathroom
cabinets for Ibuprofen or Tylenol, anything to ease
the pounding in her head, but came up empty.
Back in the family room, she paced anxiously,
arguing with herself as to whether she should obey
the instructions to stay or leave and go back
upstairs. *Why should I listen to someone I don't
even know and who might never come back?* She
pondered. Then again, he did help her so she could
assume he gave her the instructions with her best
interest in mind. *Where are Andrew and Tony?*
Worry hollowed her insides. *Where is Olga?*

Unable to stand it any longer, Angel opened
the apartment door and peeked outside. There was
no one in the hallway. She darted across the hall
and into the emergency stairwell, running up one
flight to the landing and then the second flight to
the steel door. She grabbed the handle and
noticed a small piece of silver duct tape was
wrapped around the door, keeping the automatic
lock from engaging. Her rescuer must have put the
tape there to ensure he could go up and down
without getting locked out. *But how did he get up
here the first time? He must have taken the elevator
which meant he was up here before the explosion,
when the elevator was still running.* She shook her
head and shrugged it off. It didn't matter. What
mattered was getting to Andrew and Tony and
finding out what happened to Olga.

Stepping into the lobby area adjacent to the
penthouse door, Angel shivered as a cold breeze
swept through. The penthouse door was blown
apart. Some of it was still attached to the hinges

but most of it was lying on the foyer floor. The
thick smoke was gone, but as she stepped inside,
she breathed in slowly, making sure there was no
burning sensation in her lungs. The air was clear
with only a hint of what smelled like sulfur.
Looking straight ahead, Angel gasped at a blood
stain on the wall between the kitchen and the
dining room and a pool of blood on the floor below
it. She put her hand over her mouth, trying not to
think of whose blood it could be. She remembered
hearing two gunshots while trapped in the smoky
kitchen. Someone was obviously hit and she hoped
it was one of the people who broke in and not
Andrew or Tony. Shattered glass lay everywhere
and she tiptoed in her bare feet, careful to avoid
the chunks of glass. Her hands were trembling,
partly from fear and partly from the cold air
rushing through what was once the balcony door.

"Andrew? Tony?" She hollered, but there
was no answer.

She made her way to the kitchen and found
her 9mm on the floor next to the refrigerator. She
checked the clip, and snapped it back in,
mustering up the courage to walk through the rest
of the penthouse; afraid of what or who she might
find. When she got to her bedroom, she quickly
slid into a pair of jeans, a black pull-over
sweatshirt and her black, knee-high Uggs. With
the 9mm out in front, she then searched the rest of
the penthouse, but no one was there.

Stepping onto the balcony, Angel
remembered hearing helicopter blades shortly after
Olga was taken from the kitchen. *Could someone
have actually landed a helicopter on the rooftop*

balcony? She wondered. The answer came when she rounded the corner from the covered balcony to the open-air patio section, where it now looked like a bomb had gone off. Chairs were overturned, potted plants broken and the umbrella in the center of the table was shredded. Rage welled up and she swallowed hard, trying to control the anger, as she knew this confirmed her worst nightmare; someone had flown off with Olga.

Angel jumped and shrieked as something in the darkness brushed her leg. It was her cat, Midnight. She bent down and scooped him up, stroking his ears and squeezing him to her chest. "Oh, you poor baby," she said, kissing the top of his furry head. "You must have been scared to death." As she hugged him, Midnight began to purr and Angel couldn't hold the emotion back any longer. She clutched Midnight close and broke into sobs. *I can't believe I'm crying over a cat.* Though she knew the floodgates were releasing over more than just affection for her furry feline. The tears pouring out of her were over everything from Olga to a fear of a never feeling safe again.

Angel suddenly remembered her other cat, and held Midnight so she could look at his face. "Where's Mo?" she asked, as if he would answer back. Setting her gun on the table, Angel began to search for Mo. "MO-Oh," she called out, "here kitty, kitty, kitty." She kept Midnight snuggled in her arms while she walked the length of the rooftop balcony. Midnight wasn't normally the cuddly cat type, but tonight it didn't seem to bother him. He acted as though he wanted to be held. Mo finally peeked his multi-colored face from behind a broken flowerpot, and let out what sounded like a low, agitated meow. Angel rushed toward him, scooping him up and simultaneously kissing both their little furry heads. Mo's meowing quickly switched to a deep, loud purr as he buried his face between her neck and shoulder.

Angel saw flashing lights reflecting in the adjacent building windows and she peered over the edge of the balcony. The street was filling with cop cars and EMT's were loading someone into an ambulance; someone with a sheet over his head. Angel gasped silently. *Oh, God, please don't let it be Tony or Andrew under that sheet,"* she prayed, fighting back tears. She watched as officers got out of their cars and headed for the front doors of Heavenly Towers. She squinted her eyes, trying to see if Andrew was one of them, but she was too far up to tell. It was a long shot that they could hear her from way up here, but she screamed his name anyway. She saw one officer look up and point and another man take off in a dead sprint toward the doors. *Is that Andrew?* Her heart raced. She started to set Midnight and Mo down, but remembering the broken glass, she carried them into her bedroom and locked them in the master bath. It was a giant bathroom, almost the size of the family room in her old apartment, so they would be comfortable and safe from all the debris. She then ran back to the patio and retrieved her 9mm from the table. *Just in case,* she thought. It was possible the man rushing up here wasn't a cop, or wasn't a good cop. *Better to be armed and safe than vulnerable and dead,* she told herself. She made a beeline for the foyer and stood in the center of the doorway with her gun pointed at the emergency exit staircase. If anyone except Andrew or Tony came through that door, Angel was prepared to pull the trigger.

When Andrew's face appeared in the doorway, Angel's gun lowered and her heart leapt into her throat. Tears poured out as he rushed to her and wrapped his muscular arms around her waist, lifting her up against him and squeezing tight.

"I'm not letting go," he exhaled breathlessly, "I'm never letting go." Angel melted into sobs. "I thought they took you," Andrew said, setting her down and pressing his lips against the top of her head. "I thought they took you." He exhaled and his body shook with hers. "I'm so sorry," he whispered. "I should have seen it coming." His voice cracked with emotion and Angel felt him take a deep breath, trying to regain composure.

"It's not your fault," she said, "none of us saw it coming. Not me, you or Tony…" her voice tapered off. "Is Tony with you?"

She pulled back and glanced into the lobby, half-way expecting Tony to be standing there. When she returned her gaze to Andrew and saw the look on his face, tiny darts of fear stabbed at the back of her neck. "Angel," he slid his hands around her shoulders, "Tony was hit."

Angel felt as if she might throw up and she took several steps back. *Omigod, it was Tony under that sheet.* All of a sudden her chest tightened and breathing became more difficult. Her heart beat wildly and she shook her head from side-to-side and said "nN, no, no" over and over again; as disbelief encompassed her.

"Sweetheart ..." Andrew tried to console her, but she cut him off.

"He's dead? He was covered by that sheet?" Her whole body trembled.

"No," Andrew said, shaking his head, "he was alive when we got him to the hospital, but that's all I know."

"Then whose body was being loaded into the ambulance?" she asked.

"The sniper."

"Who killed the sniper?"

"We don't know yet," Andrew replied.

"Where's Olga?"

Andrew shook his head and lowered his eyes. "They must have taken her."

All of a sudden Angel went crazy with rage, spewing out every curse word she'd ever known and Andrew tried to grab her flailing arms. "Who did this?" she screamed. "I want to know who did this and I want them dead! I want them dead!" With her fists clenched, Angel fell against Andrew's chest and sobbed. Never had she felt the depth of rage that burned in her now. Never had she wanted revenge the way she wanted it now. Andrew held her tight while Angel screamed into his chest at the top of her lungs, spewing agony, rage and fear until her voice went hoarse.

She could see the concern in Andrew's eyes when she pushed back from him abruptly and blurted, "I want to see Tony right now."

"Okay," he hesitantly agreed. "But I think you should take a few moments to calm down."

"I want to see Tony NOW!" she screamed at him, feeling the veins on the sides of her neck protrude.

Andrew blinked slowly. "I'll take you."

She knew what he was thinking. She could see it in his face. He was thinking she was out of control and had lost all rational capacity for thought. Maybe he was right, but she was completely justified in losing control. Her family was under attack. Olga was taken. Tony was shot. She had a right to lose control, she told herself. She also possessed Giovanni's genetic make-up for revenge, and she thought that probably worried Andrew more than anything.

Andrew held open the stairwell door. "The elevators aren't running yet," he said. "It's going to be a long walk down."

Angel slid past Andrew and started down the first flight. "Why did they shoot Tony and not you?" She didn't mean for it to come out so flippantly, but the anger she felt seeped into her inflection.

"They did shoot me." Angel stopped abruptly, shocked by his answer; she turned to face him. "I was wearing a vest."

She lowered her eyes and felt her shoulders slump. "I'm sorry, I didn't know." Andrew nodded but Angel could see her tone had hurt him. He started to pass her on the steps and she reached out and stopped him with her arm. "I'm sorry."

He pushed her arm down. "It's okay. Let's go."

His aloofness intensified her guilt until she couldn't stand it. "Andrew," she yelled, but he continued past her and down the steps. Stress-driven adrenaline surged in her and Angel flew down the steps, jumping four steps past him and turning with her arms out in front. "Stop!" she yelled.

He exhaled loudly, "What are you doing?"

It was a good question. She didn't really know what she was doing. There were too many emotions bouncing around in her head and heart. Her senses were on overload and she knew it. "Please just wait a second," she breathlessly uttered. "I just need you to wait for a second."

Andrew sighed and stared down at his black boots.

With her heart racing, she crept slowly up the stairs until she was on the same step with him. She reached out and touched his arm, letting her fingers run down his arm to his hand and interlocked her fingers with his.

"Sweetheart," he uttered, "what are you doing?"

She knew he was the voice of reason, but in this moment she didn't want to listen to reason. Olga was missing, Tony was shot and she'd almost lost Andrew. There was no logic for handling this, at least none she could find. She leaned up, tilting her head slightly to the right and whispered, "I want to kiss you."

Andrew took her by the shoulders and stared into her eyes. "Why do you want to kiss me?"

Emotion choked the words in her throat. "Because I need to feel you." She inched closer, her words breaking with quiet sobs, "I need to feel..."

Before she could finish her sentence Andrew's lips closed on hers and passion exploded between them. Her stomach trembled with butterflies as his kiss grew deeper and spoke everything she needed to hear. *I'm with you,* it said. *You're safe now. I've got you. I won't leave you.* Angel wrapped her arms around his neck, and Andrew gripped her around the waist with one arm and held the back of her head with the other. He lifted her down several steps to the landing and leaned her against the wall, pressing their bodies together. The heat between them intensified and lent itself toward a progression they both knew shouldn't take place in the stairwell or under these circumstances.

Andrew pulled away but the longing tugged at Angel. "Don't stop," she whispered, reaching for his jacket to pull him back close.

"Sweetheart…" Andrew said, holding her face and giving her a light kiss on her lips, "we can't do this now and we can't do this here." Angel closed her eyes. Her mind knew he was right but her heart wanted to stay in the security of his arms. When they kissed, for a brief moment, the fear subsided and the chaos calmed.

She slid her hand in his and they started down the steps. Neither spoke but both knew even the depths of passion didn't have the power to protect them from the reality they were forced to face.

CHAPTER EIGHT

Tony's hospital room was heavily guarded. When Angel and Andrew arrived, there were two large men wearing dark suits, standing at the entrance of his room and two men standing further down, on each side of the hallway. Angel was certain they were mafia, and sure they were armed, though no weapons were visible. Several policemen walked the halls as well. Andrew motioned to an officer, "What's up?" he asked.

"Andriachini," the cop answered, and no other explanation was needed. The Andriachini boss was here and his presence, felt.

As they approached Tony's room, Andrew turned to Angel. "You'll have to ask permission to see him. As an act of respect."

"Okay," Angel nodded.

"Don't be shocked if he won't let you in. You're not exactly his favorite person."

"I'm not exactly anyone's favorite person," Angel grimaced.

"You're one of mine." Andrew winked at her and a tiny fraction of her heart melted, though she masked it with an eye roll and a pursed-lip smirk. No point in showing any sign of emotional weakness. It was already bad enough she literally begged him to kiss her in the stairwell. She didn't need him seeing that one comment could make her heart dance and her stomach flutter. *A girl has to have some pride.*

Andrew's cell buzzed and he excused himself down the hall, leaving Angel to face the suited guard dogs on her own. She took a deep breath and exhaled. Even if she wasn't allowed to see him, she was already feeling relieved to have learned that the bullet missed Tony's heart and lungs. It ripped through his left shoulder, causing tissue and muscle damage, but he would eventually be all right. Approaching the two men, Angel raised both her arms, anticipating the usual pat down. They grinned at her.

"We don't need to search you, Ms. Maratinzano," the man to her right explained, while the man to her left opened the door to Tony's room and motioned her inside.

Angel tried to hide her surprise, and act as if being recognized was a regular occurrence, though she felt certain the shock shown in her eyes. Stepping inside the room, Angel was overcome with nervous emotion. How should she greet the Andriachini boss? Should she call him by his first name, Charlie, or address him as Sir or Mister? Should she bend and kiss his hand? Her mouth went dry as he rapidly approached.

"Michelangela Maratinzano," he uttered in a low tone, then gripped her face and lightly kissed each cheek. "It is good of you to come."

Angel acknowledged the boss but her eyes were drawn to Tony. "May I?" she asked, inching her way closer to his bed, unable to look away.

"Yes, come, sit, he would want you here."

"Thank you," she said, and sat in the chair at the side of the bed, sliding her hand beneath Tony's fingers. "His fingers are so cold."

"He has lost a great deal of blood."

Angel fought the lump rising in her throat. It was hard to see Tony so frail. His face was a pale shade of gray, like death and his brown hair was matted with dried blood. She squeezed his fingertips hoping for a squeeze back, but he was stiff-like. "The nurse said he was going to be okay," she uttered as both a statement and a question.

"We were told the prognosis is good. The bullet passed through." Angel nodded and quickly wiped a tear that had escaped her left eye; hoping the Andriachini boss hadn't noticed. She needed to appear strong, able to handle anything, even though seeing him like this weakened her.

The door swung open and one of the suited guard dogs spoke in Italian and then the boss excused himself from the room, leaving Angel alone with Tony.

"Tony," she fought back tears, "I don't know if you can hear me, but I promise I'm gonna find whoever did this and they're gonna pay for it." The anger rose from her belly and formed tears that ran down her face. "I swear to you, they're gonna pay for this." Her jaw clenched tighter and she buried her face on top his hand, kissing it tenderly.

"Angel," he whispered almost incoherently, "Shark," and his eyes rolled back into his head.

"Shark?" Angel squeezed his fingers to try and wake him up again. "Tony, please wake up. Focus on my voice." She stood and hovered over him. "What about the Shark? Did you see him?"

Tony's head nodded slightly.

"Yes?" She studied his face for any sign of confirmation. "Yes, you saw the Shark?" He lay perfectly still. "Did the Shark help you?" No movement. Angel slid back into the chair. "I don't know what's happening, Tony," she confessed more to herself than to him. "I'm not sure how to handle this or what to do next. I need you to tell me everything will be fine, like you used to tell me at school whenever I was stressed out." She wiped her face on the side of his sheet. "Remember when we were in college and we'd sit in the back booth at Shakespeare's Pizza and talk about life." The memory filled her heart. "We'd stuff ourselves on pepperoni pizza until it hurt and no matter how upset I was, or how stressed out, you'd say, 'Babe, it's small beans in the grand scheme.'" She smiled through tears. "Sometimes I hated that expression, but you were right, it was all small beans back then." She stroked his fingers and rubbed the top of his hand. "Tony, I need you to be okay." She kissed his fingers. "I need you to be okay."

Tony's fingers twitched, as if he were fighting against the sedating effect of medication and trying to squeeze her hand.

"Please say something," she closed her eyes and fought the urge to break into sobs.

"Babe," he murmured almost inaudibly.

Angel's eyes widened and she stood and kissed his cheek. "Yes?" The door swung open and the boss entered with Andrew behind him.

"Again, my apologies Don Andriachini," Andrew said, dipping his head slightly.

Angel's eyes bulged and she mouthed to Andrew, "His name is Charlie."

Andrew looked like he wanted to burst out laughing, but he narrowed his brow, licked his lips and focused his attention on the Andriachini boss. "We should have seen this coming."

"Who is responsible for this?" the boss's voice elevated and his nostrils flared.

"We don't know."

"When you find out, I am the first to hear." He grit his teeth and Angel could see his jaw clench even from behind. "I am the first to hear. Capisce?"

Andrew lowered his voice. "With all due respect, sir, I think the police need to handle this investigation first."

"Bah!" He threw up his arms. "The police have no power here. You know this as well as I." He leaned in closer to Andrew. "I want to know what bogata is behind this personal attack on my son." The Andriachini boss paced in front of Andrew.

"You have my word we are looking into it." Andrew motioned with his hand for Angel to get up and head toward the door. "Giovanni will be calling a meeting as soon as he can get to Chicago." Angel's ears perked up at the mention of her grandfather's name.

"When?"

"Soon," Andrew said. "As you know the FBI arrests in New York have left many of the families unsettled."

"You believe this is connected?" he asked.

"I don't know, sir." Andrew shook his head, "Just keep your men on Tony until we know who is responsible and what these people are after."

Andrew led Angel toward the door. She turned and looked at Tony over shoulder. "If he doesn't remember, please tell him I was here."

The boss nodded.

"Grazi," Angel said as Andrew pulled her out of the room. Once outside Andrew took Angel's hand and walked briskly down the hall. "Why did you call him Don when his name is Charlie?"

Andrew looked sideways at her. "Sweetheart, Don is a respectful way of addressing a boss. You never call him by his first name." He shook his head. "You have so much to learn."

Infuriation flared inside and she felt her face flush. She hated being talked down to, even when Andrew was right; especially when he was right. Andrew sped up, making it difficult to keep up, as his stride was considerably longer than hers. "Why are we rushing?" she blurted, half out-of-breath.

"Because."

Angel stopped abruptly and pulled her hand from his. "Because why?"

"We don't have time for this." Andrew grasped her wrist and started pulling her down the hallway.

"It's four o'clock in the morning. Where do we have to rush off to at this hour?"

Andrew didn't answer. His eyes were widely alert and filled with what Angel could only surmise to be panic. He peeked around the corner at each hallway intersection, darting his eyes up and down and then dragging Angel quickly behind him.

"Who are we running from?" Angel whispered as Andrew peered around a corner.

"Everyone," he said, gripping her arm and moving her quickly by a nurse's station and through a stairwell door.

In the stairwell Andrew pushed Angel against the wall and leaned in close. She anticipated his lips closing on hers at any second, but instead he spoke. "Listen," he said, "I spoke to Giovanni and his people have reason to believe someone is coming after you." Angel opened her mouth to speak but Andrew put his fingers on her lips. "Sweetheart, this isn't a mob fight so we're not dealing with the usual rules." She didn't know what that meant. "I'll fill you in on the details but right now we've got to get out of this hospital."

"Why?"

"They know we're here."

"How do you know?"

"They didn't kill Tony."

Angel was puzzled. "They tried to kill him."

"No," Andrew whispered, "close range shooters don't miss. If they wanted to kill Tony they would have shot him through the head or the heart."

"What does that mean?" Angel grimaced at the thought.

"It means they used him to lure you here, into an open place where you are an easier target." Angel couldn't breathe as Andrew grabbed her hand and pulled her down the next flight of steps.

Voices from the stairway above echoed downward and Andrew put his fingers up to his lips to indicate Angel should be quiet. Several of the voices were thickly accented, but it wasn't an

Italian accent. Andrew mouthed softly, "Where's your gun?"

"In the back of my jeans," she mouthed back.

"Get it."

Angel's heart raced as she reached back and pulled the 9mm from her waistband, gripping the gun with a white knuckled hold. Andrew leaned down and placed his lips directly against her ear and shoved the car keys into her front jean pocket. "Go quietly down the stairs and out the bottom floor door. If I'm not at the Tank in five minutes, drive away."

Angel opened her mouth to speak but Andrew cut her off...

"If someone approaches you, shoot them. Got it?"

She heard it but she didn't get it. Terror was rising and her voice quivered, "Where do I go?"

"If I'm not out there in exactly five minutes, you leave." He pulled back and looked in her eyes. "You leave, Angel." She nodded. "Drive to Venito Barone's property outside the city. I'll find you there. Go."

He nudged her down the steps and then ran up one flight and through the door marked, *Third Floor*, letting it slam behind him. The voices and footsteps that had grown louder tapered off as they seemingly followed his trail through the third floor door. Angel's hand shook as she crept down the final two flights and out of the building.

Climbing into her black Chrysler Town & Country, Angel crouched down in the driver's seat, hiding behind the tinted windows. She breathed a little easier; after all, they didn't nickname her vehicle the "Tank" for nothing. Before giving it to her, Giovanni had outfitted it with bullet resistant windows and multi-layered nylon armor which she was told created a ballistic defense against bomb fragmentation. Someone could conceivably fire on her with a machine gun and she'd be safe in the vehicle, though she wasn't anxious to test that theory.

Watching the clock and peering out the windows, Angel hoped to see Andrew. Four minutes passed and Angel gnawed on her fingernails, not wanting to leave without him. *Where is he? Who are the people following him? Why are they after me?* The clock clicked over to the fifth minute and Angel turned the key to the ignition. She wanted to use the phone in her car to call him, but he had specifically told her not to call. He said if he was compromised and they had his phone, her call alone could be used to track her location. She didn't understand how it all worked, but she promised she wouldn't use her phone. She sat for two more minutes debating what to do. Past experience taught her the importance of following Andrew's instructions implicitly. He'd never steered her wrong and the times when she ended up in the most trouble were when she didn't listen to him. Her stomach knotted as she pulled the drive shaft into reverse, backed out of the spot, and sped out of the hospital lot.

The last place she wanted to go was to Venito Barone's old property. Ironically, it was once her favorite place on earth. It was there that Tony proposed to her, which was one of the happiest moments of her life. It was also there that he later dumped her, and there that she found Grayson's body in the pond. It brought back painful memories, some that were too fresh to re-visit and others that were old, but not healed.

Driving out of the city, Angel tried to focus on all that had happened and who could be responsible; but her thoughts kept drifting. *Who might benefit from kidnapping Olga* slipped into *how did life get so crazy?* Three short months ago she was sharing the occasional one-nighter with Grayson and her biggest concern was how she looked the next morning. Now, Grayson was dead, Tony had been shot, Olga was missing and she didn't want to think about what was happening with Andrew. *Not that I could figure it out anyway,* she berated herself, *I didn't even know Don was a title of respect for a boss. How could I possibly know anything of importance if I can't even get a title right?*

Angel pulled onto the gravel road that led to Venito's old house, hoping Andrew had miraculously beaten her here and would be waiting with open arms. The night was pitch black and a fourth of the way up the long gravel drive Angel pulled off near a clump of trees to wait. It was the same spot where Andrew had parked on the night she, Andrew and Tony came here and discovered that Venito was pretending to be her father's Compare. Climbing into the back seat, Angel set the 9mm next to her and fought heavy eyelids. She waited for what seemed like hours, dozing a couple times, and startling herself awake when her head fell to one side. Exhaustion was winning and Angel finally surrendered.

The distinct sound of gravel under slow moving tires thrust Angel's eyes open and jolted her senses back to life. The sky was still dark but beginning to give way to the earliest hints of dawn. She grabbed the 9mm and crouched down in the seat, peaking carefully over the top and out the back window. There were no headlights, but Angel could make out the outline of a white pick-up inching its way closer.   Angel ducked down when she heard a car door slam and footsteps approaching. Her mind was trapped somewhere between terror and panic as she held her gun steady.

"Angel?" He hollered out in a hushed tone. She bolted up, and seeing him through the back window, she thrust the door open and hurled herself out of the Tank and into his arms.

"Andrew," she gasped.

The pick-up's headlights blinked once and Andrew raised his arm in the air, motioning it to move out.

"Who was that?" Angel asked.

"A friend," he answered and wrapped his arms around her for a moment, letting go sooner than Angel was ready. "Sweetheart, get in the car," he instructed, opening the back door and pushing her in. He then took the driver's seat and started the ignition. "I'll explain everything on the way."

"On the way where?" Angel asked, crawling into the passenger seat and fastening her seatbelt.

"To find your mother."

CHAPTER NINE

Frank Vilachi paced in front of Sophia, who sat on the bed with her knees drawn up to her chin. "I'm going to ask you one more time, Sophia," he seethed, "where did you get that shirt?"

"I told you already. I found it in the back of the closet last night," she whimpered, only to be met with another backhand to her cheekbone. It was the third slap and the stinging was beginning to numb.

"You liar!" He spat on her but Sophia set her jaw and her mind. She was not going to ruin what could become her only chance of escape by telling him Stefano gave her the shirt. No matter how many times Frank hit her, she stuck to her story.

Stefano poked his head in the doorway, "Frank?"

Frank whirled around, obviously angered by the intrusion. "What?" He clenched his teeth and squint his eyes.

"Someone's here to see you."

Frank grunted and stormed passed Stefano and down the hall. Sophia's head was resting on her kneecaps, but she could feel Stefano's eyes on her. "Thank you," he whispered, "for not ratting me out."

This was the opportunity for which she had hoped and prayed. She looked up at his youthful face and pleaded, "Please don't let Frank kill me. Please Stefano, protect me." She put on her most desperate face and poured as much emotion as she could muster into every word. She knew she needed to appeal to his deep-rooted male ego, the male force in him that was biologically driven to protect and defend a helpless female. She spoke his name to ensure he felt a more personal connection to her. "Stefano, please help me," she cried, "help me." She looked up and saw the fear in his eyes and she knew she had touched him. She could tell he was trying to figure out a way to help her without getting killed. He was in too deep and she knew it. He was a good boy, probably sucked in by Frank's promise of money and power, unaware at the time of Frank's disregard for human life. He was perhaps even unaware of the depth of Frank's insanity, until it was too late to get out.

Stefano swallowed hard and opened his mouth to speak, just as Frank paraded down the hall and back into the bedroom. "Are you sweet on my honey?" Frank asked Stefano, whose eyes grew bigger with fear. "I see how you look at her," he sneered, "you want a piece of that don't you?" Frank pushed Stefano against the door. "You want to taste my sweet honey don't you?"

Stefano shook his head, "No, sir."

Frank leaned closer into Stefano's face. "You liar!" he yelled. "Why wouldn't you want to taste that?" He grabbed Stefano's head and forced it in the direction of Sophia. "Why should I believe you don't want her?"

Without pausing or stuttering, Stefano rendered an answer either of truth or of sheer brilliance. Sophia wasn't sure which. "She reminds me of my mother," he blurted.

Frank immediately released his grip on Stefano's head, backed up and shut up, dismissing Stefano from the room. Sophia breathed a sigh of relief, aware that Stefano, whether by a stroke of genius or an admission of truth, had literally dodged a bullet with his answer. If she did remind him of his mother, the chances of him helping her escape were that much greater.

Frank glared at Sophia. "I wish I could trust you."

"I wish you did trust me," she answered.

Frank pulled her hair, forcing her head back and upward. "I'm going to get you something pretty to put on and tonight you will pleasure me."

Sophia felt a sick twinge in her stomach. She wanted to cry, scream and throw up at the mere thought of sexual contact with him. He leaned down and sucked on her neck, leaving red marks from her collar bone to her ear lobe. "And I will pleasure you," he grinned with a sadistic glow.

Frank locked her back in the closet and Sophia lay down on the pillow and silently prayed. When she heard voices coming from the basement, she scooted the pillow out of the way and set her ear directly against the floor. Frank was speaking to another man whose voice she didn't recognize. "It's working perfectly," Frank said, "all the players are lining up nicely."

"You've spoken to Giovanni's people?" the deep-voiced man asked.

"Not yet," answered Frank, "but I have word they're scrambling like be-headed chickens." He laughed a wheezy, smoker's laugh. "Not only did we dismantle his organization in New York, but we've just taken his sister and threatened to kill his granddaughter."

"And Salvatore?"

"As soon as Salvatore learns Sophia has been kidnapped, he'll come to the States to negotiate. We'll tell Salvatore he can have Sophia back, but it will be at the expense of Giovanni's sister, Lucia. We'll tell Giovanni he can have his sister back, but it will be at the expense of Salvatore's daughter, Sophia. They will decide who dies and who lives."

"Which one will get to live?" the man asked.

Sophia could hear the clicking of their shoes on the concrete floor and assumed Frank was pacing as usual while he spoke. "Both Giovanni and Salvatore will waste time trying to negotiate the safe return of their loved one, and both will be sorely disappointed."

Sophia gasped, the words ringing through her ears. Frank was talking about her father, Salvatore Buscetta, head of the Cosa Nostra in Sicily. Ever since Sophia fell in love with Joseph Maratinzano, Salvatore hated the Maratinzanos and blamed Giovanni for allowing his son to propose to a woman outside their own family. When Sophia left Sicily to be with Joseph, Salvatore disowned her.

Suddenly Sophia realized this was bigger than just saving Denny and herself. It was bigger than rescuing Angel. Frank was plotting to take down the two most powerful Mafia families on the globe and establishing himself as a respected leader among the families that remained. He must have people high up in various organizations helping him. Panic ensued. She had to escape and get word to her father or to Giovanni or to Angel. She had to reach someone.

"Are you certain Salvatore and Giovanni will be unable to locate Sophia and Lucia?" the man asked.

"Positive," Frank spewed confidently. "Last night we took out the only two reliable men Giovanni had in Chicago. Trust me, they will never find them."

"Which men did you kill?"

"Tony Andriachini and Andrew Venturini, but we didn't kill them, just wounded them enough to cause an uprising of anger among the bogatas."

"You know the man doesn't want the other families involved," his voice grew louder. "He only wants Salvatore and Giovanni."

"Calm down," Frank seethed, "we're just having a little fun. We'll frame another bogata for the attempts, hit a Galante and a Cullato tonight and cause so much chaos in the city no one will even notice our people coming and going."

"What about Angel?" he asked.

Frank chuckled a low laugh. "Angel is my icing on the cake." Sophia pressed her ear to the floor, trying not to miss a word. "We almost had her last night at the hospital, but she got away. It won't happen again," Frank sneered. "She's a peacemaker like her father, and those are the weakest and easiest to eliminate." Frank paused and Sophia listened closely. "I look forward to killing that one," he grunted.

"Your instructions are not to kill her until he has seen her."

"I'm aware," Frank seethed. "Once he is pleased I will cut her down the middle and send one half to Giovanni and the other half to Salvatore."

The deep-voiced man laughed. "You're a sick man."

"Thank you," Frank said with pleasure in his tone.

"I will let the man know everything is on track."

"Yes, tell him I'm so good, Giovanni and Salvatore will murder each other by the end of the week."

Sophia's stomach wrenched into knots of agony. She didn't know how Frank was going to pull this off, but he was right about one thing. Giovanni and Salvatore were both men of deep revenge, capable of terrible acts in the name of restitution. If either believed the other was responsible for Olga, Sophia or Angel's death, they would most assuredly avenge it. She had to get free. She began to tap quietly on the door. "Stefano," she whispered. "Stefano, can you hear me?"

The door cracked open and Stefano looked down at her. "I need to go to the bathroom," she said, "please."

"I can't ask Frank for permission right now, he's in a meeting."

"Please," she wailed, "I'll make it quick. He doesn't even have to know." Her eyes begged and Stefano caved.

"Okay, but do it fast," he uttered, "really fast."

CHAPTER TEN

"I don't know that now is the best time to start searching for my mother," Angel said while Andrew veered the Tank onto I-88 heading west toward Des Moines.

"Giovanni wants you out of the city immediately, so the way I see it, it's the perfect time to begin your search."

"Shouldn't we be looking for Olga," Angel blurted. "She's the one in danger." She was feeling edgy and irritation poured from her tone.

Andrew reached over and gave her knee a tender squeeze. "I know you're worried, sweetheart, but we'll find Olga. We've got people working on it as we speak."

They rode in silence for a few moments. Angel imagined Andrew was probably running through possible suspects in his brain, while Angel's mind filled with memories, trailed by prayers for Olga's safe return and Tony's fast recovery. All of a sudden Angel burst out, "Midnight and Mo!"

Andrew jumped, "What?"

"I locked Midnight and Mo in the bathroom at the Towers." She held her hands up to her forehead and beat on it. "They'll be starving and thirsty and need their litter box. I can't believe I forgot about them."

Angst shown on Angel's face and Andrew grinned. "You sure do love those smelly old cats, don't you?"

"They're not smelly and we need to go back." Andrew smiled from ear to ear and it made Angel fluster. "I'm serious! We need to go back."

"Sweetheart, have I ever not taken care of you and those beastly felines?"

Angel shrugged. "Can we please go back?"

"Nope."

Angel crossed her arms. "If my cats die I will hate you for the rest of my life."

Andrew laughed out loud. "That's pretty dramatic over a couple mangy cats."

"Those cats are my family." Angel choked back tears at the word family.

"Relax, sweetheart," Andrew touched her knee, "I took care of it."

"What does that mean?" She pushed his hand off her leg. "Did you go back to the penthouse, clean up all the glass so it won't get stuck in their paws, give them food and fresh water and clean their litter..."

Andrew cut her rant short. "No, I had Chase pick them up and take them to his place."

"Chase? My chef?" Andrew nodded and surprise filled Angel's face. "How do you know Chase?"

"We go way back."

Angel rolled her eyes. *Here we go again,* she thought, *a typical vague Andrew answer.* He was the master of indistinct responses. The last time he said he and someone went way back they were talking about Grayson and their connection was through the Mafia. Angel exhaled a frustrated sigh, "How do you go way back?"

Before Andrew could answer, his cell buzzed. After several "uh-huhs," "yes sirs," and a couple "got its," Andrew hung up. "That was the station," he said. "We've got a lead on your mom's possible whereabouts."

They stopped at a gas station to fill the Tank with fuel, use the restroom and get some coffee. They were four hours in with approximately two and a half more to go to reach the town of Clearfield, Iowa. According to police data, Angel's mother's letters had been processed at a post office located on Broadway Street in Clearfield, Iowa. Their best guess was that Sophia lived somewhere in or around the 50840 zip code area. It was the only thing they had to go on.

As they drove, they sipped coffee, ate chocolate covered donuts, and talked through the events of last night. The question they kept coming back to was: who had the knowledge of their whereabouts and the resources for a helicopter? Angel had just moved into the penthouse of Heavenly Towers two weeks ago so her residence wasn't exactly common knowledge on the street.

The phone in the Tank rang and before pressing the answer button on the steering wheel, Andrew said, "You answer but don't let on that you have anyone in the car with you."

Angel agreed and on the count of three Andrew pressed the answer button. Giovanni's voice filled the car. "Michelangela, I trust Andrew is with you?"

"Yes grandfather, we're both here." Angel's eyes sparkled, as it felt good to hear his voice.

"Andrew, I trust you have followed my instructions and taken my Michelangela out of the city."

"Yes sir, I have." He winked at Angel and she smiled back.

"Grandfather, has there been any word on Olga?"

"Può il Dio aiutarlo tutti," Giovanni mumbled in Italian, almost breathless.

"È ancora Olga viva?" Andrew responded in Italian, leaving Angel feeling completely left out.

"Sì."

"I'm sorry to intrude, but do you two think you could carry on this conversation in a language we can ALL understand?" Angel didn't even try to mask her irritability or hide the fact that she was pissed off. She'd been up all night and was running on nothing but caffeine, sugar and sarcasm.

"I asked if Olga was still alive and she is," Andrew explained.

"Then you've heard from her?" Angel asked Giovanni.

"I have heard from her kidnappers," Giovanni explained in his usual slow fashion. "They will spare Lucia's life at the price of another."

"At the price of another? What does that mean? Another life? " Angel scrunched up her face.

"Sì."

"Who?" Angel asked.

A moment of dead silence shot chills up Angel's spine. She knew then that the answer forthcoming was not going to be a good one. "Your mother, Sophia," Giovanni uttered.

"What?!" Angel and Andrew exclaimed in unison.

"They have Sophia too?" Andrew asked.

"Non so," Giovanni sighed in Italian, and then translated, "I don't know. Perhaps we are to bring them Sophia in exchange for Lucia."

"Well, we can't do that," Angel blurted.

The look on Andrew's face told Angel something was terribly wrong. His jaw tightened and he sat up straighter behind the wheel, gripping it with force. "This doesn't feel right."

"That's because there is more," Giovanni uttered in a low, gruff tone. "Salvatore Buscetta has been given the same ultimatum. The safe return of Sophia for the death of Lucia."

Andrew beat his hands against the wheel, "Salvatore Buscetta is in the States?"

"I don't know who that is," Angel said. "Who is that?"

They both ignored Angel's question and conversed as if she wasn't in the car.

Giovanni spoke slowly, "He is not among us yet."

"But they're luring him here," Andrew muttered half under his breath. "Salvatore has never come to the States. Why would they want him here?" Angel watched Andrew's face intently, trying to understand what was in his head. "Giovanni, do you have any idea who's calling the shots?"

"Unfortunately, my best men have been detained by the FBI, so answers are coming slowly."

"This whole thing is a little too convenient for my taste," Andrew blurted.

"Sì, for mine too." Giovanni sounded exhausted. "All I know is Salvatore will be forced to demand the life of my Lucia and I will be forced to defend."

It was the first time Angel heard Giovanni refer to Olga as his Lucia. Olga's real name was Lucia, but years ago, when she ran away from Giovanni's wrath and the Mafia lifestyle, she changed her name to Olga. The past had put such a strain on their relationship that all she'd seen them do since they reconnected was argue. She knew deep down they shared an unfailing, sibling love, but this was the first open confession of it she'd seen or heard from either of them; and it touched her.

Giovanni exhaled, "There is much bad blood between our families."

"Which is why someone is pitting you two against each other," Andrew said and bit his lip. "Someone who knows of the bad blood between you."

"What can we do?" Angel asked.

"The only chance we have is to find Lucia and Sophia and get them back into our possession quickly," Giovanni explained.

Andrew sighed, "That's hard to do with no manpower and when we don't know who can be trusted."

Silence filled the air momentarily, and then Giovanni spoke, "Si', I fear there are traitors among us; traditori tra noi."

"Speaking of traitors," Andrew mumbled. "Have you heard from the Shark? He never showed up last night."

"Yes, he did," Angel blurted, "at least, I think he did." Angel explained how she believed it was the Shark who rescued her from the tear gas and took her to the apartment downstairs. "He lifted me like I weighed one pound," she said, "and if he's as big as all of you say he is, then it had to be him."

"Did you see his face?" Andrew asked.

"No, I couldn't open my eyes because of the tear gas."

"I suppose he could have rescued you, but then why would he have disappeared and not checked in with any of us?" Andrew shook his head as if to say something didn't fit.

"Tony mentioned the Shark's name, but I don't know what he was trying to tell me," Angel explained.

Giovanni exhaled slowly. "I must go now. I will contact you when I hear something more." He expressed his gratitude to Andrew for protecting Angel and instructed him to keep her out of the city. "There is one certainty of which we know," he spoke softly. "Whoever is behind this is after you, Michelangela. You must trust no one and be very careful now."

"I will," she promised.

"Ti amo, Michelangela," Giovanni said before disconnecting.

"I love you, too."

Angel looked at Andrew, who was visibly disturbed. "We need to pull over and eat something and let me get my head around this."

It was either that she was stress eating or that this little diner in the middle of nowhere made the best omelets in the world. Angel wasn't sure which and at this point it didn't matter. She shoveled hers in almost as quickly as Andrew inhaled his. When their plates were empty, they sat in the booth with coffee and apple pie and Andrew filled Angel in on what was happening, beginning with Salvatore Buscetta.

"So, Salvatore is my grandfather on my mother's side?" Angel asked and Andrew nodded. "And he is Head of the Cosa Nostra in Sicily." Andrew nodded again. "So he's a big wig, right?"

"I wouldn't address him to his face in that manner, but yes," he mused.

"So, someone is pitting Salvatore against Giovanni, but who would do that and why?"

Andrew shook his head. "Someone crazy. Putting those two together is like taking two pissed off, rabid pit bulls and throwing them in a pen. They'll kill each other."

"I'm the granddaughter of two pissed off, rabid pit bulls?"

Andrew smirked, "Yeah, now that I think about it, that actually explains a lot."

Angel pursed her lips together, cocked her head to one side and raised her right brow. "You didn't think I was so rotten in the stairway last night."

"Sweetheart," Andrew grinned, "I've never thought you were rotten." He reached across the table and took her hands in his. "I think you're fiery, stubborn, strong-willed and a bit hard to handle."

"Gee thanks," she quipped, pulling her hand from his, "you sure know how to make a girl feel good."

"I wasn't finished."

"I'm not sure my self-esteem can take any more of your compliments," she muttered.

Andrew slid out of his seat and into the booth next to her. Moving a piece of hair from her face and tucking it behind her ear, he looked directly in her eyes and spoke softly, "You're also beautiful, funny, and you make me want to do things I don't typically walk around thinking about."

"What kind of things?" Angel taunted.

"Let me put it this way, sweetheart," he cleared his throat, "when you and I get to a point where we're not dodging bullets, blinded by tear gas or running for our lives, I'm going to lay you down and show you what a real Italian lover can do."

A warm, tingly feeling rushed through her body and Angel felt her cheeks flush with color. Desire filled her and if she had superpowers she would have frozen time, laid across the booth and let Andrew show her what an Italian lover could do, right then and there. Unfortunately, being the granddaughter of two rabid Mafia pit bulls didn't come with superhero capabilities.

"Are we good?" His chocolate brown eyes sparkled and Angel melted.

"We're good," she smiled.

Andrew returned to his side of the booth, and they both dug into the apple pie and deeper into potential suspects. He placed several calls throughout the hour they sat, requesting history of any relationship that involved both Salvatore and Giovanni or their respective family members.

"There's got to be a connection somewhere," Andrew muttered aloud.

"There can't be that many people who hate both of them," she added.

Andrew raised his brows, "Sweetheart, I mean no disrespect to you or your family, but the majority of the brotherhood hates both of them."

She leaned back in the booth and sighed, "Oh." Being new to the Mafia world, Angel knew very little about her immediate family history, not to mention extended family.

They paid the check and walked to the Tank. "You know what's bugging me," she said as she hoisted herself into the passenger seat. "I don't understand why they shot you and Tony." She closed the door and turned to face Andrew. "I know you said they didn't kill Tony because they were luring me to the hospital, but that doesn't make sense. If they wanted me they would have just taken me when they took Olga."

Andrew turned the ignition and Angel continued. "I mean, they had all this military equipment like a helicopter and explosives and tear gas; they could have easily kidnapped me or killed me. Why didn't they?"

"Maybe the Shark interrupted their plans and that's why they came to the hospital to get you?" Andrew narrowed his brow and Angel could see the wheels spinning in his mind. "You said 'military equipment' and that's what's been bothering me about this whole thing." Andrew bit his bottom lip. "From the get-go this didn't feel like a bogata hit, and it's because it's not. This is going down like a military operation, which means we need to start looking for military links, past or present, to Salvatore and Giovanni or to their families. This is someone with a personal vendetta against both, access and experience with military equipment, ops or personnel and a whole lot of dough."

Angel saw a spark of excitement light Andrew's face as he grabbed his cell and punched in a number. "Sal, it's Andrew, I need you to run a search, cross-referencing Salvatore Buscetta and Giovanni Maratinzano and their families with any military operation past or present. I want details, Sal. If either of them did so much as serve a cup of tea to a soldier fifty years ago, I want that soldier's name."

He dialed his phone again. "This is Officer Venturini; I need to speak to Ramirez." While he waited for Ramirez to take his call, Andrew looked at Angel and winked, "We're gonna find whoever is behind this. I can feel it."

When Andrew hung up the phone a plan was in motion. Sal, from the FBI, was cross-referencing contacts between the Buscetta and Maratinzano families and digging deeper into past military operations wherein Salvatore or Giovanni may have come in contact with a common third party. Ramirez was releasing to the police and the media that a small-town woman in Clearfield, Iowa had gone missing. Descriptions of Sophia would be posted and the town placed on the highest alert.

"What good will that do?" Angel asked. "We don't even know what she looks like now or even what name she's living under."

"We've got a basic physical description, albeit eleven years old, and the fact that her real name is Sophia. People in small town USA will eat this up. They're not used to living in a crime-ridden city where kidnappings and murders happen daily. This is big news to them." Andrew grinned, "These are good folk, who bake pies and look after each other. I bet they'll even form search parties and go out looking for your mom."

Angel stared out the window. "We're headed back to Chicago aren't we?"

"We have to, sweetheart. We can't do anything here." Angel slumped in the seat. She had this fantasy of knocking on the door of a cute little ranch-style home, and seeing her mother come to open the door. She pictured her pausing to look through the glass and then seeing Angel and shrieking with delight. She envisioned throwing her arms around her neck and hugging her closer and longer than she'd ever hugged her before. She wanted that moment so badly.

"What about Giovanni?" Angel asked. "Are we going to tell him we're going back to the city?"

"Not yet," Andrew said. "First, you will call a meeting of the Bosses."

"What? Why? What does any of this have to do with the Bosses?"

"We need to rule out the possibility that any of them are involved. We also need to curtail rumors that can cause fighting between our bogatas." Andrew paused and took a breath. "And lastly, we need their help to determine who the traitors are among us."

"Traditori tra noi," Angel said softly and Andrew looked impressed.

"Si," he gave her hand a squeeze, "the traitors among us."

CHAPTER ELEVEN

Sophia opened every drawer in the bathroom and looked in every cabinet. She had hoped to find a razor blade or a pair of scissors or nail clippers, anything she could use to cut through the duct tape around her wrists. There was nothing. Frank had obviously been thorough about removing any potential weapon.

Stefano tapped on the door, "Hurry it up in there."

"I'm trying," Sophia answered, "but it's hard to do this with my wrists taped together."

"I'm not falling for that," Stefano mumbled. "Hurry it up. If Frank finds out I let you out, God knows what he'll do."

Sophia opened the bathroom door a crack, just enough to be able to look in Stefano's eyes. "Please let me go."

His eyes widened. "Are you crazy? He'll kill me!"

"He'll kill you anyway, Stefano." Tears ran down around her chin and dripped to the floor. "He's going to kill my daughter. My daughter, Angel, who is about your age."

"How do you know that?" Stefano squint his eyes, as if analyzing her.

"I heard him say it just now through the floorboards." Her hands trembled as she pushed the door open a little wider and touched his arm. "Please help me."

Stefano shook his head. "Frank will kill me. He'll shoot me through the head like he did the other guy." His voice quaked and Sophia could see the fear on his face.

"Then come with me," she blurted, "escape with me."

Stefano's eyes widened again and his mouth fell half open. She could tell he was considering the idea, as much as an escape for himself as for her.

"Do you have a car?" she asked.

Stefano nodded.

"Is there someone else here with you?" Sophia panted breathlessly, "other than the man downstairs with Frank?"

"No."

Sophia opened the bathroom door the rest of the way. "We have to hurry."

His adrenaline must have sky-rocketed because Stefano grabbed Sophia by her taped wrists and walked briskly down the hall, toward the front door. As they passed the basement door, she heard Frank and the deep-voiced man still talking. Stefano quietly opened the front door and peered outside. "It's clear," he mouthed, "go."

Sophia ran down the porch steps in her bare feet and towel with Stefano on her heels. They jumped into his green Oldsmobile, careful not to slam the doors. Stefano started the car and backed out of the driveway as quietly as he could. Then, throwing the car in drive, he sped off down the street. He stared at the rearview mirror, his grip trembling atop the wheel.

"Take as many backstreets as you can and get us to a main freeway," Sophia instructed.

"Why don't we go to the police?"

Sophia looked at him with compassion. She was right, he was in way over his head. "Frank probably owns the police. Are we in Clearfield?" Sophia was trying to get her bearings but nothing looked familiar.

"No, we're on the outskirts, near Creston."

"How long before we hit I-35?"

"About 40 minutes, why?"

"We'll be safer on a major highway with more cars and less chance of being recognized." Sophia watched the side-view mirror, fearing Frank's conversation in the basement would end any minute and he'd realize they were gone.

"We could go hide out at my place," Stefano said.

Sophia shook her head. "We can't go anywhere you've been or to anyone you know. Those are the first places Frank will look."

Stefano's eyes filled with terror. "What about my girlfriend? What if Frank goes to my house and hurts my girlfriend?"

Sophia's mouth went dry. It was a valid concern. They both knew what Frank was capable of.

Stefano beat his fists on the steering wheel, spewing obscenities and fighting back tears. "He'll kill her. He'll kill her!"

"Calm down," Sophia tried to be the motherly voice of reason. "Calm down and let's think this through." Her heart raced and she silently prayed for wisdom. "It's almost noon, where is your girlfriend right now?"

"She takes classes at Southwestern Community College."

"Where is the college?"

"In Creston, off of Lincoln and Highway 25."

"Can you reach her on her cell phone?"

Stefano fumbled in his pocket, retrieved his cell and started to dial the number, when all of a sudden Sophia grabbed his phone, pressed the off button and threw it out the car window.

"What the hell did you do that for?" Stefano hollered.

"We have to assume Frank either has a tracking device in your phone or that he will trace and track any calls you make. If you call your girlfriend he'll have her name."

"How do you know that?"

"Let's just say its standard operating procedure."

Stefano shook his head. "Omigod, what have I done?"

"Do you know what classes your girlfriend takes?"

"I know a couple of them."

"Do you know where to find her on campus? Have you ever picked her up before?"

He nodded, "Yeah, it's been a while, but I think I know which building she's in."

When they arrived at the campus Stefano looked pale and sweaty with nerves. His eyes darted to Sophia, "What do I tell her when she asks why I'm pulling her out of class to leave?"

"Tell her there's a family emergency and she needs to come with you right away."

Stefano walked through the front doors of one of the campus buildings and left Sophia feeling vulnerably alone, curled up in the backseat of his car. She peered over the seat at the doors and was amazed to see Stefano walking immediately out with a cute blonde in tow, her ponytail bouncing as she walked. Her big blue eyes widened as they approached the car and she saw Sophia.

Stefano opened the door and nudged his girlfriend, Kristen, into the front seat. "Who's she and why is she wearing your jacket?" Kristen asked, nodding her head at Sophia and scrunching up her nose.

Sophia turned to Stefano, "How'd you find her so quickly?"

"She was right there in the entrance. It was perfect timing."

Sophia sat up and introduced herself to Kristen. "I'd shake your hand," she said, "but my wrists are still taped. I'm wearing his jacket because I have no clothes."

Kristen narrowed her brow, "Why are your wrists..."

Sophia cut her off. "It's a long story and Stefano will fill you in, but right now, do you have a car here?" Kristen nodded her head. "Good, we need to borrow it."

They left Stefano's car in the college parking lot and piled into Kristen's midnight blue Nissan Altima. Stefano drove, with Kristen by his side and Sophia in the backseat.

By the time they hit I-35 Stefano had given Kristen an overview of what transpired and tears streamed down her fair-skinned cheeks.

"How could you do this to us?" Kristen cried, "How could you get involved with the mob?"

Sophia leaned forward. "I don't mean to intrude, but Frank Vilachi can be a very convincing man. I don't think Stefano knew what Frank was into until it was too late."

Stefano wiped a tear that escaped his manly reigns and ran down his face. "He promised me a lot of money, enough that we'd be set for a long time. I was gonna buy that ring we saw a few weeks ago and propose to you on your birthday. I had it all planned. And then Frank blew this guy's head off." Stefano shook his head and fought back emotion, "He blew it right off and I didn't know what to do."

"Why didn't you call the police?" Kristen's voice quivered.

"Because they would have killed him," Sophia piped in. "Men like Frank own the police. They bribe cops and essentially become the law."

"That's not true," Kristen said and looked to Stefano, "is that true?"

Stefano nodded. "I think so."

"So what are we supposed to do? Where do we go now?" Kristen's eyes clouded with fear.

"We head to Chicago."

"Chicago?" Stefano blurted. "That's a good six hours away."

"I know," Sophia nodded. "I know people there that can help us." Kristen put her hands to her face, breaking into sobs and Sophia reached up and patted her shoulder with her fingertips. "We'll take this one step at a time. First, we need to cut the tape off my wrists and I need some clothing. Does anyone have any money?"

Kristen dug into her purse. "I have twenty-one dollars and some change." Stefano handed his wallet to Kristen, who flipped through it. "Forty-seven dollars, so that's sixty-eight dollars total."

"That's not enough," Stefano said, "we'll have to fill up at least twice to get there and sixty-eight dollars will barely fill us once."

"I have a Visa," Kristen smiled, holding up the credit card. "I'm only supposed to use it for emergencies, but I think this qualifies."

"Who pays the bill for that card?" Sophia asked.

"I do," Kristen answered defensively, "I have a job."

Sophia sighed, "What I mean is, where is the bill sent? Does it come in the mail to you or to someone else?"

"Well, technically, it goes to my dad, but then I just pay him whatever I owe on the card."

Sophia deflated. "We can't use it."

"Why not?" Kristen scrunched up her face. "It has a five-hundred-dollar limit and I don't have a balance on it."

Stefano squeezed Kristen's hand. "They'll trace the transaction back to your dad and it will put your family in danger."

Kristen's face drained of the little color that was naturally there. "Omigod," she said and started to cry again.

Sophia leaned back in the seat and exhaled. "Let's go as far as we can on the money we have and we'll figure something else from there." Sophia wasn't the best at math but as she tried to calculate gas mileage and prices in her head, she thought they could get as far as Sterling, Illinois. From there, they could maybe hitch hike the rest of the way. She couldn't hitch hike wrapped in a towel with no shoes. People would think she was an escaped mental patient. Somehow she was going to have to acquire some clothing. She leaned her head back and fought against the sinking feeling in her gut.

"Stefano," she sat upright and looked at his eyes in the rearview mirror. "Do you have a gun?"

He nodded.

"Since when do you carry a gun?" Kristen gasped.

He locked eyes with Sophia. "Keep it handy," she said.

CHAPTER TWELVE

It was close to 4:00pm when Angel flopped down on Andrew's family room couch and closed her eyes. They had arrived back in Chicago a little after 3:00pm, picked up Midnight and Mo from Chase's apartment and planned the meeting with the Bosses. Everything on the short-term to-do list was done, and since it was well over the five-hour mark of her 5-Hour Energy drink, Angel's boost was fading.

The meeting with the Bosses was to take place at Tetterbaum's Pub at 7:00pm tonight. Chase posted a sign on the front door explaining the pub would be closed for a private party. That gave her a couple hours to sleep before she had to get ready and rehearse the speech she and Andrew prepared. She lay her head against the arm of the couch and closed her eyes, thinking of Olga and her mother. She quietly prayed, dozing off with every word. "Our father, who art in Heaven..." her voice tapered off.

"Il nostro padre, che è nel cielo," he whispered.

"Hallowed be Thy name..." she mumbled.

"Hallowed è nome di thine," came his voice again.

Angel opened her eyes, certain she was half in and out of sleep, but aware she had heard something. "Thy kingdom come. Thy will be done on Earth as it is in Heaven," she finished the sentence.

His voice came from behind her. "Il tuo regno prossimo, tuo sarà fatto su terra come è nel cielo." She rolled onto her back and gazed up at Andrew, who was freshly showered and standing near the end of the couch. "Give us this day," he prompted.

"Give us this day our daily bread..."

"Diaci questo giorno il nostro pane quotidiano," he came closer.

"And forgive us our trespasses as we forgive those who trespass against us," she spoke softly.

"E perdonici le nostre trasgressioni mentre perdoniamo coloro che trasgredice a contro di noi." He lowered himself onto the couch.

"Lead us not into temptation..."

"Conducali non nella tentazione..." he inched closer.

"But deliver us from evil," her voice quivered.

"Ma trasportili dalla malvagità," he lay down on top of her.

"Amen," they whispered in unison and his lips enclosed on hers.

Andrew made good on his promise to show her what an Italian lover could do, and Angel melted beneath his touch. He wasn't the first Italian lover she'd had. Tony was her first. Grayson, her second. The third was definitely the charm. When the euphoric glow of passion gave way to exhaustion, Angel drifted to sleep with her head on Andrew's chest and the sound of his heart beating in her ear.

CHAPTER THIRTEEN

Kristen ripped through the duct tape around Sophia's wrists with nail clippers and a file she found in her purse. When the last bit of tape was pulled from her skin, Sophia winced. Her wrists were raw and tender from being taped so long.

"I'm sorry," Kristen grimaced, "I didn't mean to hurt you."

"You did good," Sophia said, forcing a smile. "Thank you."

Just as she figured, they made it into Sterling, Illinois but were down to seven dollars and change.

"Should we use the seven bucks for fuel?" Stefano asked.

Sophia shook her head. "I need clothing."

"What kind of clothes can we get with seven bucks?"

"Maybe a t-shirt and shorts at Wal-mart?" Kristen suggested. "Or what about a thrift store? There might be a Goodwill store or something like it."

"Good thinking," Sophia said and Kristen smiled.

"You want me to just drive around town and see what we can find?" Stefano asked.

Sophia looked around. "Let's take one pass through town, then we need to park the car in a lot filled with other cars, someplace where it blends in and leave it."

As they drove down the main street of
Sterling, a sign of salvation leapt out at Sophia.
She didn't know why she hadn't thought of it
before. "Pull over!"

Stefano veered to the right and stopped at a
meter on the side of the street. He and Kristen
turned around and stared at her.

"There's a pawn shop across the street,"
Sophia said, and before she could elaborate,
Stefano and Kristen were searching their bodies,
removing any jewelry they had. Stefano pulled a
gold cross from around his neck and Kristen took
out the diamond stud earring pierced through the
top of her right ear. Sophia slid the wedding band
Denny had given her from her left hand and
handed it to Kristen. "I fear it won't be worth
much," she sighed, "but it was all my sweet Denny
could afford and it meant the world to me." Tears
filled Sophia's eyes and Kristen touched her hand.

"Maybe it'll be worth more than you think."

Kristen sat still for a moment, staring down
at a platinum ring on her right hand. It was in the
shape of a daisy with tiny diamonds on the tip of
each petal. Stefano's gaze drifted from Kristen's
face, to the ring and back up. "No," he said, "not
that one."

"But it's worth more than all the other stuff
put together," she uttered and a single tear slid
down her cheek.

"Your great grandmother gave you that
ring," Stefano reminded her.

"I know," Kristen sniffed, "but it would
probably get us enough money to get to Chicago
and get Sophia some clothes."

Sophia reached up and squeezed Kristen's hand. "You have a beautiful heart and I'm deeply touched, but I want you to keep your grandmother's ring."

Kristen wiped her eyes and took in a deep breath. "Why can't Stefano go in with me?"

"Because we can't risk showing his face or mine," Sophia explained. "Frank knows what we look like. It's possible he doesn't know who you are or that you're even with us."

Stefano leaned over and kissed her lightly on the lips. "You can do this, Kristen."

"What if he asks me questions about where I'm from or why I'm selling this stuff?"

"You just act aloof, like it's none of his business," Stefano said.

Sophia added, "And you don't give him any information. Not your name, where you're from or where you're headed."

Kristen nodded. "I'm scared," she said.

"Don't be scared," Sophia replied. "You're not doing anything wrong. You're just going inside to sell some jewelry that you no longer want."

"Right," Kristen looked at Stefano, "I can do this."

"You can do this," he repeated. "In and out in a flash. No big deal."

"Right," she repeated, "in and out. No big deal."

Stefano moved the car further down the street and let Kristen out, jewelry in hand. They didn't want the pawn shop owner to see where Kristen came from or which way she went upon leaving.

Sophia and Stefano kept a keen eye on the pawn shop door, but it felt like it was taking forever.

"I'm a nervous wreck," Stefano blurted. "I want to go in and get her."

"Sit tight," Sophia said, "and give her some credit. She's a smart girl and stronger than you realize." Stefano grunted and Sophia reached up and rubbed his shoulder. "I'm not your mother, but if I were your mother I'd tell you she's a keeper."

Sophia saw a smile fill his face. "Yeah, she really is isn't she?"

The pawn shop door opened and Kristen stepped onto the sidewalk. The plan was for her to take a left and walk to the next corner, make another left and they would circle around and pick her up. When she hit the sidewalk, she turned right and headed in the opposite direction.

"What the hell is she doing?" Stefano blurted. "Where is she going?"

"Maybe she was so nervous she forgot she was supposed to go left. Give her a minute to realize it and turn around." Sophia watched intently, but Kristen's stride was solid and purposeful.

Stefano hit the steering wheel with both hands and spewed obscenities. "What is she doing!"

Stefano started the ignition and just as he was about to weave into the flow of traffic, Sophia grabbed his shoulder. "Wait!" she hollered, "Look!"

Two men stepped outside the pawn shop and shook hands. One was presumably the

owner, dressed in a pair of dark blue jeans and a
flannel shirt, wearing a gold ring on each hand and
a thick gold chain around his neck. He walked
back into the shop. The other wore dark slacks, a
dark t-shirt covered by a jacket and reflective
shades. He stood staunch and looked up and
down the street.

"That's one of Frank's guys," Sophia
uttered.

"How do you know? Have you seen him
before?"

"No, but just look at him," Sophia's heart
raced in her chest, "he's hard to miss." She
scrunched down in the backseat.

"How do I get to Kristen?" Stefano's voice
was laced in panic and Sophia tried to calm herself
and think clearly.

"The worst thing we can do right now is
make a move. We've got to stay calm. You've got
to stay calm, do you understand?"

"I can't be calm when she's out there with
him!" Stefano's face turned a deeper shade of red
and he had a strangle hold on the steering wheel.

"I can't sit up and look so you're going to
have to tell me what's happening." Sophia
exhaled. "Where is Kristen right now?"

"She's still walking up the street, almost to
the next corner."

"Where's Frank's guy? Is he watching her?"

"No, I don't think so. He's just standing
there."

Sophia breathed a tiny sigh of relief. "Okay,
listen, Kristen was smart enough to know this guy
was no good and she's leading him away from us.

The worse thing we can do is make any kind of move that will make him think she's with us."

"Okay, I got it. So, we just sit here."

"Sit here and watch where she goes and what he does. We'll pick her up when it's safe."

Kristen walked up another block and it was getting more difficult for Stefano to see her. Frank's guy still hadn't moved from the front of the shop. "Can I pull out and drive up there now?" Stefano wailed. "It's getting harder to see her from here."

"When you can, pull out, but don't do anything to attract attention. Don't make a u-turn or run a stop sign or..."

Stefano cut her off, "I'm not an idiot," he spewed.

"I know you're not. It's just that people make mistakes sometimes when they're worried about someone they love."

"You're right. I'm sorry. I didn't mean to yell like that."

"If you can circle around the next block up and head her off without being seen, that would be ideal," Sophia advised.

"I think I can do that." He pulled the car away from the curb and into the flow of traffic. At the next corner, Stefano turned left and then made a left down the next street, counting the blocks to try and estimate where he had seen Kristen last. He made another left onto a side street, leading them in the direction of the main street Kristen was on. Stefano pulled to the corner just as Kristen ran across the crosswalk and climbed onto a city bus.

"What the hell is she doing?" Stefano screamed. "She got on a bus! She got on a goddamned bus!" Stefano's rage shook Sophia.

"Follow the bus," Sophia said.

Stefano paused and Sophia could see his mind churning out possibilities. "What if they're onto her? What if they told her to get on the bus, knowing we would follow and it's a huge trap?" Stefano slammed his elbows against the wheel and grabbed his hair. "If it's a trap then we're all dead. They'll kill us and then do God knows what to Kristen."

"Stefano, calm down," Sophia tried to be the voice of reason.

He chewed on his thumb nail. "What if they don't know about her and she's just getting on the bus to get away? She'll be safer if she's away from us, right? If they don't know about her, then leaving us is the smartest thing she can do, right?" Stefano's voice elevated as the panic inside him grew. "If we drive away now, she'll be safe, right?"

"No." Sophia and Stefano locked eyes in the rearview mirror. "Think this through, all the way through." Sophia leaned forward. "Even if Frank doesn't know about Kristen now, he'll know about her soon."

"Why?" Stefano blurted. "How will he know?"

"When Kristen gets off that bus, she'll make her way home, to the home she shares with you; and who do you think will be at your home waiting?" The last bit of color drained from Stefano's face as he listened to Sophia. Sophia blinked slowly. "You have to believe that I know what I'm talking about. I've run from these people my whole life. They will not stop searching for you until you're dead, and they'll kill anyone and everyone in your life."

Stefano shook visibly with fear. "So, what do we do?"

"We follow the bus and trust that Kristen must know what she's doing. When she gets off we'll pick her up."

"But if it's a trap then we're all as good as dead."

"We don't have a choice." Sophia fought the lump in her throat as she saw tearful regret in Stefano's eyes. "You and Kristen can't ever go back."

Stefano beat on the steering wheel again and cried out. "I screwed up everything! I destroyed her whole life and mine and yours."

Sophia stayed low but reached up and touched his arm. "You didn't do anything to screw up my life; and you're not going to destroy yours or Kristen's either. We're going to live through this and I promise you there will be a happily ever after for you two." Stefano tightened his lip and nodded through tears. "Now, follow that bus."

Stefano made a right into traffic and followed the bus. At the first stop they watched closely but Kristen didn't get off. It was the same at the second stop, the third and fourth. "What is she doing? Why isn't she getting off?" Stefano exhaled.

"Just stay the course," Sophia encouraged. "She's a smart girl and right now we have no choice but to trust her."

They stayed behind the bus until the sixth stop, where Kristen exited the bus and made a beeline for a Thrift shop on the corner. She disappeared quickly inside the store, never looking back.

"What do I do?" Stefano blurted. "Do I park the car or drive around?"

Sophia licked her lips. "Drive up one block and pull over." Stefano followed her instructions and they sat in silence staring back at the Thrift store doors.

Fifteen minutes passed. Stefano moaned, "Should I go in after her? What if something happened to her?"

Sophia prayed for wisdom in the quiet of her mind and tried to calm her thoughts. "Let's give her more time."

Several minutes later Kristen walked out the front doors, glancing left and right up the street. She was carrying two bags as she turned right, crossed the side street and headed toward their car. When she got closer, Stefano reached over and pushed open the passenger door and Kristen jumped in. She was out of breath and shaking and she burst into tears when she saw Stefano. He hugged her tightly and they both cried, Stefano uttering repetitive apologies.

Sophia eyed the perimeter from all sides, making sure Kristen wasn't followed. When she felt certain it was safe, she touched Stefano's arm to get his attention. "You need to pull out slowly into traffic and get us out of here."

As they drove, Kristen told them she got $248.00 for all their jewelry and that she overhead the man in the black jacket telling the Pawn shop owner to keep his eyes open for two criminals; a man and a woman answering to the name of Stefano and Sophia. "He described both of you and said you were probably on your way to Chicago and would need money." She started to cry as she told them, "I was so scared I didn't know what to do. I didn't want to walk back to the car so I just got on the bus."

Stefano squeezed her fingers in his hand, brought them to his lips and gave them a kiss. "You did good. You did really good."

Sophia leaned forward and rubbed Kristen's arm. "I knew you were a smart girl," she smiled.

Kristen handed the bags back to Sophia. "I got you some clothes and shoes. I guessed on sizes so I hope they fit. I didn't get you any underwear because, well, I thought it was kind of gross to wear thrift store underwear." Kristen scrunched up her nose and Sophia laughed out loud.

"I appreciate that," she said.

Stefano drove to a gas station on the outskirts of town and filled the tank, while Sophia slipped into the bathroom and put on her new clothes. She slid on the black cargo pants, which were a little baggie but they had a drawstring in the waist so she could pull them as tight as she needed. Kristen had guessed correctly on the C bra size and on the size 8 loafer shoes. The pull over, long-sleeve black tee was a little loose, but the jean jacket covered it nicely. She looked at her reflection and sighed. It wasn't pretty but anything was better than that towel.

"Well," she smiled, sliding into the backseat, "I won't win any fashion contests, but it's not too bad for forty bucks."

Stefano started the car and pulled out. "The tank's filled so we have plenty of gas to get us into the city."

"Good," Sophia said, "now, how about some food?"

Kristen's eyes lit up, "I'm starving!"

Three cheeseburgers and two hours later they arrived in Chicago and Stefano pulled the car into a hospital lot where it wouldn't be easily found amongst the hundreds of parked vehicles. On the way to Chicago Sophia had run through all the options in her mind and devised what she believed to be a good plan. Since she overheard Frank tell the man in the basement that they had kidnapped Olga, she knew it wouldn't be safe to go to Olga's home. She surmised that since Frank knew she didn't have any money, he would have his people checking the cheap motels, so they couldn't get a room and lay low.

"Can't we go to the police now that we're here in the city?" Kristen asked.

Sophia shook her head. "I wish we could, but I have no idea who Frank is working for. For all we know half the police force are meat eaters." Kristen cocked her head to the side, obviously puzzled by the term meat eater, and it made

Sophia grin. "A meat eater is a corrupt cop, a cop paid off by the mob."

"What about your daughter?" Stefano asked.

Sophia felt a lump in her throat. "I haven't been back here for eleven years. I left to protect her from this lifestyle, but somehow she's wrapped up in it now." Angst filled Sophia's face and Kristen reached back and squeezed her hand. "I don't know how to locate Angel and even if I did, it isn't safe." Sophia took a deep breath and fought back the emotion. "The only person that can help us is the Compare. All we have to do is stay hidden until we can reach him."

"What's a Compare?" Kristen asked.

Sophia brought Kristen up to speed with a quick summary of her past with Joseph Maratinzano, how he was murdered in a car bomb and she and Angel went into hiding under the protection of Joseph's Compare. "Aside from Olga," Sophia said, "Joseph's Compare is the only person I know I can trust."

"You can trust me and Stefano," Kristen smiled.

"Thank you," Sophia smiled back. Kristen's innocence reminded her of Angel. "Now, everyone knows what to do, right?" They nodded. "Kristen, you're just a concerned citizen who's helping out some poor woman you found on the street."

"Got it," Kristen said.

"Don't forget to use an internal hospital phone when you make the call to the Compare and stay on the line for ninety seconds, so the Compare can trace our location." Kristen nodded again.

"Once you've made that call, ask the nurse to see me," Sophia instructed.

"Do you think they'll let me? I mean, I'm not family or anything."

"Try to convince them. If you don't come back within ten minutes I'll tell the nurse I want to see you, to thank you for saving my life." Sophia directed her attention to Stefano. "Stefano, you'll get us a new car and move it as close to the west entrance as you can. Then we'll all meet in the hospital cafeteria."

"Why do we need a car? I thought we were just going to hide out until the Compare found us," Kristen asked.

"The car is just a back up plan," Sophia explained. "An escape if we need it." Sophia looked at Stefano. "You know your job, right?"

"Yep. I'm gonna take this car to the hospital personnel lot, take the plates off and leave it, then scope out a new car for us from the regular lot."

"Why does he need to move the car?" Kristen questioned.

"Because the personnel lot won't empty overnight like the regular lot, so the car can conceivably go unnoticed for a couple of days." Stefano explained.

"It will buy us time," Sophia added, "and don't forget to switch up the license plates."

"I know. I'll find the car we want and exchange the back plates with another random car."

"The more plates you switch up, the more confusion you cause and the less likely people are to notice us."

"Got it," Stefano nodded.

"Okay," Sophia exhaled, "let's do this." She pulled up the left leg of her cargo pants and dug her fingernail into her knife wound, crying out in pain. Kristen gasped, covering her mouth with her palm. Blood ran down Sophia's leg and she rubbed some of the blood on her hands. Stefano then helped Sophia out of the car and she looped her arm around Kristen's neck and shoulder. They limped toward the Emergency entrance, leaving Stefano behind.

"Stick to the plan," Sophia said, "no matter what happens."

Once inside, Sophia watched Kristen perform what could have won her an Academy Award. Kristen produced real tears and her hands trembled as she walked Sophia to the front desk and told them she found this woman bleeding on the street. Sophia feigned weakness and incoherency and Kristen wailed, "I think she was mugged because she had no purse, or I.D. and I didn't know where else to take her." She quivered her bottom lip and widened her blue eyes. "I think she's been stabbed or shot or something but I was afraid to look."

Sophia was taken back to a room immediately and Kristen was told to wait in the lobby. "Can I use a phone to call my mom and tell her why I'm late? I don't have my cell phone with me."

"There's a phone over there," the nurse pointed to the corner of the waiting area, "just dial 9 and then the number."

Kristen thanked her, walked immediately to the phone and punched in the number Sophia had jotted on the corner of a torn napkin. If someone answered, she was to give the code word and wait for the code back, to ensure she was speaking to the Compare. If no one answered she was to leave the code word on the recording and make sure she kept the call connected for ninety seconds so the Compare would be able to find them.

There was no answer. Kristen left the code and hung up.

CHAPTER FOURTEEN

By the time Angel arrived at the pub the four Bosses were already inside. Chase served them wine and appetizer plates of gnocci, ravioli, warm bread and oil. He returned to the kitchen with a stunned awe on his face.

"Do you know who is out there?" he said to Angel, his face sweaty and ashen from nerves.

"I do," she answered calmly.

Chase leaned against the stainless-steel countertop and shook his head. "Wow," he exhaled, "there's a whole lot of scary ass power out there."

Angel grinned. The way Chase incorporated the word ass into every other sentence cracked her up. She leaned on the counter next to him. "I should probably tell you who I am. My full name is..."

"Michelangela May Maratinzano," he cut her off, "I know."

Angel's mouth fell open and out of sheer instinct she pulled the 9mm from the back of her jeans and aimed it at his head.

Chase threw his hands in the air and gasped, "Whoa, whoa, wait a minute."

"How do you know who I am?" she demanded.

"I told him." Andrew's voice came from the doorway and Angel whirled around, surprised to see him.

"I thought you weren't going to be here for this," she said to Andrew.

"I thought you might need some back-up or someone to pray with," he winked at her and Angel felt her face blush. As of this afternoon prayer time took on a whole new meaning.

"Can I put my hands down now?" Chase asked.

"Sorry," Angel lowered the gun and stuck it back in her jeans, covering it with the bottom of her shirt.

"How long has he known?" she asked.

"Since he took care of Midnight and Mo." Andrew grinned, "I thought it only fair to warn him they were mob cats."

Angel rolled her eyes.

"Yeah," said Chase, "those are some mean ass cats."

"They are not," she objected.

"So, listen," Chase spoke excitedly, "I was gonna ask you eventually but now's as good a time as any, so here goes." He took a deep breath. "I want in." Angel and Andrew looked at each other and then back at Chase. "You know, I want to be in the fam, part of the bo-ga-ta." He over-emphasized every syllable and gestured with his hands like a gangster rapper.

Angel couldn't hold back a giggle.

"I'm serious," Chase continued, bouncing up and down like a spiky haired Chihuahua, waiting for someone to throw a ball. "I want to be made. I'm loyal. I'm strong. I've got a good head on my shoulders and I've had weapons training. I'd be a real asset to the family."

"Let's get through tonight and we'll talk about it," Andrew pat Chase on the back and then turned his attention to Angel. "Are you ready to go out there?"

"Not even a little," she admitted.

"You'll do fine; just remember to show confidence and strength."

"Right." *Easy for him to say.* "I'd feel better if Giovanni knew we were here and meeting with the Bosses. I feel like we're doing this behind his back."

Andrew put both hands atop her shoulders. "I spoke to him, sweetheart, and he's not happy about it."

"Great," Angel moaned, "what did he say?"

"He's on his way."

"On his way here, to the pub, or on his way to the city in general?" Angel's heart was pounding harder and faster now.

"He can't make it to the pub in time but said he'd meet us afterwards at the Towers."

"Does he know the penthouse has been pretty much destroyed?"

Andrew leaned down and planted a kiss on the top of her forehead. "Sweetheart," he exhaled as if frustrated, "you need to stop worrying about all this other stuff right now and take one thing at a time. The Bosses are waiting."

I hate it when he's right, she moaned inside and then took a deep breath. *You can do this.* She told herself. *Just focus on the meeting and we'll worry about Giovanni and the penthouse later.* Hard as she tried, the pep talk wasn't working and her stomach knotted. Before entering the dining area, Angel peeked from behind the bar and saw the Bosses surrounded by their bodyguards. She estimated that each Boss arrived with at least one or two men. All were large and all heavily armed. *I certainly hope we're all on the same side,* she thought, and then darted back to Andrew. "I don't have a bodyguard," she breathlessly sighed.

"It's your restaurant, sweetheart; you don't need a bodyguard here."

"I don't feel like they'll take me seriously if I just waltz out there alone."

Andrew took out his .22 and handed it to Chase. "You wanted in, here's your chance to prove yourself worthy."

Chase's face lit up like an excited little kid. He pulled off his apron and shoved the gun into the front of his jeans where it was in plain view. "Let's rock," he said and paraded cockily in front of Angel.

"Gentlemen," she announced, breezing confidently into the dining area and nearing the table, "thank you all for coming this evening and on such short notice. I realize your time is valuable so I will get right to it."

Charlie Andriachini and Joseph Venturini stood up out of respect until Angel was seated. Vincent Galante and Carlo Cullato did not. Angel made mental note of their blatant display of disrespect. "Please be seated," she said, eyeing Galante and Cullato. "I have asked you here tonight because I need your assistance."

Cullato chuckled aloud and mumbled under his breath, "As if we didn't see this coming."

"She lasted all of two weeks without Giovanni here," Galante sarcastically quipped.

"Yes, why isn't Giovanni leading this meeting?" Cullato sneered.

Joseph Venturini slammed his palms on the table, shaking the wine glasses. "Let her speak."

"Thank you." Angel took a deep breath and rose from her chair. "I will not pretend to be educated in all past or even present bogata business. Admittedly, I am half your age."

"And you expect us to teach you?" Cullato seethed.

"No," Angel raised her voice, "I expect us all to work together to help find the person responsible for the recent attacks against our families." She began to pace around the table. "I didn't ask you here for a lesson. I asked you here so we could develop a course of action together." Angel took a deep breath. "We may run our businesses independently, control our territories separately, but we are stronger in combating an outside attack if we work together." Angel returned to her seat and glared at Cullato. "And to answer your question, Giovanni has been delayed in New York."

"I have heard of no attack," Cullato spat. "This is a waste of time."

Charlie Andriachini stood. "My Tony was shot last night and we have few leads as to who is responsible. Tony is recovering, thank God." He made the sign of the cross over his body and kissed the tips of his thumbs.

Joseph Venturini joined him in standing, "My Andrew took a bullet last night, as well. Thank God he was wearing a vest."

Vincent Galante hesitantly rose to his feet. "I lost a good man today by a sniper shot through the head. God rest his soul."

"My condolences," Angel said, lowering her eyes. Andriachini and Venturini offered their sympathies and they all took their seats.

Carlo Cullato abruptly stood up and cleared his throat. He was by far the gruffest and most arrogant of the Bosses. "I thought one of you hit my man this morning. It was a rifle shot through the head. We were able to locate where the shot came from but not the shooter. My guy left behind a young wife and three small children." He sat back town as abruptly as he had stood.

They all mumbled their condolences and Angel rose from her seat. "We are under attack and whoever it is would like us to wage war against one another instead of seeking them out."

"None of your people were hit," Cullato pointed out.

"She doesn't have people," Galante uttered under his breath.

Angel tightened her jaw and clenched back the anger rising inside her. "My aunt, which some of you know as Lucia and some of you know as Olga, was kidnapped last night. My mother, Sophia, has also been taken."

"Why didn't they just take you?" Galante spouted.

Joseph Venturini leapt to his feet. "Why don't you shut the hell up Vincent!" he yelled, and several of the bodyguards drew their weapons, including Chase. "As usual, you fail to understand the magnitude of this situation," Venturini stared down Galante.

Angel interjected, speaking poignantly toward the Galante Boss. "It was my error in assuming you would all understand. Let me help you." Sarcasm seeped through her voice. "Someone is attempting to pit Salvatore Buscetta and Giovanni against one another by kidnapping Salvatore's daughter, Sophia and Giovanni's sister, Lucia.

The room filled with low grumblings and Angel continued. "The person responsible has contacts and resources in high places. We have reason to believe the FBI bust in New York stemmed from a tip-off from this same party. It is a person with upper administration level information about each one of our businesses." Angel circled the table. "We are assuming his goal is to take down Salvatore, Giovanni, myself and each one of you at this table."

The room grew quiet.

Angel exhaled and slid back into her chair. "This person cannot operate alone, which means one thing. Ci è un traditore fra noi. There is a traitor among us. Search your organizations, gentlemen, and find any disloyal members."

"How did someone reach Sophia and Lucia, surely they were under heavy protection, were they not?" Carlo Cullato asked.

"We were in process of setting up protection when we were hit. Lucia was taken by helicopter..."

The Galante Boss interrupted, "Helicopter?" He pursed his lips and sneered, "What bogata flies around in a goddamned helicopter, kidnapping people?"

Angel stared at him. "I didn't say we were necessarily dealing with another bogata here. The resources these people have are impressive and it appears there are no boundaries to how far they can and will go."

Cullato pound his fist on the table, "Bratva!"

"That is a possibility," Andriachini nodded. "Bratva is the Russian brotherhood and they deal in heavy weaponry."

"What about the Chinese Triads or Tongs?" Galante raised his eyebrows.

Andriachini shook his head. "They deal in small items and their presence here is minimal by comparison."

Joseph Venturnini folded his hands on the table and looked at Angel. "Exactly what resources do we know they have?"

"We know they have a helicopter, military grade explosives and tear gas." Angel took a breath, "We know they have snipers and that they seem able to locate any of our people with ease." Angel drew in a deep breath and exhaled. These were topics she never dreamed she'd be discussing. "And their deadliest resource is inside information about our organizations."

You could hear a pin drop as the Bosses stared at one another.

"Michelangela," Andriachini broke the silence, "have you found a common enemy of Salvatore and Giovanni?"

"You mean other than the fact that her father married a damned Zip," Galante gruffed.

Carlo Cullato chuckled, "That's enough to cause a war right there isn't it?"

Angel didn't know what a Zip meant so she breezed over it in conversation but made mental note to ask Andrew later.

"We are still researching this angle." Andriachini and Venturini shot each other a glance and Angel met their eyes. "I would hope that anyone who has information that may be helpful will offer it openly," she said.

"Back in the late 1960's," Andriachini spoke slowly and reminded Angel a little of Giovanni, "there was a Mafia war between the American organizations and the Sicilian Cosa Nostra, the Zips.

Aha, Angel noted in her brain, *a Zip is a member of the Sicilian Mob.*

"Both Buscetta and Maratinzano families were involved in causing the war."

"What were they fighting over?" Angel asked.

"A shipment. The Buscettas controlled the majority of heroin in and out of Sicily at that time."

"Heroin?" Angel tried not to show surprise on her face.

"It was the sixties," Venturini noted, "big money was in big drugs."

Angel made mental note to ask Giovanni about that later.

Andriachini continued, "A large heroin shipment was arranged to come to the States and the Maratinzanos were due to receive the shipment, by way of a mediator named Moloney. Upon receipt, the Maratinzanos claimed the shipment was short and paid less money. Moloney accused the Maratinzanos of defrauding him and the Buscettas accused Moloney of embezzling the missing heroin in an attempt to become powerful enough to grow his small clan. Moloney was ultimately murdered, though I don't believe any family claimed responsibility for the hit."

"So how did this trigger a war?" Angel asked.

"First," Venturini added, "it caused bad blood between the Buscetta and Maratinzano families, both unsure if the other could be trusted."

"That bad blood was obviously intensified when my mother left her family to be with my father," Angel said, understanding now.

"Si," Andriachini nodded. "For a while we thought Salvatore would wipe out all Giovanni's people for no other reason than to keep his daughter."

"So after Moloney was killed, wasn't the argument over?" Angel shifted in her seat.

"Moloney's small clan attempted retaliation on both families, resulting in the death of a handful of cops and many innocent bystanders. Public outcry from the excessive violence brought a law enforcement crackdown and hundreds of arrests," Andriachini explained.

"What became of the Moloney clan?" she asked.

Venturini piped in, "They weren't heard from again, at least not in a publically organized fashion."

"It may result in nothing, but I think it's a piece of history between the two families that's worth a deeper looking into," Andriachini said.

"I agree," said Angel, "grazie."

When the last Boss left, Angel locked the front door and then joined Andrew and Chase in the kitchen for a large plate of spaghetti and meatballs, some warm bread and oil, and a glass of Cabernet.

"Being your bodyguard was kick-ass," said Chase, grinning ear to ear. "How'd I do?"

"You did great, a kick-ass job," she smiled, teasingly mimicking his lingo.

"I'm gonna need my .22 back," Andrew said.

"Oh, yeah, right." Chase jumped up and pulled the gun from his pants. "Hey, I got lots of guns at home I can bring if you think we'll need them."

"Oh yeah?" Andrew's cop ears perked, "what do you got?"

"I got a sweet little Beretta, a .38, a Glock, a 357 magnum and an M-16 rifle just off the top of my head," Chase gloated. "I can pretty much get my hands on anything you want."

"You got licenses for all those guns?"

Angel elbowed Andrew as if to say shut-up and turned her attention to Chase. "Ignore him," she said. "Thanks for being my bodyguard tonight. I felt better having you in there with me."

Chase's face glowed with obvious excitement. "Any time, seriously, count me in. Hey, do you want me to ask around on the street about this Moloney guy?"

"We'll take it from here hot shot," Andrew winked.

Leaving the pub, Angel followed Andrew to the Towers. The elevators were working again and they rode to the penthouse floor. When the elevator doors opened, three men faced them, each pointing a gun at their heads.

Andrew lifted his arms and locked his fingers behind his head. "Boys," he nodded, stepping off the elevator. They patted Andrew down, removing his .22 and his .38 and instructed him to face the wall. They started to do the same to Angel, and Andrew said, "You boys know who she is don't you?"

The tall, blonde-haired man, with the square shoulders, square head and jagged jaw-line spoke, "We've been instructed to trust no one and search everyone, which is what we're going to do."

They removed Angel's 9mm and instructed her to face the wall. She didn't like being told to face the wall, as it brought back memories of Grayson and the last time she saw him alive. She hesitantly turned. "I'd like to see my grandfather now."

"Soon as we get clearance," the square, blonde answered.

When they were finally allowed inside the penthouse, Angel was taken back by how different it looked. The front doors were repaired and no one would ever be able to tell they were once blown apart. The glass door to the patio and the glass windows that had been cracked and shattered were all replaced. The dining room table sat upright with no scuff marks or bullet holes to be found. There were no broken frames, no blood stains on the walls and floor and no stench of sulfur in the air. It looked as if the entire incident never happened.

Giovanni sat in the family room in the big armchair in front of the fireplace. He rose when he heard Angel and Andrew enter. "Michelangela," he reached out and she filled his arms with a tight hug, kissing him on both cheeks. He made the sign of the cross over his body, touching his forehead, chest and each shoulder, then kissed his thumb and uttered, "Thank God you are safe."

Andrew looked around the room. "Do you have confidence in all these men," he asked.

"Si," Giovanni nodded, "these are ones recently released by the FBI. Most have been with me a substantial time."

Andrew nodded, but bit his lip. "Then they won't mind if we take our weapons back?"

Andrew's .22 and .38 lay on the dining room table next to Angel's 9mm. Giovanni waved his hand toward the guns, "Go, take." Andrew grabbed the guns, handing Angel hers and slipping one in the back of his pants and the other under his jacket.

Angel sat down on the couch across from Giovanni's chair. "How did you get the place cleaned up and repaired so fast?"

"I've had people working on it round the clock since it occurred. The windows have all been replaced with bullet proof, tinted glass. No one can see in and a standard sniper rifle cannot break through it." Giovanni breathed in slowly and leaned back in the armchair. "Now, tell me about your meeting."

Angel filled him in on every detail of the conversation, including which men were respectful to her and which were not. At one point Giovanni grinned, "Michelangela, you mustn't take their sarcasm personally."

Her defenses flared. "It IS personal."

"Only to you," Giovanni said, "to them it is business."

At the mention of the Moloney clan, Giovanni's expression turned morose and Angel could see anger building in his chest and filling his face. "The Moloney clan no longer formally operates, at least not in the States."

"Did we kill Moloney?" Angel asked.

"Bah," Giovanni waved his hand in front of his face, "that is, as they say, ancient history."

"History has a nasty habit of repeating itself." Angel looked at him and raised her right eyebrow.

He wiggled his finger at her and grinned. "You have your aunt's spunk."

"Yes, and I want to get her back, so please..." Angel scooted to the edge of the couch cushion and leaned forward, "...please tell me everything about Moloney, no matter how terrible it is. I can handle it."

Giovanni inhaled deeply and sighed loudly. As he told Angel the story, she began to see the difference between the man he was back then and the man he had become today. There was a certain measure, albeit a small measure, of compassion in him that she was sure didn't exist fifty years ago. To become the Capo di Tutti Capi he had to be strong, ruthless, claw his way to the top, demand loyalty and mercilessly punish the disloyal.

Andrew's cell buzzed and he excused himself from the conversation and stepped out onto the patio. When he returned, Angel could see excitement behind his eyes.

"What's up?" Angel asked.

Andrew looked at Giovanni, "With your permission sir, I need to leave." Giovanni gave a nod and Andrew turned to Angel, "I will see you tomorrow."

"Andrew?" Angel glared at him. "What's going on?"

"There's no time to go into detail right now, sweetheart." He gave a wink, "I'll fill you in tomorrow."

"What about Midnight and Mo?" Angel wasn't really concerned about her cats. She knew they were fine at his house. Before learning that the penthouse had been restored, she assumed she'd spend the night with Andrew, and now that he was rushing off she felt a sudden let down. "Maybe I should go with you and pick them up tonight?" She blurted and thought, *way to play hard to get, moron, why don't you just throw yourself at him!*

"Tomorrow." Andrew hurried toward the door and left Angel in the sinking throes of curiosity.

"Andrew," Giovanni's voice rang out and Andrew moved back into the family room.

"Yes sir?"

"Keep me apprised of any information relevant to our situation, regardless of the hour. Capisce?"

"Capisce."

CHAPTER FIFTEEN

It was almost 11:00pm and Angel couldn't sleep, though she wasn't trying very hard. Her mind was a jumble of thoughts. She missed Olga and longed for one of their late-night conversations over a slice of cheesecake or Cannoli. She tried not to focus on the worst-case scenario for her mother or Olga and forced herself to think in terms of when they find them and not if they find them. She wondered why Andrew left in such a hurry and if their afternoon together, wonderful as it may have been, was a mistake.

She grabbed her laptop from the desk, propped herself up in bed and started researching the late 1960's incident between the Buscettas, Maratinzanos and Moloney. She read about the heroin shipment, the possible embezzlement and the inevitable war it started. It was all just as Andriachini described. Dozens dead. Police crackdown. Hundreds arrested. She printed out a list of the names of people arrested during the incident and began to look up each name, searching for anything that might point to the person behind the recent attacks. Wikipedia offered the most information, though she was aware it could be tainted with inaccuracies. After all, anyone could add their spin to it.

Thirty minutes later, she rubbed her eyes and started pacing around the room. There was no way she could fall asleep now, even though she was exhausted and it was close to midnight. She had a nagging feeling that she was onto something and her mind wouldn't shut down. She went to the kitchen, made a cup of instant coffee in the microwave and headed back to her room to delve deeper into research.

There wasn't much information on Moloney's clan. They weren't regarded as a real or respected organization and once Moloney was accused of defrauding the heroin shipment, they were written off as a joke by every well-respected crime family. After Moloney was murdered, his right-hand man named Finnegan was also found dead, as was the third in line, Selovich. The group dissipated after that and Angel couldn't find anymore information about them.

She dialed Andrew's cell. No answer. She text him: Can u run a check on the names Moloney, Finnegan, Selovich? Angel hoped the text would prompt Andrew to realize she was still awake and call her, but he didn't.

She wasn't sure what time she actually dozed off but when she awoke it was 4:30am and she heard voices coming from the family room. It was Giovanni, Andrew, Chase, the blonde square and several other men she didn't know. Angel crept quietly from her room to the hall where she could hear what they were saying. *Why am I not in on this conversation?* She wondered and then felt her temper flare. *I should be in on EVERYTHING!"* She was tempted to walk out, but then realized she might learn more by eavesdropping.

"When we confiscated everything in Venito Barone's office, we decided to leave the telephone line open, redirecting the calls to the station."

"What was the purpose?" Giovanni asked.

"Because Venito was an imposter, pretending to be Joseph's Compare, we thought it would be beneficial to see who contacted him regularly. Who was he working with, if anyone? We thought it was a proactive means of helping us head off future problems."

Chase shook his head, "See, man, it's when you guys do crooked-ass shit like that, that makes people not respect the cops no more."

Andrew shrugged, "Maybe so, but when you're dealing with people like Venito Barone, ethical action isn't always the logical choice."

"And logical action isn't always the ethical choice," Giovanni added.

"Our unethical decision paid off tonight when Venito's old phone number received a call from the emergency waiting area of Northwestern Memorial Hospital."

Angel's ears perked up. *That's the hospital Tony is in.* She leaned in closer and listened.

"The caller was a young woman and she stated she was calling for Joseph's Compare and then she mentioned a word, calling it the 'code word.'"

"What was the word?" Chase asked.

"Clint."

"That's a weird-ass code word," Chase said.

Silence filled the room, as each of the men tried to determine what the code word meant. Angel's pulse quickened. She knew exactly what it meant.

"What does this Clint mean?" Giovanni asked.

Andrew shrugged, "We're running it through our database but so far we're coming up empty."

"Clint Eastwood," Chase blurted, "maybe it's a Dirty Harry reference?"

The blonde square man spoke, "Maybe it's an anagram and the letters are mixed up to form another word."

They all thought on that for a few seconds and then Andrew shook his head. "I don't know what it means, but whoever made the call knew to stay on the line long enough for us to trace the location."

"Or was too dumb-ass to know NOT to stay on that long," Chase quipped.

Andrew shook his head, "No, she stated she was instructed to keep the connection for ninety seconds."

"Instructed by whom?" Giovanni asked and Andrew shrugged.

Angel left the hallway and crept back to her bedroom. She was filled with nervous excitement as she quickly dug a shoebox out of the back of her closet and retrieved a small, white stuffed elephant. The elephant's trunk sagged, he was missing one eye and his body was marked with stitches indicating he had been sewn together numerous times. She shoved him under her pajama top and walked to the family room.

When Giovanni saw her, he reached out his arm, "Michelangela," he said, "I am sorry we have awakened you."

"Grandfather, Andrew, may I speak with you privately please?"

Before they could answer, Angel breezed out of the room, walking passed the dining room and the kitchen and into the sitting room that led to the master suite. She heard Giovanni and Andrew mumbling to the men that they would return in a moment.

"What's going on, sweetheart?" Andrew asked but she waited until Giovanni had entered the room to acknowledge his question. After all, she was still ticked off that she was not invited to the big pow-wow in the family room.

As soon as Giovanni came in, she pulled the stuffed elephant from under her top and said, "I'd like you to meet Clint."

They stared at her like her head just spun and she sprouted antennae.

"This is Clint," she repeated.

"Oookaaay," Andrew said with his eyebrows raised.

Giovanni lowered himself onto the sofa. "I'm afraid I am not following you."

"You said the caller left the code word 'Clint.'"

"You were eavesdropping?" Andrew asked and crossed his arms over his chest.

Angel narrowed her eyes. "Had I been invited to the conversation, as I SHOULD have been, I wouldn't have HAD to eavesdrop."

Andrew threw up his hands the way you would if you were held at gunpoint. "Whoa there, sweetheart, take it easy."

"Don't tell me to take it easy," she gritted. "There's nothing easy about this whole situation; and I don't appreciate being left out."

"Let us all calm down and…," Giovanni began and Angel interrupted him.

"I'm not going to calm down and I'm not going to take it easy and I'm NOT going to tolerate the two of you having little meetings behind my back or talking in Italian right in front of me so I can't understand what you're saying!" Angel panted. "You two piss me off!"

Giovanni's eyes were wide and Angel was quite sure no one had ever spoken to him in this manner. "Angel," Andrew said, but she cut him off.

"Don't Angel me!" she yelled.

"Lower your voice," Andrew said, his jaw tightening.

Giovanni cleared his throat and gestured for her to continue, "What information do you have about this elephant."

Angel exhaled, trying to get rid of the anger she felt, but it was undeniably there, tugging at her insides. She plunked down in the armchair across from the sofa. "This," she held up the stuffed elephant, "was the equivalent to my blankie as a child." They stared at her like deer in headlights and she rolled her eyes. "You know how children have that one special item when they're little?" she asked and they nodded. "Well, my special item was Clint, my elephant. I carried him everywhere. I slept with him, prayed with him, told him my secrets. Clint was my best friend."

"And…" Andrew's voice tapered off.

"And…" Angel sighed, "…only three people in the world knew his name was Clint."

Giovanni sat up straighter and Andrew uncrossed his arms and looked more intent.

"Who knew?" Giovanni asked.

Angel smiled. "My dad, my mom and Aunt Olga." You could hear a pin drop in the room as both men's minds churned. Angel continued, her voice growing more excited, "Since Olga knows my dad's Compare is dead, she wouldn't call him; but my mother doesn't know he's dead. She probably doesn't know anything about Venito Barone at all."

"And the Compare would have been the one person in the city she knew she could trust to help her," Andrew added.

Angel nodded and smiled at Andrew. "I think the call you intercepted with the code word Clint confirms my mom's alive and she's here. We've got to find her."

"Il mio Dio," Giovanni exhaled and then translated, "My God." He looked at Andrew. "Are there friends of ours on the force you can trust to locate Sophia?"

"It would help to know if any of the families are involved. That would tell me who can be trusted."

Giovanni spoke low. "Because of your relationship and Tony's relationship to Michelangela, let us bring your two families into the search; but neither Cullatos nor Galantes are to be involved."

"Until we know who the traitors are..." Andrew began but Giovanni interrupted.

"Choose two members from each family. I will deal with their Bosses." Giovanni stood. "As my men are released by the FBI, I will have more help for us."

"What about me?" Angel asked.

"You and Clint stay here," Andrew said and Giovanni nodded in agreement.

Angel rolled her eyes. "I can help," she protested. "I know what my mother looks like better than the two of you."

"You haven't seen her in eleven years," Andrew said.

"And you've never seen her," Angel rebutted. "I'm not just going to sit here and twiddle my thumbs. Besides, she won't know she can trust you unless I'm with you."

Giovanni looked at Andrew. "Bring her back safely."

Angel smiled and kissed Giovanni's cheek. "I'll not only come back safely, I'll come back with my mom and then we're going to find Aunt Olga."

"Il mio Dio."

CHAPTER SIXTEEN

As the sun started to shed light on the city, a plan was set in motion and so was a processional of tinted-windowed, black SUVs. Andrew and Chase were in front in Andrew's Chevy Equinox, Angel was next in the Tank, followed by two of Giovanni's men, then the Venturini men and the Andriachini men brought up the rear. They headed toward Northwestern Memorial Hospital where they would divide up and search their assigned quadrants of the hospital and surrounding streets.

Andrew, Chase and Angel entered through the Emergency entrance. Andrew flashed his badge at the main desk and began asking questions about Sophia. A plump nurse with round green eyes and short, blonde hair punched some keys on the computer. "Looks like we treated a Jane Doe last night."

"Treated for what?" Angel blurted, causing the nurse to look up with a 'who the hell are you' expression.

"She's with me," Andrew interjected. "What was our Jane Doe treated for?"

"Stab wound to the left thigh."

Angel grimaced.

"I assume she was treated and released?" Andrew asked and the nurse nodded. "Is the treating doctor or nursing staff still on shift?"

She tapped some keys on the keyboard. "No. Well, wait, it looks like Nancy might still be

here, but she's on break. You could try the
cafeteria."

"Does Nancy have a last name?" Andrew
asked.

"Taggert. Short, dark brown hair, brown
eyes."

"Thank you." Andrew smiled, "You've been
a big help."

Locating Nancy Taggert was not difficult.
The cafeteria was almost empty and Nancy was the
only one dressed in rose-colored scrubs. She sat
at a table over by the window and sipped a cup of
coffee. She was personable and remembered
Sophia.

"Yes," she answered Andrew, "I remember
our Jane Doe. She was a lovely lady with a stab
wound that we estimated was a couple days old.
She didn't remember who she was or when she
had been stabbed or who stabbed her."

"Did she come in alone?" Andrew
questioned.

"No, she was with a young blonde girl. The
girl said she found her on the street with no
identification and thought she'd been mugged,"
Nancy explained.

"About how old was the blonde girl?"
Andrew asked.

"I'd guess early twenties. She had pretty
blue eyes and wore her hair in a ponytail."

"Did the blonde girl go into the treatment
room with Sophia?"

"No, we don't typically allow that unless
they're family." Nancy took a sip of coffee.

"Actually, she asked to use the phone to call her mother and tell her she'd be late."

"Did Sophia and the blonde girl leave together?" Andrew asked.

"No, I didn't see the blonde girl when we released the woman." Nancy narrowed her brows. "But now that you mention it, I saw them together in the cafeteria later and they were with a young man."

Andrew raised his eyebrows and glanced at Angel. "Can you describe the man?"

"Young, cute, he had on blue jeans and a jean jacket," Nancy said and shrugged. "Sorry, I didn't really pay that much attention. I just assumed they were buying her something to eat since she apparently had no identification or money or anything."

They thanked Nancy and left the cafeteria, heading upstairs to Tony's room. Stopping in the hallway, Andrew gave Chase and Angel new instructions. Angel was to go to Tony's hospital room and wait there. Chase and Andrew were going to search every floor for Sophia, the blonde girl and the mysterious young man.

"What makes you think they're still in the hospital? Angel asked.

"If we're right about your mom having the young girl make the call to the Compare, then she knew he would trace her location and come to meet her. She will stay where he can find her, or she'll call to give a new location."

"Then she's got to be hiding in a place where she can see him when he comes in, right?" Chase said.

"Presumably," Andrew answered.

"Why can't I search with you?" Angel asked.

"Sweetheart, for all we know we're not the only ones who intercepted the phone call and are here searching for Sophia." He put his hands on her shoulders and looked in her eyes. "We have to assume they have access to the same information we do, so I can't have you waltzing around the hospital unprotected."

Andrew planted a kiss on Angel's forehead then handed her over to Chase to be escorted to Tony's room. When they walked in Tony was out of bed, peering out the window. "What are you doing up so early?" Angel asked. "Should you be out of bed?"

Tony extended his good arm for a side hug and answered without taking his stare from the window. "Babe, I'm fine, just a little sore."

Angel leaned into him. "What are you looking at?" Tony didn't answer but motioned with his hand.

Chase and Angel peered out the window, which overlooked the personnel parking lot and part of visitor parking. "Look," Tony pointed. "Several guys are walking the rows of cars looking for something or someone."

Chase squinted his eyes. "Those don't look like our guys," he said to Angel.

Tony pulled his gaze from the window and stared at Chase. "Who's Mr. Military? You replace me already?"

Angel smiled, "Well, if you're gonna lay down on the job…" she teased.

Chase extended his hand. "Name's Chase. I'm her bodyguard."

Tony laughed and Chase frowned. "Oh, sorry man, I didn't know you were serious."

"It's a long story," Angel said and rolled her eyes. "But, yes, for now he's sort of like my bodyguard."

"Where's Andrew?" Tony asked.

"Searching the other floors," Chase answered. "Which is what I should be doing, but I'm a little worried by the weird-ass guys in the lot."

"Why?" Tony quipped, "They lookin' for you?"

"We've got men searching the hospital but those aren't our men," Angel explained.

"You're sure those aren't your guys? They look like brotherhood."

"Positive," Angel and Chase answered almost simultaneously.

Angel filled Tony in on the phone call, the code word, the trace to the hospital phone and their search for her mother. "They also have Olga," Angel said, but we have no lead on where she's being held.

Tony walked into the bathroom and talked to Angel through the door. "Babe, call Andrew and tell him to find out if anyone has reported a car being stolen from this hospital."

"Mr. Bodyguard," Tony hollered to Chase. "What kind of weapon you got on you?"

".38, why?"

"Anything else?"

"I got my Glock in Andrew's car."

"Babe," Tony uttered and then walked out of the bathroom, dressed in blue jeans, a black t-shirt and dark boots. "Call Andrew and tell him to grab a couple rifles from his car and the bodyguard's Glock and meet in my room." Tony then grabbed a weapon from one of the thugs guarding his hospital room.

"Are you going to tell me what you're thinking?" Angel asked.

Tony checked the clip on the .38 he borrowed and snapped it back in. Then he went to the window and peered out. "How many men you guys got out there?"

"Two of Giovanni's, two from your family and two from Andrew's family," Angel answered. "Why?"

"Well, eventually your guys are gonna run into these guys and the outcome ain't gonna be pretty."

"This is kick-ass!" Chase exhaled excitedly. "So, are we gonna pick them off from up here? I wish I had my M-16."

Tony glanced at Angel. "Is he always like this?"

"Pretty much," she nodded. "He's over-zealous."

Andrew entered the room with two rifles and Chase's Glock. "What's the plan?" He asked Tony. Andrew looked out the window and saw the men searching the lot. "You recognize any of them?"

"Nope," Tony said. "I don't know everyone, but I know the main guys in the Chicago bogatas, and these aren't any of them."

"Looks like they're carrying multiples," Andrew exhaled aloud.

"I saw that too," Chase blurted and pointed. "The big dude with the goatee has an ankle holster; probably a .38 or .45 in the back and it looks like a shoulder strap with something a little bigger." Chase's eyes were wide, "That's some heavy-ass firepower."

Tony looked at him. "You scared?"

Chase shrugged. "More excited than scared. Weapons don't scare me. You just have to know what you're up against and respect what it can do."

Andrew grabbed his phone and read a text. "You were right," he said to Tony. "A doctor called in reporting a stolen car. He worked the night shift and his car was gone when he came out this morning."

Tony stared out the window. "Babe," he looped his arm around Angel's neck. "Tell me about your mom."

"What do you want to know?"

"Is she street smart? Does she have a lot of common sense? Is she athletic and strong or fragile and weak?"

Angel shrugged. Those were strange questions. "Um," she licked her lips, "I haven't seen her in eleven years. She was definitely street smart. The last time I saw her she was pretty athletic. She always looked a lot younger than she was." Angel tried to think back. "I don't ever remember seeing her cry so I wouldn't call her fragile or weak."

Tony looked at Andrew. "I'm guessing your stolen car is still in one of the lots with a different license plate."

Andrew smirked. "I haven't seen that done in years." He peered out the window. "It would work though, if she thought she was being followed."

"What are you talking about?" Angel asked.

"The old license plate switcheroo," Tony grinned. "Take an average looking car from a huge lot and move it to another lot where the owner won't think to look. Switch the plates with another random car. The owner will get frustrated and call the police to report the car stolen. Then, randomly switch the plates of several other cars and move them to various locations."

"It used to be an old college prank," Andrew explained. "And trust me, it wraps the police up in paperwork until they want to pull their hair out."

"Why would my mom pull a license plate switcheroo?"

"To flood the lot with policeman," Chase said.

"In your mom's case, she probably escaped here in a car with Iowa plates, so her motive may have been to mask the vehicle she used. Particularly if the vehicle belonged to someone who helped her escape and she wanted to protect their identity," Andrew explained.

"Or maybe she just wanted to cause some wild ass chaos," Chase grinned.

"Give me your rifle scope," Tony blurted.
Andrew handed it to him and he peered through
the lens. "Gotcha," Tony mouthed.

"What?" Tony handed Andrew the scope.

"Fourth row up, thirteenth car over from
the right. Two men standing guard by it."

"I see it," Andrew said.

"Look at the plates."

"Iowa," Andrew exhaled.

Angel ran to the window. "So, my mom is
still here?"

"Probably," Andrew said. "But we can't be
certain. If she did the license plate switcheroo she
could have taken a different car and left."

"But then the Compare couldn't find her..."
Angel's voice tapered off, "And neither could we."
She fought a lump rising in her throat as her faith
was beginning to fade.

"Babe," Tony wrapped his good arm around
her shoulders. "We'll find her."

Chase was busy staring through the rifle
scope while Tony, Andrew and Angel were talking
through a plan of action. "Hey guys," he called out.
"I think I see something."

They rushed to the window. "What?" Angel
asked.

"There," Chase pointed. "Six rows back,
right in the middle. It looks like there's someone
squatting down between the cars."

Andrew grabbed the scope and peered
through. "It's Giovanni's men." He scanned the
lot. "The Venturinni's are coming on the left and
the Andriachini's are to the right."

"I told you this was gonna get ugly," Tony quipped, pulling the .38 from his waistband.

Andrew looked at Tony, "Where the hell do you think you're going?"

"Down there to help."

"No," Angel gasped. "You're in no shape to go down there."

Andrew handed Tony the rifle. "You can help from here." He then text one of Giovanni's men: "I need at least one of them alive and able to speak."

A text came back: "Got it."

Tony opened the window a crack and stuck the rifle out. "Fine, you guys go and search the building. I'll help our guys from here."

Chase grabbed the Glock and Angel pulled the 9mm from her jeans. Andrew took off his Kevlar vest and draped it over Angel's shoulders. "We'll start from the top floor and work our way down. We stay together and check every room, every closet, and every storage area. Got it?"

"Got it," Chase said and Angel nodded.

"If we get separated for some reason, we meet back here with Tony." They nodded.

Andrew's eyes pierced through Angel with more feeling than she'd ever seen from him. "Someone approaches you, you shoot first and ask questions later." Angel nodded.

"Like Olga always says, '=Better to be judged by twelve than carried by six.'" She smiled and tried to swallow the fear that was trying to grip her. She'd never shot anyone and she wasn't one hundred percent sure she'd be able to pull the trigger if and when the time came.

"Go," Tony said. "If they get through our guys out there, they'll be coming in to find Sophia themselves and then we're in a real mess."

Andrew, Chase and Angel ran up the stairs to the top floor. Before opening the stairwell door that led to the hallway, Chase held his palm up indicating they should be quiet. "What's that noise?" He whispered. "Do you hear that?"

"It sounds like a ...."

"A helicopter!" Chase interrupted Andrew and dashed up the last flight of steps to the door leading to the roof.

"It's probably just where they fly in emergency patients," Andrew said, but Chase was already gone. "Wait!" Andrew yelled as they ran up the steps after him. Chase peeked out the door.

"What's going on?" Andrew asked.

"That's not a hospital helicopter," Chase said. "I need to get a closer look. You guys stay here."

Before Andrew could argue, Chase slipped through the door and around the side of the wall. "Damnit!" Andrew blurted, "Didn't I say we were to stay together."

In under a minute Chase slid back through the door, out of breath. "That's what I thought," he panted. "It's Selovich."

"Selovich?" Angel gasped, and smacked Andrew's arm. "That's one of the names I text you to look up last night."

"I did. He's part of the Russian mob and deals in arms."

"Yeah, he's scary-ass crazy too," Chase uttered. "But if you want the good stuff, he's your man."

"You've done business with this guy?" Andrew asked.

"Yep, a couple times, but I'm telling you, he's a real scary-ass nut job."

"Why does the Russian mob need a helicopter at the hospital?" Angel asked.

Andrew pondered for a few seconds. "They must know Sophia's here waiting for the Compare, which means they had to have intercepted the phone call to the Compare or our traitor is someone closer than we think."

CHAPTER SEVENTEEN

Chase took the right side of the hallway and Andrew and Angel took the left side. They pushed open every door and called out Sophia's name. Each time they were confronted by hospital personnel, Andrew flipped his badge and Angel put her fingers to her lips to indicate they should be quiet. That pretty much shut everyone up. The eighth floor was clean. No Sophia. Half-way down the hallway on the seventh floor Andrew opened a door that looked like a storage closet. He peeked inside and was about to close the door when Angel grabbed the side of the door. "Did you hear that?" She asked.

"No, what?"

"A shuffle sound." She reached around and turned on the light switch. It was a small room, lined with tin shelving that held cleaning supplies, towels and toilet paper.

"I don't hear any..." Andrew stopped when he heard the noise. He held up his hand to indicate to Angel that he heard it and she shouldn't speak. Andrew backed out of the storage closet and stared at it from across the hall. It sat between two normal sized hospital rooms, but it didn't go as deep as the rooms on either side of it. He walked into the room to the left and then to the right, both were vacant. He was calculating in his mind how much space lie between the two rooms when Angel stuck her head into the hall. "I found a latch on the inside of the shelving," she whispered.

He shook his head, "You and your latches." She grinned, remembering it was a tiny latch on the floor of the stainless-steel shelving in the pub that led her and Andrew to the Tetterbaum tapes.

When Andrew felt the latch and figured out how it opened, he motioned for Angel to get Chase, which she did.

On the count of three, Andrew threw the latch and a section of shelving popped loose from the wall, displaying a doorway. Chase stepped through with the Glock out in front and Andrew close behind. Angel closed the hallway door and then stepped through the opening. It was pitch black. Chase found a light switch on the left side of the doorway and flipped it, and a dim overhead light filled the room. It was a little smaller than a standard hospital room but there were no windows. In the front left corner, there was a metal ladder that rose to a moveable panel in the ceiling. Chase immediately climbed the ladder, sliding the panel out of the way and peering upward.

"It looks like an old elevator shaft, but it goes up to the roof," he hollered down.

"See if it leads directly to the roof or if there's another room up there," Andrew instructed and Chase climbed out of view.

Andrew made a beeline for a desk that sat in the far corner to the right. He began opening drawers and scanning through papers on the top. A hospital bed sat against the wall just down from the desk. There was an IV set up and it was obvious by the rumpled sheets and pillow indentation that someone had recently laid in the bed.

"What is this room used for?" Angel asked.

"It's not used for anything good," Andrew responded, pulling a prescription pad from the top drawer and tossing it to Angel. She read the name on the pad and her jaw dropped: Dr. Manzini.

"I was told he left the state," Angel shook her head. "His office and the hospital told me they had no way to reach him."

"Well, sweetheart, he's definitely here and he's working for someone."

Chase dropped back down the ladder. His eyes were wide. "You gotta see this crazy-ass shit, man," he exclaimed, "You won't believe it!"

"What?" Angel and Andrew said in unison, heading for the ladder.

"It looks like an old elevator shaft up there." Chase was out of breath. "The ladder leads to the roof through an access door near where the helicopter set down. When I put my ear to it I can hear the blades," he panted. "On my way back down the ladder I noticed there was a landing to the left and then a door." Chase exhaled. "It's crazy dark, but there's definitely a door."

"Did you open it?" Angel asked.

"No, I thought about it but thought it was better to get you guys first." Andrew and Angel shot each other a glance and Andrew smirked. "What?" Chase blurted. "I wasn't scared or nothin', I just thought you guys would want to be in on it."

Angel touched his arm, "It's okay, we do want to be in on it."

"Yes, it was a good move," Andrew grinned and headed up the ladder.

"You want me to go up first?" Chase stammered, "'Cuz I'm not scared to go first. I like going first."

"Why don't you bring up the rear," Andrew said over his shoulder.

"Good idea, that way Angel's in the middle of us."

Angel rolled her eyes and started up the ladder. She was feeling both fearful and excited. The prospect of finding her mother made butterflies dance in her stomach. When they were all on the platform, Andrew clicked the handle on the door and pushed it open. With his gun in front, he entered and angled left while Chase pushed through to the right and Angel stood in the doorway. The room was pitch black.

Andrew grabbed Angel's arm as the door closed behind her. "You stay right here until we find a light switch."

Andrew released her arm and Angel heard both of them walk away in different directions. She hated standing there alone, not being able to see her hand in front of her face. It reminded her of finding Antonio dead in the cellar and she tried to shake those images from her mind. The darkness felt suffocating and Angel forced herself to breathe slowly. *The room can't be that big and one of them should bump into a light switch soon,* she told herself.

All of a sudden Chase hollered and crashed to the floor.

"Chase?" Angel called out.

"I'm okay, I tripped over something or..." he paused. "Someone." There was fumbling in the darkness. "Aw geez, it's a person. I'm touching the foot of a person."

Angel felt her breath catch. *Not my mother. It's not my mother.* She frantically chanted inside her mind.

"Stay where you are," Andrew instructed. "Stay with the body and I'll come to you."

Angel heard scuffling of feet then Andrew yelped and a tingly feeling of fear crept up the back of her neck. "What's going on?" She inched a few steps to the right until she could place her back against the wall.

"You didn't tell me the body was sitting in a wheelchair," Andrew said to Chase. "I just tripped over the chair."

"You said not to move so I haven't moved," Chase blurted. "I've got my hand on a foot that feels like it's inside a fuzzy slipper or a furry-ass sock or something."

Angel's breathing quickened when she heard Chase describe the foot. All she could picture in her mind was Olga sitting in her big bird yellow robe and matching fuzzy slippers. Panic started to grip her chest and she moved faster along the wall, searching for a light switch.

Andrew must have heard Angel moving and barked, "Angel, where are you? If you're moving you need to tell us. I don't want anyone accidentally taking a bullet."

"I'm looking for a light switch," she answered, circling the room to the right of the door.

"Holy…" Andrew stopped abruptly.

"What is it?" Angel cried out, fearing the worst. "Is it Olga?" Andrew didn't answer. "It's Olga isn't it?" Angel's voice elevated as panic took hold and she sped up her search for a light. "Omigod, please tell me it isn't Olga." A lump formed in her throat.

"Chase, I want you to get Angel out of here." Andrew's voice was stern. "Take her back to Tony's room."

"Sure thing," Chase said and Angel could hear him moving around the room. "Angel, where are you? Let's meet by the door we came in. Okay?"

Angel didn't answer. She didn't want to be escorted out. She wanted to find a light and see what was happening. She quietly continued around the edge of the wall, feeling up and down.

"Angel!" Andrew yelled in a loud whisper, "Answer us!"

Angel kept moving. She knew if she answered, Chase would take her back to Tony's room and as scared as she was she didn't want to be escorted out like a child. Whatever it was, or worse yet, whoever it was in the wheelchair, she could handle it. Three quarters of the way around the room Angel's fingers bumped against the crack of a door. She felt up and down until she found a knob and then she twisted and tugged. The door opened and light flood the dark room causing all of them to squint. Angel turned her head toward the wheelchair and gasped as she saw Olga taped to the chair with her head slumped downward. She moved toward Olga just as Andrew stood up and fired his .22 in the direction of the opened door. Angel screamed and hit the floor stomach first, catching herself with her hands before her face smacked the floor.

"Stay down," Andrew yelled, and fired a second shot, moving quickly through the doorway.

A man yelped from the other room. "Son of a ..." he was interrupted by Andrew's hand around his throat.

"You better save your breath," Andrew seethed, lifting him by his neck. "You have a lot of explaining to do."

"You shot me," Dr. Manzini winced, gripping his leg. "I can't believe you shot me."

"You should be thankful I didn't kill you."

Angel scurried to her feet and she and Chase wheeled Olga through the door and into the room where Andrew had handcuffed Dr. Manzini. In the light Angel could see there was color in Olga's face and her chest moved up and down as she breathed. "She's alive," Angel blurted and shook Olga gently. "Aunt Olga," Angel said and shook a little harder. "Olga, wake up." Olga didn't move. Angel stared at Dr. Manzini. "What's wrong with her?" When he didn't answer Angel grabbed her 9mm and shoved it in Dr. Manzini's face. "What did you do to her?" She yelled.

"She's sedated," he whimpered almost breathless. "I had to sedate her because she wouldn't keep quiet."

"When will she wake up?" Angel pushed the gun against his chest.

"In a couple hours." His voice shook. "She'll be fine, I swear."

"She'd better," Angel seethed, pulling her gun away and sticking it back in the waistline of her jeans. "Or you're a dead man."

"I'm a dead man anyway," Dr. Manzini exhaled.

"Why?" Andrew asked, "Who will kill you for losing Olga?"

Dr. Manzini shook his head, "Oh, no, I'm not talking until I have an iron clad deal of protection."

Andrew grabbed him around his throat and put his gun to his temple. "How about I put a bullet in your head right now?"

"Go ahead!" Dr. Manzini screamed, startling Angel and making Chase's eyes bulge out. "Go ahead and do it!"

Andrew stared Dr. Manzini down. "Fine, you help us get out of here and give me the information I need and I'll make sure you have protection."

Dr. Manzini expelled a defeated chuckle. "There's no way out now. There are men crawling all over this place looking for Sophia and her people. You'll never get passed them. We're all as good as dead."

"What about the chopper?" Chase interjected.

Angel watched Andrew mull it over in his brain, probably calculating the odds of success and weighing them against the almost certain guarantee of failure.

"You'll never get passed Selovich," Manzini scoffed. "We're all dead."

"I can get passed Selovich," Chase blurted.

"It's not a matter of getting passed him, we need him to fly the helicopter," Andrew piped in as the voice of reason but Chase shook his head.

"I can fly it, man," he grinned ear to ear and nodded his head up and down. "I can fly it." Chase bounced up and down on his heels. "All I need is a diversion, man, and we're home free."

"When have you ever flown a chopper?" Angel asked.

"I was in the Army for a while."

Andrew raised his eyebrows, "But you're not still in the Army?"

"Discharged." Chase exhaled and shrugged. "Dishonorable discharge."

"It wasn't for crashing a helicopter was it?" Andrew quipped.

Chase grinned. "No, I had no trouble with the choppers. It was the smart-ass Sergeant that I had issues with."

Andrew glared at him. "What were your issues?"

Chase cocked his head to the side, "No big-ass deal. He had a chip on his shoulder and I took upon myself to shoot the chip off."

Andrew gawked at Angel and shook his head. "Why are you looking at me?" she asked. "I didn't know he was in the Army?"

"Don't you reference check your employees?" Andrew held up his hands and Angel grinned.

"I checked the references that pertained to his cooking abilities, not whether he could fly a helicopter."

Andrew and Chase bantered back and forth for a few moments, devising a plan of action. Manzini would gimp through the roof access door, drawing Selovich's attention while Andrew and Chase would come through the access panel on the other side.

Manzini piped in, "Selovich will take me out as soon as he sees I've been shot."

"I'll take care of Selovich," Andrew said with confidence. "Chase, you take control of the chopper and make sure you can fly it."

Andrew turned to Angel, "As soon as we have control of the chopper, I'll text you, then you bring Olga up."

"I can't get her up the steps by myself." Angel threw her hands in the air as if to say "duh."

"Damnit," Andrew ran his fingers through his hair. "Okay, un-tape her and I'll come back down and help carry her up the steps."

"Okay."

Andrew grabbed Manzini by the arm, "One wrong move and you're dead. You signal him of danger in any way and …"

Manzini cut him off, "And I'm dead, I get it."

Though he appeared agitated, Angel saw a bead of sweat run down the side of his cheekbone and she knew Manzini was nervous. Compassion tugged at her heart but anger won the battle, as she reminded herself what he had done to Olga. When Andrew, Manzini and Chase left the room, Angel began the daunting task of pulling the duct tape from Olga's wrists and mouth. Her seventy-year-old, thin skin was red and bruised from the tape and Angel's hands shook as she tried to gently pull it from her face. It tore the skin in several places and bled. Angel dabbed the blood with her t-shirt. "I'm sorry," she winced, thankful Olga was sedated so she wasn't feeling any pain.

Moments later Andrew appeared in the doorway. "We're clear, let's go." They wheeled Olga to the stairway door that led to the steps. Angel locked the wheels on the chair and on the count of three Angel helped lift Olga onto Andrew's back where she hung like a wet blanket.

"Don't drop her," Angel whispered, running ahead of him to open the roof access door. Stepping onto the roof, Angel gasped at the sight of Selovich's body. He had been shot in the back of the head and was lying face down. Angel's stomach instantly knotted and she fought her gag reflex.

"Don't look at him," Andrew hollered. "Just keep moving."

It all felt surreal, like she had left her body and was watching everything happen from somewhere above. She leapt over Selovich's legs, headed for the chopper and pulled open the back door to help Andrew lift Olga in. Once she was in, Angel climbed into the front seat next to Chase and Andrew rode in the back between Olga and Dr. Manzini, who was handcuffed to a metal support rod.

"You sure you can fly her?" Andrew yelled up to Chase, who gave a nod and lifted the helicopter from the roof.

Angel's heart was pounding violently and she took deep breaths and tried to mentally talk herself beyond the fear. Hard as she tried, she couldn't peel her eyes from Selovich's body and the pool of blood surrounding his head. It wasn't the first body she'd seen up close. Markus Cullato's brains were blown off in her lap, she had tripped over Antonio's body and fell in his blood and Grayson's dead stare still haunted her. Though this was the fourth body she'd seen, the brutal reality of violent death was something to which she was not yet accustomed. She wondered if she would ever become desensitized to it.

Since it was too loud to place a phone call Andrew sent a text to Giovanni, telling him they were going to land a chopper on the penthouse patio in a few moments. "Tell your men to stand down" he text. "Olga and Angel on board."

Angel pulled out her phone and text Tony. "Found Olga. Leaving in chopper. Be back to find mom."

CHAPTER EIGHTEEN

Chase set the chopper down on top the Towers and Dr. Manzini was given an immediate escort by Giovanni's men. "Keep him alive," Andrew hollered as they led him away. "We need to know who he's working for?"

Dr. Manzini shot Andrew a hateful glance. "You promised me protection."

"When I get the information I want, you'll the get the protection you need."

Two men lifted Olga from the chopper and carried her to her bedroom in the back of the penthouse. "Be gentle with her," Angel instructed, as she and Andrew made their way to the family room to join Giovanni.

Chase barged in with bulging eyes and a wide grin, "That was kick-ass righteous!" His face was glowing like a kid who'd just learned to ride a bike. "Did you feel the power up there? Whoo-hoo!" he howled, "That was a sweet-ass ride!" Angel giggled at his enthusiasm and it felt good to laugh. She couldn't remember the last time she had laughed.

Andrew chuckled out loud and bumped knuckles with Chase. "It was cool. Well done."

Giovanni entered the family room and lowered himself into the armchair by the fireplace. "I trust our Lucia has been unharmed," he said.

"As far as we know," Angel sighed. "She was sedated when we found her."

"I pity the person in her presence when she awakens," Giovanni put his hand to his forehead and shook his head. "Il mio Dio."

"Yeah, she's gonna be pissed," Angel agreed.

The two men that had carried Olga to her room entered the family room and stood behind Giovanni's chair. Three others joined them, as if awaiting instruction. "Looks like you got some of your men back," Andrew said to Giovanni.

"Yes, the FBI has been releasing them slowly. My sources tell me we should be back to full capacity within the next forty-eight hours." Giovanni leaned back in his chair. "Tell me about this Manzini."

Angel filled him in on how Dr. Manzini was the one who treated her after her car accident, who forged the death certificate for Grayson, who told her to see Venito "The Therapist" Barone and then mysteriously disappeared.

Andrew told him about the hidden office in the hospital and how he suspected Manzini worked for anyone willing to pay. "I don't think he has loyalty to any one family or group in particular," Andrew explained.

"What information do you need my men to extract?" Giovanni placed his fingertips together and rested his elbows on the arms of the chair.

"We need to know if he knows anything about Sophia, his connection to Selovich and who's calling the shots."

"Selovich?" Giovanni's expression grew dark. "What does Selovich have to do with any of this?"

"Selovich is a Russian arms dealer," Andrew began.

"Yeah, he's a real crazy-ass, too," Chase interrupted and Giovanni raised an eyebrow at him.

"Do you know Selovich?" Giovanni questioned.

"Yes, sir. Well, sort of, sir," Chase pandered. "I've done business with him before. He's a real whack job but if you want the good stuff, he's your guy." Chase eyed Andrew, "Well, he was your guy."

Giovanni followed Chase's eyes to Andrew, who exhaled loudly. "We needed to borrow his chopper and he wasn't keen on the idea."

"I see," Giovanni nodded and gestured two of his men over with his hand. "Interroghi Manzini e scopra chi sta lavorando per," he instructed. "Don' la t lo uccide fino a che non lo dica." His men gave a nod and left.

"What did you tell them?" Angel asked.

Giovanni grinned. "I told them to find out who Manzini is working for and not to kill him until I give the word."

Angel swallowed hard. *This is probably not a typical conversation going on in family rooms across the country,* she thought.

"Any information on Sophia's whereabouts?" Giovanni asked.

"No, grandfather," Angel replied. "But we didn't get to finish our search because we found Olga instead. We know she must be hiding out in the hospital, waiting for dad's Compare, so we need to hurry back and find her before someone else does."

"Si, go, I will oversee the Manzini interrogation and get the information you require."

Angel bent down and kissed Giovanni on the forehead. "Grazie grandfather," she whispered and then hurried toward the patio door.

Giovanni called out to Andrew and he stopped and turned around. "Andrew, proteggere la mia Angel."

Andrew smiled, "I'll protect her with my life."

Chase flew Angel and Andrew back to Northwestern Memorial. By the time they arrived there were several police cars and two men dead in the parking lot. Andrew went to talk to the policemen while Chase and Angel went to Tony's room.

"Babe," Tony grinned as Angel walked in. "How's Olga?"

"Sedated, but otherwise okay." Angel peered out the window. "What's been going on here?"

Chase stared down at the two bodies in the parking lot. "Did you drop those guys?"

"Nope," Tony shrugged. "It's the weirdest thing, I had them in my scope, but I never had a chance to fire. Someone beat me to the punch."

"Who?" Angel's eyes grew wide.

"Dunno, babe." Tony draped his arm around her shoulders and pulled her close, leaning down and whispering in her ear, "I missed you."

A sense of guilt rushed over her as the visual memory of being in Andrew's arms filled her mind. *I have nothing to feel guilty about,* she told herself. *Tony left me. We haven't been a couple in a really long time.* Her mental justifications didn't help. She swallowed hard and looked up at Tony. "I missed you too." He leaned down, kissed her lightly on the neck and sent chills dancing up her spine.

Chase gawked at them. "I didn't know you two were an item. I thought for sure you and Andrew were together." He shrugged, "Weird, huh."

Angel's face flushed and she stepped awkwardly away from Tony. "Oh, no, we're not an item. I mean, we used to be," she stammered. "I mean, Tony and I used to be an item, not me and Andrew. But then he left, Tony I mean, not Andrew, and now he's back but he's not back with me. He's just back in general." Angel's voice faded and she nervously cleared her throat.

"Babe," Tony grinned. "It's good to know I can still get you flustered."

"I'm not flustered."

Chase raised his eyebrows. "That was some crazy-ass flustered right there."

Angel rolled her eyes and re-directed her attention to the window. "So, who do you think hit those guys?"

Tony shrugged, "Dunno, but we probably ought to find out so we know who's side they're on."

Andrew came in, followed by one of the men guarding Tony's door. "I'm borrowing one of your guys to help us look for Sophia," he said to Tony. "We'll divide up and search floor by floor, but keep your weapons concealed. This place is crawling with cops."

"Says the cop," Tony teased.

Andrew raised his eyebrows and pointed toward the window. "Did you drop those two?"

"Nope," Tony said. "Somebody beat me to it."

Andrew looked at Chase who threw his palms up. "Don't look at me. I didn't do it."

"Who did?"

Tony threw up his hands. "No clue, man."

Chase stuffed his Glock into his pants and pulled his shirt over it and Angel did the same with her 9mm. Andrew had a .45 in his shoulder harness and a .22 in the back of his jeans, hidden by his leather jacket; and Tony shoved a .38 in the back of his jeans.

"Tony, me and Angel will go together and you and Chase will go together," Andrew said, pointing at the guard. "What's your name?"

"Dane," he answered with a deep voice.

"Cool-ass name," said Chase. "What's it mean?"

"Great Dane."

"'Cuz you the dawg, right" Chase grunted and held his fist up for a knuckle bump, but Dane just stared at him, expressionless.

Dane and Chase were instructed to begin their search on the top floor and work their way down. "But we already covered the top two floors," Chase argued.

"I want them re-checked. We're not seeking a stationary object," Andrew explained, "There are three people who could be hiding together or separately. Chances are they are not staying in one location but moving around to different parts of the hospital. For right now we are going to assume that Sophia will stay in the Feinberg Pavilion, near the Emergency Department where she placed the call so the Compare can easily find her."

Tony shuffled his feet. "How many men do we have outside, checking the surrounding area in case she left the main building?"

"We've got two guys on Erie Street in front of the main building and two guys on Huron Street behind the main building; but it's a big area to cover and my guess is Sophia won't trust anyone unless it's the Compare."

"Let's do this," Tony slapped his hands together.

"If you find anyone, text immediately," Andrew said. "And we meet at the chopper in 45 minutes with or without Sophia."

Once Chase and Dane left, Andrew turned to Angel. "I want you to stay between myself and Tony." Angel bit her lip. *If he only knew how the mere thought of that toys with my emotions,* she thought, *not to mention my desires.* "The only reason I'm letting you search with us is so your mom will see you and know it's safe to come out."

"The only reason you're LETTING me..." Angel repeated and felt her jaw tense. She narrowed her brow and glared at him. "You're LETTING me?" She over-emphasized the word letting to drive home her point; the point being he had zero authority over her. She could do whatever she wanted.

"What I mean is..." Andrew began and Angel cut him off.

"I know what you mean," she huffed off down the hall, toward the steps.

Tony smirked at Andrew as he walked by. "Nice one, Ace."

"Shut up."

They entered the stairwell with a plan to take the stairs down to the bottom floor and search the emergency area first. "Logic tells me she is in a place where she can see the Compare come through the doors," Andrew said.

"Or maybe she's higher up and can see him get out of his car in the parking lot," Tony pointed out.

When they approached the door that led to the first-floor hallway, Andrew took a deep breath. "We stick together," he reminded them. The entire floor was bustling with people. Cops were milling around taking statements from people who either saw or overheard the shooting in the parking lot. The men's bodies were being carted through the emergency entrance, with their faces covered and blood staining through the sheets. Angel swallowed hard at the sight.

They searched the emergency treatment rooms, the waiting area and the adjacent hallways. No Sophia. Only Andrew, with the wave of his badge, was allowed to peak at any vacant surgery and surgery prep rooms. Tony and Angel had to wait in the hallway.

Angel leaned against the wall and slid down until her butt hit the floor. She was beginning to lose hope of ever finding her mother. She rested her chin on her kneecaps and sighed, while Tony slumped against the wall next to her and crossed his arms over his chest. "Don't worry, babe, we'll find your mom."

Several people walked by and Angel gave them a quick once-over. None of them were her mom so she lowered her eyes back to the floor. "She's got to be around her somewhere," Tony consoled.

"I didn't mean to eavesdrop," came the voice of a young woman in mauve colored scrubs and a matching surgical cap covering her head. "But who did you say you were looking for?"

Angel ran her eyes from the woman's feet to her face and hope filled her heart. "You don't work here, do you?" Angel blurted and the woman became visibly nervous, rocking her weight back and forth between her feet and wringing her fingers.

"Yes, I work here," she lied.

Angel slid up the wall to a standing position. "How come your shoes aren't standard hospital issue? I've never seen a nurse wearing sandals."

"I'm not a nurse," she stuttered. "I'm an x-ray tech.

Suddenly a young man in blue scrubs poked his head out of a door down the hall and gave the young woman a deliberate stare down. "Kristen." He raised his eyebrows, "Could you help me? Now, please?"

The young woman nodded and turned to Angel and Tony. "It was nice to meet you and I hope you find whoever you're looking for."

Out of desperation, seeing Kristen start to walk away, Angel hollered, "I'm looking for my mother, Sophia. She's in danger."

"Stefano," Kristen cried out and Stefano burst into the hallway with his .38 drawn.

"Whoa,whoa,whoa," Tony berated, quickly pulling the .38 from his waistband and aiming it at Stefano.

Kristen threw her hands up to her face and muffled a scream, then dropped to her knees and trembled. "Please don't shoot him," she started to cry. "We know where Sophia is."

Tony grabbed Kristen up by one arm and held the gun under her jawbone. He glared at Stefano. "You tell me where Sophia is and I give you back Kristen, here, with her head still attached."

Angel gasped. She'd never seen Tony like this and even though she was ninety percent sure he wasn't going to blow Kristen's head off, her stomach knotted from the ten percent doubt. "Tony," she whispered, but he didn't acknowledge her.

"What's it gonna be, Ace," he said to Stefano. "Head on or off?"

Stefano stepped out into the hallway, lowered his gun to the floor and held his hands up. "Good choice," Tony said, releasing Kristen and pushing her toward Stefano. He nodded his head at Angel. "Get the gun, babe," and then turned his eyes back to Stefano. "Lead the way."

Stefano was breathing hard. "How do we know you're not just going to kill Sophia and us?"

"Sophia's my mother," Angel said. "And she was kidnapped."

"Yeah, by Frank Vilachi, I know. I was there." Stefano grimaced.

"Vilachi?" Tony shook his head. "No way Frank Vilachi pulled this off by himself."

"Who's Frank Vilachi?" Angel asked.

"A big fat nobody, that's who," said Tony. "They call him 'Crazy Frankie' and he's a real loser."

"How do I know you two don't work for Vilachi and you're just pretending Sophia is your mother?" Stefano asked.

"If I worked for Vilachi you'd already be dead." Tony didn't miss a beat, "Now start walking."

"How do I know you're not lying?" Stefano's face turned red and Angel saw fear behind his eyes. She felt sorry for him and tried to think of a way to convince him that they were on the same side. "I can prove it to you. I'm assuming Kristen is the one who made the call to the Compare, right?"

"Yeah," Kristen sheepishly answered.

"I know the password for the Compare," Angel said and Kristen stared at her. "The password is…"

"Clint," came his voice from behind her, cutting her sentence short. Angel whirled around and stood face-to-face with Frank Vilachi and two large men with guns. "Well, well, well," a sinister grin slid across his lips. "If this isn't convenient." He chuckled as his men removed Tony's gun, stripped Angel of her 9mm and Stefano's .38 she had picked up from the floor. "Stefano here will take us to Sophia and I'll not only get to kill the three of you, but I'll get to deliver the mother and daughter together."

"Deliver them to who?" Tony blurted.

Frank laughed. "Didn't my men already try to kill you once this week? I'll make sure we finish the job this time." Frank and his men pushed them down the hall and through the stairwell door. Angel wanted to look over her shoulder and see if Andrew was anywhere in sight, but she was too afraid it would be obvious that she was looking for someone. He could be their only chance of survival, and if he was there, she didn't want to risk giving away his location. She bit her lip and inched her way closer to Tony.

"Stop here," Frank ordered. "Now, let me see, normally I'd start by killing the traitor in the group." He placed the barrel of a .38 against Stefano's forehead. "But since we have a new member, I think it only fair that I introduce myself properly." He grabbed Kristen around the throat and pulled her away from the rest of them. Kristen cried out and Angel could see her hands trembling. Frank grabbed her blonde ponytail and pulled her head back. He rammed his tongue into her mouth, brutally forcing a French kiss. Kristen's body convulsed as she cried and tried to twist her face away.

Stefano leapt forward but Tony grabbed him back as Frank's men raised their guns and took aim. "You son of a bitch," Stefano yelled and it echoed up the stairwell.

Frank dropped Kristen to the floor in front of him and petted her hair like a dog. "Women like Sophia and Michelangela and this pretty little one here," he stroked Kristen's face, "just need to be put in their proper place."

Anger burned in Angel's stomach and all the way down to her toes. She wanted to leap on top of Frank and claw his eyeballs out with her fingernails. She could only imagine how Stefano was feeling. His face was bright red and his hands were clenched into fists. Angel looked at Tony, searching for some sort of reassurance that they would live through this moment, but Tony never took his eyes from Frank and he appeared eerily calm. His eyes were set so firmly on Frank that Angel thought lasers might shoot out and zap Frank's head right off.

"You kill us all here and you'll never get out of the building alive," Tony said to Frank. "This place is crawling with cops and brotherhood."

Frank's smile broadened. "We own most of the men here, but thank you for your concern." He placed the barrel of his .38 against Kristen's temple and stared at Stefano. "Now take me to Sophia."

Stefano's voice cracked, "She's one floor up."

Stefano led the way up the stairs, followed by Tony, then Angel, then Frank and Kristen and Frank's two armed thugs. Angel glanced up the stairway between the railings and thought she saw someone peeking over the railing. She did a quick double-take but whoever it was had disappeared. They rounded the first flight of stairs when the whirling sound of bullets through a silencer sent everything into slow motion. Someone was shooting between the railings from the stairwell above. Stefano dove to the right, toward the wall, and Tony pushed Angel to the floor atop Stefano. One of Frank's men took a bullet through the forehead and fell backwards on the landing. Blood and pieces of brain splattered on the wall. The other thug took a bullet in the throat and sputtered to his knees, trying to speak, but falling face forward and spewing blood all over the staircase and railing. Kristen's shrill scream echoed through the stairwell as Tony scrambled to grab a weapon. Frank pulled Kristen in front of him and used her as a shield as he began to back down the stairs. Tony took aim.

"Let him go!" Stefano yelled to Tony. "You'll hit Kristen."

Tony's hand was steady and his jaw, tight and Angel stood breathless as the intensity in Tony's eyes deepened. "I'm gonna give you one chance, Frank. Tell me who you're working for."

Frank chuckled insanely, "Go to hell. I work for myself."

Tony took one step closer. "Last chance Frank."

"If you shoot me, I'll shoot her," he seethed, digging the gun into Kristen's jawbone.

"Please don't kill me," Kristen sobbed. "I don't want to die. I don't want to die."

"Don't shoot her," Stefano wailed.

Tony spoke to Stefano but never took his eyes off Frank. "If I let him walk out with her, she's as good as dead." Before Stefano could respond

Tony pulled the trigger and sent a bullet right through the middle of Frank's forehead. He dropped like a wet sack, pulling Kristen down on top of him. Kristen screamed, scrambling away from Frank and curling into a fetal position in the corner. Without hesitation Angel dashed down the steps, trying not to look at the gaping hole in Frank's forehead or the pool of blood filling up the landing. She leapt over his legs, grabbed the gun that had fallen next to him and put her arms around Kristen.

"It's over," she whispered. "You're alive and Stefano's alive and it's over now."

Kristen clung to Angel, shaking uncontrollably in her arms and sobbing out incoherencies. Angel knew the feeling all too well. It was shock, terror and relief flooding the body all at once.

Tony yelled down, "Babe, we gotta go. Now!"

Angel helped Kristen to her feet, though her knees were wobbling. "Don't look at him. Don't look at any of them," she told Kristen as they stepped over Frank's legs and inched passed the thugs. "Look up at Stefano," she said. "Keep your eyes on him."

Stefano was on his knees at the top of the staircase in what appeared to be a state of shock. His eyes were glassed over and his mouth half-opened. Tony grabbed him and pulled him to his feet, slamming his back against the wall. "Look in my eyes," Tony yelled just a few inches from his face. "Focus on what I'm telling you. If we don't get out of here right now, we're all dead." Tony grabbed Stefano's face. "Do you want to be the next body at the bottom of these steps?" Stefano moved his eyes to meet Tony's stare. "Do you get what I'm telling you, Ace?" Stefano swallowed and nodded his head. "Get moving, all the way to the top, straight up."

"What about Andrew?" Angel asked.

"He'll catch up."

"Tony," Angel wailed. "What about my mom?" Tony stopped and stared at Angel and she could see his mind calculating options. "We can't leave her here," Angel pleaded.

"Damnit," Tony exhaled, then ran down the steps and picked up two more guns. He handed Angel's 9mm to Kristen and grabbed a .38 for Stefano. Angel was already holding Frank's gun. Kristen's hand shook uncontrollably against the gun. He grabbed Angel around the waist and pulled her close. "Listen, babe, we have to split up if we're gonna try to get your mom out too." Angel nodded. "You take Kristen to the chopper and have Chase fly you to the Towers. Then send him back for us." Angel opened her mouth to argue, but Tony kept talking. "If anyone confronts you, anyone at all, you shoot." Angel nodded but deep down she feared she would not be able to pull the trigger.

Tony and Stefano disappeared through the second-floor door and Angel and Kristen dashed up the steps just as the police entered the stairwell and found the bodies of Frank and his two thugs.

"Holy Mary, Mother of ...." an officer blurted and another one cut him off.

"Get Detective Venturini over here. He's got to see this."

CHAPTER NINETEEN

Angel and Kristen dashed up the stairs as quickly and quietly as possible. They could hear voices in the stairwell, drifting up from below, as the police tried to ascertain motive and decipher what had happened. Angel motioned for Kristen to stop running while she strained to listen.

"This was a frickin' blood bath," one cop said.

"This is how the mob bathes," another responded. "Real pretty lifestyle, ain't it?"

"Where's Venturini? Anyone reach him yet?" A general grumbling indicated no one had seen him. "Don't move anything until he sees this."

"Can we at least pull ID's so we know what bogata we're dealing with?"

"Go ahead but keep them here for Detective Venturini to inspect."

Angel exhaled and motioned for Kristen to continue moving up the stairs. *Where is Andrew?* She wondered. *Why hasn't anyone seen him?* Angel's mind was whirling with questions. *Who shot Frank's thugs? Was it Andrew? Was it the same person who killed Frank's men in the parking lot? How did Frank know the code word for the Compare? He either intercepted the call himself, which would mean he was somehow linked to Venito Barone all along; or someone told him.* The second option shot fear up her spine. There were only a few people who knew that code and they were all very close to Angel.

As they approached the door to the roof, Angel grabbed Kristen's arm and put her fingers to her lips to indicate they should be quiet. She placed her ear against the door and listened. She couldn't hear the whirling sound of helicopter blades, which she surmised meant Chase and Dane hadn't made their way to the chopper yet. Angel pushed the door open just a crack and peered through. She didn't see anyone, but fear kept her from pushing it all the way and walking out into the open.

"Why aren't we going to the chopper?" Kristen whispered.

"The pilot's not there yet," Angel whispered back.

They heard a door open a couple flights down and then slowly shut with a click. There were no voices but a faint scuffle of footsteps and Angel couldn't tell if the person was walking up the stairs toward them or down. Whoever it was, they were trying to be very quiet. Angel's heart beat rapidly against her chest and she reminded herself to breathe slowly. *Stay calm,* she told herself, but her palms were already getting clammy. She gripped the .38 a little tighter and moved toward the railing, motioning for Kristen to stay put. Angel peeked over the top of the railing, but she didn't see anyone on the stairs.

There was another scuffle sound and Angel's stomach somersaulted. She turned and motioned for Kristen to open the rooftop door. Kristen grabbed the handle and leaned against the

door just as it was yanked open from the outside
and she fell flat against the rooftop. Angel looked
up in time to see a man's arm draw back and a
canister of tear gas hurl through the air toward
her. She dove forward as it clanged against the
wall behind her and rolled across the landing,
spewing out tear gas. She dove for the door,
slamming her elbows and knees against the
concrete, but he had already closed it. Despite
how she fought to keep them open, her eyes
clamped shut from the burning. Through the door
she heard Kristen scream and then several rapid
gun shots.

Angel scrambled to her knees and tried to
find the handle to open the rooftop door but the
tear gas rendered her eyes inoperable. She tried to
call out, but the stinging in her throat strangled
her. Still clutching the .38 in her right hand, Angel
banged it against the door until the burning in her
lungs caused her to slide back to the floor and
gasp for air. She could hear the whirling of the
helicopter blades from outside and footsteps of
someone approaching from the stairs below; but
she was powerless to escape. Tears and mucus
covered her face as she lay flat on her belly, at the
mercy of whoever was coming up the stairs. All of
a sudden she felt his arms around her mid-section
as he lifted her off the landing in one quick motion
and carried her through the rooftop door. The cool
air hit her skin and began to soothe the burning.
Her head landed on Kristen's lap as he tossed her
into the back of the helicopter.

"Take her up," he yelled to the pilot with a deep voice that Angel recognized, and then he pounded two times against the side of the chopper.

Once in the air, Angel's vision began to clear and she could see Chase was flying the chopper. "Are you okay?" Kristen hollered. Angel sat upright and nodded, trying to clear her throat, but her mouth was void of all saliva. Mucus poured from her nose and she wiped it on the bottom of her t-shirt.

When they arrived at the Towers, Angel jumped out and made a beeline for the kitchen, sticking her face under the cold running water, flushing her eyes and letting the water run into her mouth and down her throat. The stinging was beginning to subside. After she dried off with a clean dish towel, she joined Chase and Kristen in the foyer. They were discussing the man who had rescued them.

"He was the biggest dude I've ever seen," Chase said. "I'm talking big-ass mammoth type dude." Chase flexed his arms outward to indicate someone huge. "He came out of nowhere, man. It was like he just appeared there, carrying you like a suitcase."

Kristen nodded, "He was huge. He carried you like you only weighed a pound."

Chase's eyes grew wider, "I wonder who he is."

"Whoever he is, he saved us," Kristen said.

"YOU saved yourself," Chase blurted. "That was some wild-ass shooting you did."

Angel looked at Kristen. "You shot someone?"

Kristen raised her shoulders and held up her hands. "Tony said if anyone confronted us we should shoot them."

"She didn't just shoot him," Chase shook his head. "She loaded that mother with six rounds of lead." Chase used his hands to imitate Kristen holding the gun. "She was all wild-ass screaming and ran right at him. Bam. Bam. Bam. Bam. Bam. Bam!" Chase grinned. "It was hot."

Angel's eyes were wide with disbelief. She couldn't believe Kristen, who not even twenty minutes ago was in fetal position, trembling in the corner, actually aggressively shot someone. *It must have been a fear-driven adrenaline rush from all the stress,* Angel thought. "Who was he? Who did you shoot?"

"He was the dude who threw the tear gas into the stairwell. I don't know who he was, but he wasn't one of our guys," Chase explained.

"How did he know we were in the stairwell?" Angel asked.

Chase shrugged. "Dunno, but he did NOT know who he was messing with." Chase grinned and gave Kristen a playful punch on the arm, then mimicked her screaming and firing rapid shots into the guy. "You were like Annie Oakley meets Rambo up there. It was awesome!"

Angel rolled her eyes. Deep down a part of her felt intimidated, insecure and even a little jealous. *How can SHE, with not an ounce of mafia blood in her veins, shoot someone and I can't?* The truth was Angel didn't know if she had it in her to pull the trigger and take someone's life. She wanted to believe that, in a life-or-death situation, she could do it; but there was this underlying fear that she could not. Andrew's warnings played in her head. "If you hesitate on the trigger, you die," he told her. *If Kristen didn't hesitate than surely I won't either,* her mind rationalized but her heart wasn't buying it. She wanted to believe that she had the strength to do whatever the situation called for at the appropriate time; but insecurity robbed her of any confidence.

Chase left to take the chopper back to the hospital and Angel took Kristen into the family room to meet Giovanni, who was resting in the armchair by the fireplace.

"Grandfather." Angel kissed his cheek, "Has Olga awakened yet?"

"No, the house is still peaceful," he said with a smirking twinge of humor.

"Did you learn anything from Dr. Manzini?"

"Only that he was contacted by Frank Vilachi and instructed to keep Olga until further notice. My men are locating Vilachi now."

"That won't be necessary." Angel took a deep breath and sat down on the couch, exhaling the stress of the morning. She motioned for Kristen to sit next to her, but Kristen lowered her eyes and shook her head no. *She's afraid to meet Giovanni but she can shoot a stranger six times,* Angel thought, *that's ironic.*

Angel filled Giovanni in on all that took place at the hospital. She told him how Tony killed Frank and how a mystery shooter killed Franks thugs in the parking lot and again on the stairs. "I think our mystery shooter is the Shark," Angel said.

Giovanni raised his eyebrows and tightened his lips. "The Shark has failed to check in with me."

"I have a hunch he was the one who pulled me out of the tear gas and took me downstairs the other night, and the one who saved us in the stairwell and again on the roof."

"If this is true, why would he not respond to my order to check in?" Angel could see the anger on Giovanni's face, as his jowls grew tighter. He did not like disobedience. "There has never been so much mistrust and disloyalty." He pounded his fist on the arm of the chair and Kristen gasped, drawing Giovanni's attention. "Who is this woman lurking near my chair?" Giovanni pointed in her direction.

"This is Kristen. She helped my mom escape and she probably saved my life on the roof today."

"Come, sit," he motioned Kristen toward the couch and by the look on her face Angel surmised she was almost immobilized with fear. Kristen inched her way to the couch and sat next to Angel. Her hands were shaking. "Do you know who I am?" Giovanni interrogated her with his eyes.

Kristen shook her head no and cowered, "But I've seen the Godfather movies and you seem pretty high up in the ranks." This made Giovanni chuckle out loud.

"What is your family name?" He asked.

"My last name is Warren," Kristen's voice quivered. "My family isn't in the mafia. We're just farmers in Iowa."

"How did you become involved in this conflict?" Giovanni positioned his elbows on the arms of the chair and pressed his fingers together in front of him.

"My boyfriend worked for that Frank guy, but he didn't know Frank was bad. He just needed money to buy me an engagement ring and..." Kristen's voice cracked and tears flowed freely down her cheeks. "I don't know who I can trust..." her voice was cut short by emotion.

This struck an all too familiar chord with Angel and she reached over and squeezed Kristen's hand. A couple of weeks ago Angel had been in the same boat, wondering who, if anyone, she could trust. In many ways, she still felt she had to analyze everyone's motives and scrutinize every action. It was a horrible feeling. Not knowing who you can trust is a mentally exhausting, emotionally draining existence, and Angel knew the feeling all too well. "I promise you," Angel said. "You can trust us."

"But you're Mafia, right?"

Angel stared blankly, unable to answer the question. How could she explain something she scarcely understood herself? How could she say yes we're Mafia but we're the good guys when there was plenty of evidence throughout history to indicate otherwise? She bit her lip and looked at Giovanni.

"We are a family," Giovanni answered, "a bogata."

"But you kill people, right?"

"Bah," Giovanni waved his hand in front of his face. "We protect that and those which we consider our own."

"And we consider you and Stefano to be our own," Angel piped in, "since you helped Sophia escape."

"Stefano," Giovanni repeated. "Is your boyfriend of Italian descent?"

Kristen nodded, "Yes, but he's not mafia."

"What is Stefano's last name?"

"Carlachi."

Giovanni leaned his head back and repeated the name, "Carlachi. Carlachi. I knew a Carlachi family many years ago in New York." He inhaled through his nose and cut his eyes to Angel with a glance that spoke volumes. His eyes told her that he doubted Stefano's interaction with Frank Vilachi was merely coincidental. "Where is your boyfriend, Stefano, now?" Giovanni asked.

Angel piped in, "He's with Tony. He said he knew where my mom was hiding."

Giovanni directed his attention back to Kristen. "Did he know Sophia's location?"

Kristen nodded. "Yes, she was in a small storage room on the second floor. Stefano and I came down to the first floor to steal some hospital scrubs and find a gurney. That's when we ran into you and Tony."

"Why did you need a gurney?" Giovanni questioned.

"Sophia was worried her limp would be obvious to Frank's men."

"Is she limping badly?" Angel asked.

Kristen shivered. "Frank stabbed a pretty big hole in her thigh and she's in a lot of pain."

Angel grew angrier. Even though she already knew about the stab wound, it bothered her to hear that her mom was in pain.

Giovanni sat quiet for a moment, and then spoke with a very deliberate tone. "You are not to contact your family or Stefano's family until this conflict is resolved. Do you understand?"

"Yes," Kristen answered, wiping tears on the back of her hand. "Sophia told me I would put my family in danger if I contacted them."

"Good," he nodded. "You are a smart girl to listen to Sophia. You will stay here under my protection until it is safe for you to return home. Michelangela, take her to your room to rest while we go over some business."

She led Kristen to her bedroom, gave her a change of clothes and then returned to the family room. "Kristen is going to take a hot shower and lay down for a while," she said, sitting down on the couch across from Giovanni.

Giovanni exhaled slowly and pursed his lips. "The Carlachi family has been around for many generations. They are mid-tier, working mainly with the Cullato clan of New York. Though they are small, they are powerful and not to be dismissed. Back in the day when Moloney was trying to make a name for himself, he teamed up with the Carlachis."

Angel listened with wide-eyed anticipation of what Giovanni would say next.

"They dabbled primarily in small weapons and drug trafficking." Giovanni rubbed his fingers down his jowls and around his chin. "When Moloney stole from our heroin shipment, attempting to pit Salvatore and myself against one another, it was with the assistance of three men. Finnegan. Selovich. And Michael Carlachi.

"I read about this on the internet and it said that Moloney, Finnegan and Selovich were all murdered, but there was no mention of Carlachi."

Giovanni nodded. "Carlachi was not killed because the Cullatos backed his innocence. We let him live as a gesture of peace among our bogatas."

"But?" Angel narrowed her eyes, "There has to be a but or it lacks relevance."

"BUT," Giovanni over-emphasized the word by bulging his eyes, "we put Carlachi out of business and drove his family out of New York."

"And there's the but," Angel sighed. "Giving the Carlachi family motive for revenge."

"Si."

Angel stood and paced in front of the fireplace. "I just have one question." She faced Giovanni and crossed her arms. "Is there anyone from the past that doesn't hate us?"

"Power and popularity do not often dwell together."

"I'm beginning to see that," Angel grimaced and pulled out her cell phone. She was hoping to see a text message, but there was nothing.

"Grandfather, have you heard from Andrew?"

"He was supposed to be keeping his eyes on you," Giovanni gruffed. "No, I have not heard from Andrew, but I have spoken to Salvatore Buscetta personally this morning."

"What did he say? Is he coming here? Does he know Sophia escaped and we're trying to find her? Does he know we have Olga back?" Her questions came rapid fire and Giovanni held his hand up, signaling her to stop.

"Breathe, Michelangela." Giovanni grinned. "You have your father's tenacity." He then cleared his throat and said, "I spoke to Salvatore about our theory on Moloney and his followers." Giovanni took a breath and Angel fought the urge to scream, *Spit it out! You're talking too slowly! You're making me crazy!* "He is working on some leads in Sicily but believes he has found the identity of the person orchestrating this charade."

Angel's eyes widened with wonder. "Who is it?"

"Moloney's son. A man named Sean Michael Denarius Moloney. We are not certain of his location or involvement yet." Giovanni hung his head, "But it seems the past is once again tormenting our present."

I knew it! Angel silently chanted to herself. *I knew this was linked to Moloney!* She tried not to outwardly gloat though she was giving herself an inward pat on the back. "So, what's our next move?"

"To get Sophia returned safely. Salvatore is holding me personally responsible for her well-being." Giovanni made the sign of the cross over his body. "Il Dio mio," he exhaled.

"Why is he holding you responsible? You didn't kidnap her." Angel's temper flared. "That doesn't seem right."

"Let's just say Salvatore is sensitive with the topic of his daughter and our family. He will be with us tomorrow evening and for everyone's sake Sophia better be present and unharmed."

All of a sudden one of Giovanni's men rushed from the hallway into the family room. His face was flushed and he appeared flustered. "Giovanni, sir," he paused as if trying to find the right words, "Lucia is…" but he was interrupted.

"Get out of my way!" She snapped. "Merciful Heavens, why are all these gorillas in my hall!" Olga stormed down the hall and into the foyer with her hands on her hips.

"Aunt Olga," Angel jumped up and ran to her, throwing her arms around her neck and squeezing tight. "I was so worried about you."

"What are you blubbering about child?" Olga scanned the room until her eyes landed on Giovanni. "Humph, what the devil is HE doing here?"

"Speaking of the devil," Giovanni muttered.

"I'm not the devil you old goat, you are!"

"Lucia…" Giovanni began but Olga was off on a rant.

"I don't care if you are the Cappo di Tutti Capi, you don't scare me one iota," Olga snorted and then grabbed her stomach with both hands. "Merciful Heavens, I'm starving. How long have I been sleeping? When was the last time we ate something?"

"Aunt Olga, don't you remember what happened?" Angel asked.

Olga stopped on the way to the kitchen and narrowed her brows as if she were trying to force a memory. "I don't remember where, when or what I last ate," she put her index finger to her face, "but it must have been something sticky because I've gotten it all over my face." Olga didn't realize that the stickiness was from the duct tape that had been on her mouth. She waddled into the kitchen and Angel turned to Giovanni with surprise.

"Do you think she honestly doesn't remember being kidnapped?" Angel sat back down on the couch, "I mean, could they have had her sedated the whole time?"

Giovanni's eyes twinkled, "If I were going to kidnap her, I'd surely keep her sedated." He grinned and pointed to his forehead, "That tells me we're dealing with someone with smarts."

CHAPTER TWENTY

Angel sat at the dining room table with Olga and Giovanni and chewed on her thumb nail. The waiting was driving her mad. She had text Andrew three times but never received a response. She tried Tony twice but he hadn't responded either and she didn't have Chase's cell number in her phone. Olga opened the fridge and pulled out two left-over Cannoli and cheesecake that she had baked prior to being kidnapped. Angel and Olga sipped coffee while Giovanni nursed a cup of hot tea.

Two of Giovanni's men stood guard at the front door and Olga turned around and gawked at them. "Merciful Heavens," she shook her head, "I feel like a prisoner, under lock and key."

Giovanni cleared his throat, "You can leave anytime you'd like." He raised his cup and gave her a wink of sarcasm and Angel giggled.

"Oh, you think he's funny, do you, Missy?" Olga shook her finger at Angel, then picked up her spoon and chucked it across the table at Giovanni.

"Omigod," Angel's mouth fell open. "Did you just hurl your spoon at him?"

"I don't know what you're talking about," Olga grinned and feigned innocence.

Giovanni picked up the spoon and with a quick flip of his wrist, he sent it airborne and bounced it off Olga's forehead.

"Merciful Heavens!" Olga exclaimed and rubbed her head, scowling at Giovanni. "Lucky shot."

"I was always the best shot," Giovanni said to Angel. "Your aunt here could not hit the broad side of a barn."

"You were good but you weren't great."

"Bah," Giovanni waved his hand in front of his face. "You refuse to see greatness."

"After all these years you're still a pompous ass."

Angel scooted her chair back from the table and stared at the two of them. "You're like two little kids."

"She started it," Giovanni taunted and pointed his finger at Olga, who grabbed the spoon and raised her arm to chuck it at him again; but Angel intervened.

"Give me that!" She took the spoon from Olga and huffed off into the kitchen, mumbling under breath. She returned a moment later with two white plastic spoons. "There," she said, setting a spoon in front of each of them. "When you learn to play nice you can have real utensils again."

They began bantering in Italian and Angel rolled her eyes, grabbed her cup of coffee from the table and stepped out onto the patio. The air was crisp but the sun warmed her skin. She plunked down in a patio chair, pulled her cell phone from her pocket and checked text messages again. Nothing. Neither Tony nor Andrew had made contact, and that was beginning to worry her.

Angel leapt to her feet when she heard the whirling of helicopter blades overhead. "They're here!" She yelled inside and Giovanni's men came running with guns drawn.

First out of the chopper was Dane. He was built like a brick house and the name Great Dane was fitting. His size and stature were certainly great. He reached into the chopper and lifted Sophia from the back. Angel gasped at the sight of her mother. She looked small in Dane's arms and frail. Stefano climbed out the other door and ran toward Angel.

"Where's Kristen?"

Angel never took her eyes off her mother, but pointed toward the patio door and mouthed, "My bedroom." Stefano ran inside and found his way to Angel's bedroom while Dane carried Sophia into the family room and set her on the couch. Then he and Chase flew back to the hospital.

"Mom," Angel gasped, and she couldn't hold back the flood of emotion. She knelt in front of Sophia and hugged her, sobbing uncontrollably.

"I'm so sorry, baby," Sophia cried. "I'm sorry for everything."

"I never got your letters," Angel sobbed. "I never knew you tried to contact me."

Sophia stroked Angel's hair. "I know baby, Tony told me about your father's Compare and about Venito Barone. He told me everything." She wrapped her arms around Angel and kissed her on top her head. "I've missed you so much and longed for this moment."

"Me too," Angel whispered and a rush of joy engulfed her. She was with her mom again, something she was afraid would never happen. All the unknowns that once hindered their relationship vanished as Angel came to understand the sacrifices Sophia had made through the years to protect her. Her mother loved her and that's all that mattered at the moment.

Sophia held Angel's face in her hands and looked in her eyes. "I never wanted this lifestyle for you. I wanted to protect you from it. You understand that right?"

Angel nodded. "I know, mom, but no matter what lifestyle we have, we're better together."

"Sophia inhaled a deep breath, "I should have trusted you to be strong enough to handle the truth."

Angel wiped away the tears that dripped from her chin. "It's okay now," she smiled. "Everything is going to be okay now."

Olga waddled over from the dining room. "Don't I get some lovin' too?"

A big grin filled Sophia's face. "Lucia," she caught herself, "I mean, Olga." Sophia stretched out her arms and squeezed Olga tightly. "Thank you for taking such good care of my Angel," she muttered through tears.

"Merciful Heavens," Olga chuckled and pointed at Angel, "this one here can take care of herself, that's for sure." She patted Angel's cheek, "She's got her mama's beauty, her father's strength and," she made the sign of the cross over her body, "God help us, her grandfather's stubbornness."

Sophia's expression grew more serious at the mention of Giovanni. "Are you and Giovanni on speaking terms?"

"Against my better judgment," Olga rolled her eyes, "but someone, and I won't mention any names," she pointed to Angel, "brought him into our lives and now we can't get the old coot out."

"Where is he?" Sophia asked, "I need to speak with him. It's urgent."

Angel started to get off the couch to find Giovanni, but Olga stopped her. "You stay here with your mama," she said, pushing Angel back down. "I'll get him." She looked over her shoulder as she walked across the family room. "Merciful Heavens, what a blessed reunion this is," she clapped her hands together. "I'm gonna make a big batch of Cannoli to celebrate."

Olga waddled off and Sophia laughed. "She hasn't changed a bit in eleven years."

"She's a handful alright," Angel laughed.

"Does she still drive big brown Bessie?"

"Yes!" They both laughed.

Sophia patted Angel's leg, "Olga hasn't changed, but you sure have. My girl has become a woman."

Angel sighed. *A woman who still feels as lost as a little girl,* she thought.

"Any men in your life?" Sophia asked.

Angel shook her head. "Not really. Not anymore."

"What about that Tony? He's a real looker," Sophia wrinkled her nose when she smiled.

"Tony's the 'not anymore' I was talking about."

Giovanni entered the room and interrupted their conversation. "Sophia, È buono da vederlo.

Sono felice che siete illeso." He kissed her hand and then sat in the armchair across from them.

"Grazie per tutti che abbiate fatto per proteggere me ed il mio angelo. Sono obbligato a voi," Sophia said.

"Siete famiglia," Giovanni nodded.

Angel cleared her throat as loud and obnoxiously as she could and they both stared at her. "Oh, pardon me," she said, "was that rude?" She put her finger to her chin, tilted her head and scrunched up her nose. "Was that as rude as talking in Italian in front of someone who doesn't speak the language?" She pursed her lips and threw up her hands.

Sophia's eyes widened. Angel guessed her mother was probably amazed that she copped an attitude with the Cappo di Tutti Capi. After all, to Sophia he was a dangerous force that commanded respect, but to Angel he was a grandfather who, despite his power, loved her.

Giovanni rubbed his forehead, "Il Dio mio," he sighed. "I told her I was happy she was safe and unharmed."

Sophia joined in, "And I thanked him for protecting you and told him I was indebted to him."

"Bah, there is no debt," Giovanni waved his hand, "we are family."

"Wow," Angel sat back and crossed her arms, "it sounded more interesting in Italian."

Giovanni called for one of his men to come over. "Get me Dr. Manzini to inspect Sophia's wound and find me an Italian instructor for Michelangela."

Sophia kept her leg propped on the coffee table but sat up a little straighter. "Before the doctor arrives, I need to speak with you." She told Giovanni about her husband.

"You were re-married?" Angel couldn't believe it. It was like her mother had a whole separate life the past eleven years. A life without her.

"Frank Vilachi showed me a picture of my sweet Denny, bound and gagged, lying on a concrete floor..." her sentence broke with emotion. "I have no idea where they took him or what they've done to him." Tears flood her face and she looked to Giovanni. "Will you send some of your men to find him? Please?"

"Where was the last place you saw him?" Giovanni asked, concern and anger igniting his eyes.

"At our home in Clearfield, Iowa. It's a small ranch-style house. I went outside to work in the garden when Frank's men came." Sophia's voice cracked, "It all happened so fast."

Giovanni rested his elbows on the arms of the chair and pressed his fingertips together. Angel noted this was a position he often took when he was deeply concentrating on what was being said. "You said Frank showed you a picture?" Sophia nodded. "How much time passed between the time you were taken and you saw the picture?"

Sophia tried to remember. "I'm not sure. I was in a basement and it was dark. Maybe a couple hours?"

"When Frank's men kidnapped you, did they transport you by car or helicopter?"

"Car," she said with certainty. "I never heard a helicopter."

Giovanni inhaled and exhaled slowly. "Then for now we will assume that your husband was transported the same way and begin our search in proximity to your home in Clearfield."

Tears ran down her face and Sophia tried to control the quivering of her lip. "Giovanni, my husband doesn't know who I am," she said quickly as if confessing to something awful. Sophia wiped her tears with her fingers and met Giovanni's eyes. "He doesn't know who I really am."

"Si," Giovanni nodded, "I will take care of it. When we retrieve him safely, you will be the one to explain your identity."

"Grazie," she whispered.

Angel leaned over and hugged her mother. "We'll find him, mom, don't worry."

Dr. Manzini was brought from the apartment below to look at Sophia's stab wound. "It's infected," he blurted. "She needs antibiotics."

"Then you will call in a prescription for her," Giovanni told him. Manzini glared at him and clenched his jaw. "Allow me to be clear Dr. Manzini, your only asset is the medical attention you offer. If you are no longer an asset I will have you removed."

Everyone in the room knew what removed meant. It meant he would join Hoffa somewhere, buried deep in concrete or swimming with the fishes. Manzini softened. "I will gladly call in a script for an antibiotic and a pain killer." He made the call and then Giovanni's men escorted him back to the apartment below.

"Grandfather, what will you do with him?" Angel asked.

"That will be determined later," Giovanni answered in a tone that let Angel know this was a topic he was unwilling to discuss.

Angel helped Sophia settle into the guest room to rest while Giovanni's men left to pick up Sophia's prescription and, against Olga's wishes, bring in food for everyone. When Olga learned food was being brought in, she waddled over to Giovanni, with her hands on her hips and a scowl on her face. "What's the matter with my cooking?" She demanded.

The corners of his mouth turned up slightly, as if he were trying to hide a smile. "I do not have time to answer that question. The list is extensive."

She shook her finger at him and huffed back to the kitchen.

Angel shook her head, "Why do you intentionally taunt her?"

Giovanni could no longer hold back a smile. "Non so," he said in Italian. "It brings me pleasure."

Giovanni placed a call to Salvatore and informed him that Sophia was safe and would remain under his protection until Salvatore arrived. Salvatore expressed gratitude and offered his men to assist with the search for Moloney's son.

"Upon your arrival we will hold a meeting and discuss search tactics. I have brought two families in to help us," Giovanni told him.

When he got off the phone Angel asked, "What did he say?"

"He is not pleased by my decision to bring in the Andriachinis and Venturinis to assist us."

"Why?"

"Salvatore Buscetta is not a man who lends himself to trust other men."

"Yes, but did you explain to him that we are shorthanded because of the FBI busts in New York and..."

Giovanni held his hand up and Angel stopped mid-sentence. "Salvatore is not interested in my excuses."

"He sounds like a real nice guy," Angel mumbled sarcastically under her breath.

"Salvatore is a decent man. He is a man of little tolerance for error and thus, his organization does not have the problems with traitors that we have here in the States."

"Why?"

Giovanni's face hardened. "Because he tolerates no disloyalty and is not swayed by compassion or excuses."

"Yeah, he even disowned his own daughter because she fell in love with someone outside the family." Angel rolled her eyes. "Real nice guy. Can't wait to meet him."

"Michelangela," Giovanni leaned forward and tightened his lip and she could feel his eyes pierce through her. "You do not have to like him but you will show him respect. Capisce?"

Angel lowered her head. "Capisce."

"Good. Now, we move on from this." Giovanni leaned back in the chair.

They sat in silence for a moment, and then Angel asked, "Did Finnegan have a son?"

"I do not recollect," Giovanni answered. "Why do you ask?"

"Well, Moloney has a son that we think is involved. Selovich had a son that Andrew killed on the hospital roof, that we know was involved. I just wondered if there was another player; somebody from Finnegan's family?"

Giovanni looked at her with a sparkle in his eye. "You are a thinker, just like your father. He was always thinking one step beyond everyone else."

"I bet Andrew can get that information," she said and the words caught in her throat. *Where is Andrew? Why isn't he answering my texts?* Her thoughts bounced from concern to frustration to anger and back to concern again. *Mom said Tony explained everything to her, so why didn't Tony come back on the chopper with Dane and Chase?* She had to stop the questions from controlling her thoughts, or it would drive her crazy. She had to force herself to think about something else.

"Michelangela, I would like to have a meeting with this Stefano," Giovanni said.

Angel's eyes widened, "You're not going to hurt him are you?"

"I want to know who put him in contact with Frank Vilachi. I believe Stefano's actions were misguided by the ignorance of his youth, and that is something I am willing to overlook, if he will tell me who sent him to Frank for a job in the first place."

"Do you think the Carlachi family is working with Moloney?"

Giovanni's eyes grew dark. "I think there are very few coincidences in this world."

Giovanni's cell buzzed and he held up his finger for Angel to wait. When he disconnected the call he said, "That was Andrew. He and Tony are coming back by car, driving your vehicle and Andrew's vehicle. They are stopping to pick up your cats and will be here shortly. We will belay my talk with Stefano until later."

Angel rolled her eyes. "Why hasn't Andrew responded to my texts? Why did he call you instead of me?" She stomped her foot and crossed her arms, scowling at Giovanni.

"Now who is acting like a child?" Giovanni grinned.

Angel grunted and huffed off to her bedroom. She opened the door and peeked in, hoping she wasn't disturbing Stefano and Kristen. They were snuggled up like spoons on the top of her bedspread. Stefano had his arms wrapped around her and their fingers on both hands were interlaced. They were such a cute couple and Angel hoped Giovanni would go easy on them. After what they went through this morning, a brutal interrogation was the last thing Stefano needed.

Angel took an extra comforter from the top of her closet and draped it over them. Then she slipped into a clean t-shirt, one not filled with mucus, grabbed her laptop and headed for the patio. She decided she didn't need to wait for Andrew to look up whether or not Finnegan had living relatives. She could search online without him.

She Googled the Moloney clan and then clicked on the highlighted name Finnegan. Not having a first name or initial to go on made the search more cumbersome, but she finally narrowed it down to the right Finnegan. He had two sons. The oldest was ten when he died and the youngest was eight. That would mean they were both in their fifties now.

She jumped up and carried her laptop inside when she heard the helicopter approaching. The air was brisk as it was, but downright cold with the chopper blades blowing it around at high speeds. Angel set her laptop on the dining room table and continued reading about Finnegan. Chase and Dane walked inside. "We're gonna need to fuel her up soon if we want to take more trips," Chase commented to anyone who might be listening, but no one responded. He looked at Angel, "Where's Annie Oakley?"

"She's lying down with her boyfriend."

"Story of my life," Chase pouted, "another perfect woman out of reach."

Andrew and Tony came through the front door. They talked to Chase, Dane and Giovanni, and even Olga came from the kitchen to greet them; but Angel never looked up from her laptop. She was too angry at them, especially at Andrew. When Tony finally walked over she glanced up at him and saw that his arm was in a dark blue and white sling. "Is that a new injury or a precautionary sling from the previous gunshot?"

"Precautionary," Tony sank down into the chair next to her, "so I don't use it too much too soon."

"So, I guess you shouldn't use it to, oh I don't know, text people back?" Her tone dripped sarcasm.

"Babe," Tony reached for her hands but she took them off the keyboard and crossed them in front of her. "Is that why you're so pissy? Because I didn't text you back right away?"

"You didn't text me back at all!" Angel spoke louder than she intended, drawing the attention of everyone in the room.

Tony grinned. "I'm really flustering you lately," he said, as if it was an accomplishment of which one should be proud.

"I'm not flustered, I'm pissed off."

"C'mon babe, you know I'm bad at texting."

"I was worried sick," Angel blurted. "You or Andrew should have contacted me."

"Okay, calm down. I'd think you'd be happy I found your mom instead of busting my balls about a text."

Angel closed her laptop and stormed into the sitting room between the master suite and the kitchen. She felt guilty for being mean to Tony when he wasn't the real reason she was upset.

Andrew left Chase and Dane recanting the hospital events for Giovanni and stepped into the sitting room. Angel was on the far end of the couch with her laptop on her knees. "Can I come in?" Andrew asked.

Angel didn't acknowledge his presence until he sat down next to her and closed her computer. "I'm sorry I didn't text you back," he said. "I was being pulled in a hundred different directions."

"Where were you when we met Frank? You conveniently disappeared while the rest of us almost ended up dead." Tears were welling in her eyes and she fought back the lump rising in her throat. The truth was she wasn't that upset about him disappearing, she was upset about his non-responsiveness. She was upset about him not taking her to his apartment last night. She was upset about feeling ignored, blown off and abandoned by him, especially after what happened between them. She was upset that the whole dynamic of their relationship seemed to have shifted in a direction that made her feel vulnerable and insecure.

Andrew abruptly stood up. "Come with me to my apartment to pick up your demon cats."

"I thought you already picked them up?"

"No, I decided it would be better for them, and for me, if you were the one who transported them home." Andrew raised his eyebrows.

"You're just afraid to touch them aren't you?"

"Yes," Andrew shook his head, "very much afraid. So, will you come with me?"

They drove the Tank over and Angel couldn't escape the awkwardness she now felt being alone with Andrew. She stared out the window most of the drive while Andrew mulled over details about the six bodies at the hospital. "It didn't take long to ID them," Andrew explained, "they all had criminal records."

"I'm not surprised," Angel commented.

"And none of them were bogata brothers."

"Really?"

"All independently hired." Andrew ran his hand through his hair, "Whoever is orchestrating this has an unbelievable amount of contacts and resources." Andrew pulled into his driveway. "You know what I find interesting?"

"What?"

"The two guys from the parking lot and two of the guys in the stairwell were shot with the same gun; a rifle. Frank Vilachi was shot with a .38 and the man on the roof was shot six times with a 9mm." Andrew cocked his head, "Anything you want to tell me about that last one?"

"It was my gun but I didn't do it."

"Ah," he chewed on his bottom lip, "you didn't do it?"

"No. According to Chase, Kristen is some sort of wild combination of Annie Oakley and Rambo."

Andrew narrowed his eyes in disbelief. "The little Iowa farm girl shot a guy six times?"

Angel held up her hands, "I swear, just ask Chase."

Angel reached for the door handle with her right hand just as Andrew took her left hand and held it. "Before we go inside I have something I want to say." He shifted in the seat to face her and Angel suddenly felt nervous.

"If you're going to talk about what I think you're going to talk about, you don't need to say anything," she rambled nervously.

"Yes I do."

"No, really," she ranted, "I understand. What happened the other night was a big mistake and we can just forget it ever happened and move on."

Andrew inched closer. "That's just it..."

She cut him off, "I know, right. It was just a big, fat, humongous mistake. So, let's just forget about it."

Andrew leaned closer and put his index finger over her lips. "Don't speak," he whispered, "just listen." He lowered his finger and looked intently in her eyes. "I don't want to forget about it. I can't forget about it even if I tried." Her heart beat wildly. "It's just that this whole thing is so damn complicated."

Angel lowered her eyes to the seat and sighed, "I understand." The last thing she needed was another man telling her their situation was complicated. Tony called off their engagement because it was too complicated. Grayson faked his own death to get away from her because it was complicated. Hearing the word complicated was the kiss of death in any relationship.

"You don't understand what I'm saying," he hung his head and let his shoulders slump.

"Yes, I do. I get it, and I knew it was coming. It's totally fine." She forced a fake smile and reached for the handle to open the door.

"You are stubborn woman," Andrew said, leaning back and staring out the window.

"What?"

He pound his fist on the steering wheel. "You're not listening." He reached over and pulled her chin toward him. "Let go of the door handle. Look at me and listen. Don't speak, just listen." He took a deep breath. "I think about you all the time.

When I wake up, you're in my head and when I go to sleep I'm holding you in my heart. I'm scared to death to lose you and I'm scared I'll never have the chance to call you mine."

He was breathing as hard as she was. "Right now there is nothing more that I want than to take you inside and make love to you." Chills danced up the back of her neck and she felt her face flush. "The trouble is I don't know how or even where we fit, so doing that doesn't seem like the wisest choice."

He let go of her chin and ran his hand through his hair. "My life is complicated. I'm Joseph Venturini's son and at the same time I'm a Special Detective on the Chicago police force, which has more meat-eaters than anywhere in the nation." Angel stared at him.

"Are you a meat-eater?" She was almost afraid to ask.

"Technically, yes. I'm on the Venturnini payroll, which means I look the other way sometimes. But that doesn't make me a bad or unethical cop." Andrew angled his body to face her. "It's like this," he licked his lips and narrowed his eyes as if he were trying to choose the best way to make her understand. "I took an oath to protect and serve, and I also swore by the Omerta to be loyal. Sometimes that loyalty demands that even in the workplace I protect and serve my family first."

Angel hadn't thought of it that way, but she could now see the loophole. It was definitely a gray area. "Will you ever be the Venturini Boss?"

"I hope not," Andrew exhaled loudly. "My older brothers are next in line and if I were presented with that opportunity it would mean both of them were dead. I love being a cop. I don't want to be head of my family because it would mean I'd have to stop doing what I love to do."

"So, are you a cop first and then a Venturini or the other way around?"

"I'm both, sweetheart, which gets complicated." He smiled at her and mouthed, "Complicated."

"I make it even more complicated because I'm a Maratinzano, huh," Angel rubbed her pinky against his.

"You have no idea," he teased.

"Is there *really* that much pressure on you because of me?"

He squeezed her fingertips. "The pressure isn't because you're from another bogata. There have been peaceful relationships between members of other bogatas. The pressure comes from the fact that you are the granddaughter of the Cappo di Tutti Capi."

Angel gnawed on her bottom lip. "So, if I was just a random member of the Maratinzano family would you protect me the way you do?"

Andrew slowly shook his head no. "Well, not at first anyway. I protect you now out of personal investment, not obligation." He released her hand and put his arm across the back of the seat. "When you first came to Tetterbaum's Pub, I was instructed to keep my eyes on you."

"Instructed by who?" Angel sat upright, curious to hear more.

"Giovanni."

"I don't understand. You were already working at Tetterbaum's when I started there…" her voice tapered off. "I guess I've never really understood why you were working there in the first place."

"It's complicated," he grinned.

"You can't use that to explain everything."

"Agreed," he smirked. "My job there was two-fold. I was there as a cop to investigate the rumor of the Tetterbaum tapes and to protect Ernest Tetterbaum from a potential hit. I was also there as a Venturini to find the tapes and destroy any evidence against my family." Andrew grinned, "When you showed up and I got a call from the Cappo di Tutti Capi instructing me to protect you, my job became three-fold."

"You could have just said no."

Andrew laughed out loud. "Sweetheart, when the Cappo di Tutti Capi tells you to do something, it's an offer you don't refuse."

"So, what you're telling me is that I've pretty much been a pain in your ass from the get-go."

His smile grew bigger. "What I'm telling you is …"

She joined him in saying, "it's complicated."

Angel rolled her eyes. "You're a Venturini. I'm a Maratinzano. You're a cop. I'm being groomed to be head of a Mafia family. We might as well be the Capulets and Montaques."

He took his hand and brushed a piece of hair from her cheek. "I don't like that ending."

"What happens now? Are we just friends?" Angel looked at him and felt desire burning inside her. They weren't just friends. She wanted to kiss him, not all the time, but sometimes. How could they be just friends when there was obviously a mutual attraction begging to manifest itself in the warmth of physical touch?

Andrew stroked her hand with his fingertips. "There's one more thing." He paused as if it was awkward to say. "Tony." Angel dropped her head down and a sudden guilt rushed over her. "I know you still care about him and maybe even still love him. I can see it in you and I don't want to get in the middle of something unfinished between you two."

Angel looked at him and bit her lip. "It's complicated," she whispered and he nodded. She leaned her head back against the seat and sighed. "What do you want to do? Pretend this never happened?"

"No," he exhaled, "definitely no. I want to treasure what happened. But I don't think we should let it happen again until things are less complicated."

Angel gave a half-smile and nodded her head up and down. She didn't like it, but it made sense. Andrew always made sense. He was the constant voice of reason. Sometimes she liked that fact and sometimes she hated it; but even though she hated it, she knew he was right. There was too much chaos in her life to try and sort through her feelings for either Tony or Andrew; and she undeniably felt something for both.

"Now," he released her hand, "let's go inside and get your demonic cats out of my house."

"I'm beginning to understand why you're a dog person," Angel taunted, getting out of the Tank and slamming the door closed.

"Oh, yeah, and why is that?"

"Because dogs are simple and cats are..." Angel raised one eyebrow, "complicated."

Andrew smirked, "You better pray those feline hellcats didn't tear up my furniture."

"You want to pray with me?" Angel looked at him with a teasing grin.

Andrew put the key in the front door and pushed it open. "More than you know, sweetheart. More than you know."

CHAPTER TWENTY-ONE

Inside the house they found Mo first, curled up on one end of Andrew's couch. "Oh no, what's it doing on the furniture? Now I have to fumigate the couch," Andrew moaned and Angel scooped up Mo, stroking his head until he purred like a motorboat.

"Cats are clean animals," she defended.

"Sweetheart, the words clean and animal don't go together."

At the sound of Angel's voice, Midnight poked his head out from under the couch and Angel picked him up. "You're being Mr. Social," she said to Midnight, scratching behind his ears. Midnight looked at Andrew, bellowed out a low growl and hissed.

"Yeah, he's Mr. Personality all right."

They put Midnight and Mo in the Tank and went back inside to grab the litter box and cat food, which were both in the laundry room. Angel bent down and slid the litter box into a trash bag. "I just want to go on record as saying it's gross to put their food and water bowl next to their litter box."

"They don't care," Andrew shrugged.

"That's like you sitting on the toilet while you eat."

Andrew grimaced. "That was a visual I could have lived without."

"You and me both," Angel laughed.

They walked from the laundry room, through the kitchen and into the family room when Angel abruptly stopped and Andrew crashed into the back of her, spilling cat food all over the floor.

"What the...?" Andrew exclaimed and then he realized why Angel had stopped.

They both stood frozen for several seconds, staring at him. He was the largest man she'd ever seen in real life. He looked a little like Andre' the Giant, except he was bald and more muscular. He had deep brown eyes that looked almost black and his skin was naturally olive and tanned. He held a .45 in his left hand, though Angel was pretty sure he didn't need a gun to scare anybody.

"You're the Shark?" Angel asked, in a slow tone of mesmerized awe.

"Yeah," he answered in the deep voice Angel remembered from the rooftop and the apartment.

"You saved my life a couple times," Angel spoke slowly, "thank you."

"Now I need somethin' from you in return." Angel couldn't fathom what he was about to ask. She stood wide-eyed, with her mouth half-open in anticipation. "I need your help to prove I'm innocent."

"Innocent of what?" Angel and Andrew said in unison.

Andrew convinced the Shark that he didn't need the .45 and they all moved into the kitchen and sat around the table. The Shark took up one entire side of the square table and Angel couldn't stop gawking at him. He looked so powerful. The Shark spoke for almost fifteen minutes and Angel hung on every word.

"Why didn't you go to Giovanni with this information in the first place?" Angel asked.

"Giovanni sent me to Chicago to protect you. I had just arrived when you were attacked in the penthouse," the Shark explained in a low, gruff voice. "I was walking on the sidewalk outside the Towers when the sniper took his first shot. I saw where the shot came from and I took care of the problem." He exhaled and sucked in a long breath. "I didn't realize the sniper was a decoy until the explosion."

"None of us did," Andrew said.

"I couldn't get to the chopper before it took off, but I was able to stop them from taking you." He pointed at Angel. "They had Olga in the chopper and were coming back for you. I carried Angel to safety and then went to see if I could get any information out of the sniper. That's when I discovered who was behind the attack." He shook his head and blinked slowly. "The sniper was a man named Gerald Finnegan," the Shark swallowed hard. "He was my brother."

Angel's mouth fell open. "You're Finnegan's son?" He nodded. "You're father worked directly with Moloney and was murdered after the heroin shipment incident?" He nodded again.

"Did you get any information from Gerald?" Andrew asked.

"Only that the Moloney clan had been developing a plan for over ten years; a way to avenge all of our father's deaths."

"Did he tell you any specifics of the plan?"

"No," the Shark shook his head, "my brother viewed me as a traitor because of my affiliation with Giovanni."

"If all the other members are avenging their father's death, why aren't you a part of it?" Andrew questioned.

The Shark crossed his arms over his enormous chest. "Because I know my father was guilty of stealing from Salvatore Buscetta and Giovanni."

"How do you know?"

"I was just a boy but I saw the packages of heroin stored in our basement. I watched Moloney and Selovich and my father carry them in." The Shark exhaled and his shoulders slumped. "I was ashamed to be the son of a thief."

Andrew leaned back and folded his arms on his chest. He had that look in his eye and Angel could tell his mind was churning with possible scenarios. "Can you explain to me where you've been since that night and why you haven't checked in with Giovanni?" Andrew asked poignantly.

"This isn't an interrogation." Angel shot Andrew a tense glance.

"It's okay. I'll answer your questions," the Shark said. "After I killed Gerald I set out to find the other son's of the three men. I was on my way to Iowa but when I heard you two were there, I feared Giovanni already knew of the Moloney clan's plot and already assumed I was a part of it. The only way I could think to clear my name was to find ..."

"Wait a second," Andrew interrupted, "why were you on your way to Iowa?"

"To find Moloney's son, Sean."

"He's in Iowa?" Andrew leaned forward in his chair.

"According to Gerald, his last known address was a small town in Iowa."

Andrew looked at Angel. "Well, that's a little too coincidental for my taste," he said, crossing his arms and rocking back on two chair legs. "Were you able to locate Sean?"

"Yes, but I did not speak to him. He has a base of operation just outside Clearfield. I have photographs of it."

"Where are these pictures? Can we see them?" Angel asked.

The Shark's lip curled at the corner, as if he were about to break into a smile. "They are in a safe location. You can see them if you agree to help me."

"Why didn't you try to talk to Sean while you were there?" Andrew asked.

"Like I said, I was viewed as a traitor so I thought returning to Chicago and convincing Selovich's son that I wanted to join the group would be more believable. And it worked. I pretended to be interested in the plan of revenge so he let me fly with him to the hospital. We were to wait on the roof until Sophia was found and then fly her back to Iowa."

"That's when we found Olga, killed Selovich and took the chopper," Andrew added, coming up to speed on how it all fit together.

"Yes. Since he was my last chance of gaining specific information on what Moloney was planning, I concluded my only hope was to keep you alive," he said, nodding at Angel. "By keeping you alive, maybe it would be enough to prove my innocence and loyalty to Giovanni."

"I think Giovanni will believe you," Angel uttered, "he's a reasonable man."

The Shark and Andrew locked eyes and Andrew shook his head to indicate no. "He can't afford to believe you unless you have concrete proof."

"What about Salvatore?" Angel piped in, "Will he believe you?'

"Salvatore Buscetta is more brutal than Giovanni," Andrew mumbled under his breath. "Right now, he looks like a traitor to both sides."

"You see my problem," the Shark exhaled.

All of a sudden Andrew's eyes lit with excitement. "If word were to get out that it was Giovanni's men who killed your brother, do you think that would make Moloney believe that you now have a justifiable motive to want to join in his revenge?

Interest shown in the Shark's face and he leaned forward. "Maybe. As I said, I have been viewed as a traitor to the movement all these years, but the death of my brother might be a believable scenario for me to switch sides."

"We can sell Giovanni on the notion that you have been secretly uncovering this plot and trying to stay one step ahead of Moloney. We'll explain that you've killed two of his men and saved Angel and that you are now pretending to be Moloney's ally in order to stop him, which is why you could not risk any contact with Giovanni."

"Four of his men," the Shark corrected. "I killed two in the hospital parking lot, and two in the hospital stairwell."

"That mystery's solved," Angel noted.

Andrew clapped his hands and rubbed them together. "We'll need Chase and the helicopter and some gear, but I think we can pull this off."

"Thank you," the Shark sighed. "If this works I am indebted to you both."

"If this works, we're even," Andrew said. "But I need to see those pictures first."

CHAPTER TWENTY-TWO

Chase flew the helicopter across town and set it down behind the abandoned strip mall that housed what Angel called Andrew's Bat Cave. They loaded the chopper with several weapons Chase had purchased from Selovich before he was killed and outfitted it with state-of-the-art surveillance equipment.

"Where'd you get all this cool-ass shit?" Chase said, picking up a tiny camera.

"From a trusted friend at the FBI," Andrew answered and took the camera out of his hand. "Listen," he said to the Shark and Chase, "we know Sean Moloney has men in both the FBI and local law enforcement. We have to assume they will check your weapons, which is why we're sending you with only the ones bought from Selovich."

He held up a small surveillance item that looked like the head of a screw. "These microphones are so sensitive we'll be able to hear a conversation within a fifty-yard radius," Andrew explained. He walked to the front of the helicopter and pointed to a tiny camera, no bigger than the tip of a pencil. "There are ten of these mounted on the helicopter so we'll be able to pick up every angle. When you arrive at Moloney's location make one 360 degree fly over prior to landing so we can see the size of the compound, how many structures there are and what type of resources he has."

Chase grinned and nodded. "Righteous."

Like everything else, this plan was complicated. Everything had to work precisely as planned or it could quickly turn into a suicide mission. The Shark contacted Moloney's people and requested a meeting, explaining why he wanted to join the movement. As anticipated, Sean Moloney agreed to the meeting, probably more out of curiosity than anything else. Chase's job was to fly the Shark to the location and then leave. "When you land," Andrew told Chase, "they're going to search you and the chopper so we can't risk putting a wire on you."

"No problem, Chief, I've got a steel trap for a memory," he knocked against his head, "I'll remember everything word for word."

Andrew inhaled and exhaled hard. Chase was like talking to a distracted toddler. Andrew never knew for sure if the information was sinking in. "Give me your phone," Andrew said to Chase, who dug it out of his front pocket. "I'll give this back to you when you return."

"Why can't I keep my phone?"

"Because they'll check it and find out you are somehow linked to Angel or to Tetterbaum's Pub..." Andrew's voice tapered off.

"Oh, got it, right-on."

"The less they know about you the safer everyone is," Andrew said, glaring at Chase. "You understand that?"

"Got it," Chase said.

"And you know what to do, right?"

"Yep, I know what to do. When I get out to be searched I drop the bugs onto the ground. I'll try and drop as many as possible."

"Right," Andrew said. "But take the ground into consideration. If you're in grass, you can probably drop them and not worry about it being seen. If you're in dirt you may have to dig them into the ground with your shoe."

"What if I land on pavement?"

Andrew stared at him, "Don't." Andrew spoke with intensity, "Those devices are the Shark's only means of communicating with us. If you can't plant them, he's as good as dead."

Chase's eyes bulged. "So, I should set her down on some lush-ass grass."

"If at all possible, yes."

Andrew directed his attention to the Shark. "You know what to expect." He gave a nod of his large head. "They'll take your phone, your weapons and anything else you've got." He handed the Shark a new cell phone. "This one has been programmed with names and numbers that will make your story more believable. It has contact information for Selovich, and several well-known arms dealers in Chicago and New York. Get familiar with the contact list on your way over." He nodded. "We've already input fake phone records into the system so if they run a search you should be clear."

They climbed into the chopper and Chase gave Andrew two thumbs up. "I'll see you at the meeting." Andrew gave a thumbs up and watched them lift off. When they were out of sight he dialed Angel.

"How'd it go?" she asked.
"I hope I didn't just send them off to be slaughtered."
"Don't worry, "she encouraged him. "They'll be able to pull it off."
"I hope so, sweetheart."

CHAPTER TWENTY-THREE

Sophia and Olga were at the dining room table, arguing with Giovanni when Angel walked in. "What's going on?"

"Bah," Giovanni shook his head, "these women."

Sophia explained that she wanted to be at the meeting her father was attending. "I have a right to be there," she told Giovanni.

"Si, si, I know, you think you have a right," he threw his hands into the air. "I will speak to Salvatore and see if he believes you have this right." Giovanni drudged out of the room, mumbling in Italian.

Olga shook her head, "He's such a pissy old coot."

Angel sat down between Sophia and Olga and sliced off a piece of cinnamon coffee cake. She took a bite. "Mmmm, Aunt Olga, you make the best coffee cake. Almost as good as your cinnamon pancakes."

"You don't remember your Mama's cinnamon pancakes," Olga gave Sophia a wink.

"I haven't made those in years," Sophia reminisced. "When you were a little girl that was all you ever wanted to eat. And you were stubborn about it too. You would refuse to eat at all if you didn't get your cinnamon pancakes."

"Oh, I remember you were a little stinker, you were." Olga shook her finger at her. "What am

I saying," Olga patted the top of Angel's hand, "you're still a stinker."

Angel grinned.

The penthouse was crowded. Stefano and Kristen had Angel's room. Sophia was in the guest room. Angel shared Olga's room and Giovanni had his own suite on the floor below. Angel knocked on her bedroom door to see if Stefano and Kristen were hungry for some breakfast. When she opened the door, Kristen was sitting on the bed crying and Stefano was kneeling in front of her, talking quietly.

"Is everything okay?" Angel asked, slipping in and closing the door behind her.

Stefano and Kristen stared at each other and Angel could tell he was signaling her not to say anything. "Everything's fine," Stefano said, "we're just talking."

Angel met eyes with Kristen and it was easy to see she was tormented with fear. "Can I bring you something to eat?" Angel asked. "Or some coffee?"

"No thank you," Stefano answered quickly and Kristen lowered her eyes and shook her head no.

Angel left the room and told Sophia and Olga what happened. "I think he's hiding something," Angel said. "I can tell Kristen wants to talk but she's terrified."

Sophia sighed, "They have been through a lot."

"I have a feeling there's more to this than just emotional stress." Angel gulped down the rest of her coffee, which was now lukewarm and went to find Giovanni. He wasn't in the family room or on the patio. She took the elevator down one floor to see if he was in his suite, but when the elevator door opened she wished she had stayed upstairs. Two of Giovanni's men dropped Dr. Manzini's body onto a large black, plastic tarp then lifted it and carried it toward the elevator. Angel's breath caught and her pulse quickened as she slid out of the elevator and they slipped in with the body. Angel tried not to look. When the elevator doors closed, Angel turned toward the apartment where Dr. Manzini had been held and saw Giovanni standing in the doorway.

"Michelangela, do you need something?" His eyes were hardened and lacked that tender grandfather sparkle.

Her mind reeled with questions but her lips were only able to utter a single word, "Why?"

"Come inside," he motioned her through the door and onto the couch. He sat across from her and spoke slowly and deliberately. "Manzini held no loyalty. He would both serve and turn on anyone for a price. Men like that cannot be trusted. In Italian we call them ratto, which means a rat. If I had let him go, he would have reported back to whoever hired him and sold them information about us. The only protection we had was the proactive elimination of the problem. Do you understand?"

Angel nodded, but deep inside she wondered whether Manzini was given a chance to be loyal. She wondered if killing him was premature and maybe even unnecessary. She wondered if there could have been another solution, but she didn't say anything.

"The protection of our family must come first and without compromise." Giovanni's eyes pierced through her. "Do you understand this, Michelangela?"

She nodded again.

His face softened. "I can see the doubt in your eyes. One day you will fully understand the demands and responsibilities of leading the family, but for now you must trust me."

"I do trust you," Angel spoke softly. "I just wish there didn't have to be so much killing."

"Si', it is most unfortunate," Giovanni nodded his head, "but understand we do not set out to kill those who are innocent. People make their own choices and suffer those consequences."

"What about mistakes? What about when someone accidentally makes a mistake but doesn't realize the harm it causes until it's too late?"

The sparkle lit Giovanni's eyes and his lips curled into a small smile. "You possess the compassion of your father. It is an admirable quality, but one you must learn to control. Compassion can be used against you." Giovanni leaned back in the chair. "Now, you came down here to see me about something, what was it?"

Angel bit her lip. *If I tell him about the conversation between Stefano and Kristen, will he have Stefano killed?* She blinked slowly. *If I don't tell him and Stefano really is a traitor, am I putting all our lives in danger?* She took a deep breath and lied. "I just wondered if there was anything you needed me to do to prepare for the meeting with Salvatore."

"We will meet Salvatore at 8:00pm. Inform your men I will hold a briefing at 6:00pm to prepare for the meeting. I would like all of you in attendance."

"My men?" Angel raised her eyebrows.

"The ones who have proven their loyalty. Andrew and Tony. I have checked out Chase and Dane. Dane works for the Andriachinis but has not been made yet. If he proves loyal through this, he may be one you choose to bring in. Chase has no bogata affiliation and no family to speak of. I have asked my men to keep a watchful eye on him until he proves himself trustworthy."

Angel nodded and felt suddenly overwhelmed. She started to rise from the couch and then sank back down. Giovanni's eyes were heavy upon her and her lip quivered as she started to speak. "I don't know how to do this." A single tear fell and ran down her cheek. "Everything is clouded in my head and what used to feel right is now wrong and things I know are wrong are somehow considered okay and…" her voice was stopped by the lump in her throat.

Giovanni rose and moved to the couch. "Michelangela," he held her head against his chest and rubbed her hair, "you are not to know everything now. I am here to instruct you in our ways, but that instruction will take time. You must give yourself time to learn and accept and become who you were born to be."

Angel leaned back and wiped the tears from her face. "That's just it. How do I know this is who

I was born to be?" Insecurity welled up and she burst into sobs. "I don't think I can kill people."

Giovanni pulled her close again and held her head against his chest. "My sweet Michelangela, do not fear weakness. Sometimes what you see as weakness turns out to be your greatest strength." He pulled her back and looked into her eyes. "You have more strength in you than most men." He poked her in the forehead with his index finger and smiled, "You have smarts and you have heart. Astuto e cuore." He pointed to her head again and said, "Asuto. Smart." Then pointed to her heart and said, "Cuore. Heart."

Angel repeated it softly. "Astuto e cuore."

Giovanni's eyes sparkled, "I am proud of who you are and your father would be too."

Angel took a deep breath. "It's just confusing sometimes, like when you call Andrew and Tony 'my men' but they are part of other bogatas..." she exhaled, unsure of even where she was going.

Giovanni stood up and walked to the patio door. He drew open the blinds and peered out at the city. "Michelangela, come here." She rose and joined him at the door. "When I am home and I look out at the city of New York, I see clearly. It is immovable and when I am there, I am immovable. There is respect for tradition." Angel studied him while he spoke and soaked in every word. "Alas, when I am here in Chicago and I look at the city, there is not a clear picture. Everything is moveable." He turned and stared deep in Angel's eyes, taking both her hands in his. "Your father felt as you do which is why he tried to change our ways here in Chicago."

"And he failed," Angel deflated.

"No, Michelangela, he did not fail. He laid the foundation for the work you will do. He planted the seeds of change that have begun to grow in your generation. You have already begun to unite bogatas as never before. Never before have men laid down their lives to protect a person from another family like Andrew and Tony protect you."

Angel shook her head. "That's not because of me, it's because I'm the granddaughter of the Cappo di Tutti Capi."

"Bah," Giovanni waved his arm. "It began because of me, but it lasts because of you." He draped his arm around her and led her toward the apartment door. "Trust your instincts and justify your decisions only to yourself. In time you will learn not to let compassion cloud your judgments. You will see clearly and know what must be done to protect your family." He touched her forehead and then her heart. "Astuto e Cuore."

As she walked out the door, Angel whirled around to face Giovanni. "Stefano's hiding something," she blurted.

Giovanni nodded. "I know, child."

"Are you going to question him?"

"The true character of a man reveals itself in time. If Stefano's involvement in all of this is as innocent as Sophia and his girlfriend believe, then that innocence will show itself. If not, we will deal with him later." Giovanni's lips curled at the corners into a tiny grin. "Michelangela," his eyes sparkled, "good instincts."

CHAPTER TWENTY-FOUR

When Heavenly Towers was constructed Giovanni had several conference rooms built into the lower level, and one uniquely designed meeting room two floors below the penthouse. It took up the entire floor. The windows were constructed of bullet proof glass and it was completely soundproof. Ceramic tile in tones of browns and grays made up the floor and the walls were painted a deep, rich tan. Dark brown leather chairs and mahogany boardroom tables sat over to the left with seating for at least fifty. There were bathrooms to the right and a small open kitchen area with a stainless-steel refrigerator, wine racks and a long bar with leather stools that sat ten. This was the place where they would meet with Salvatore.

There was no emergency exit doorway to and from this level and the elevator stopped on this floor only with the input of a special code; otherwise, it soared passed as if the level didn't even exist. As far as Angel knew, no one but Giovanni himself had the code.

It was nearing 6:00pm, the time for the preliminary meeting, and Angel was feeling jittery. She wasn't sure why. After all, they were holding the upper hand against Moloney. They had successfully retrieved Olga and Sophia, killed Frank Vilachi, Selovich and Finnegan and planted a mole in Moloney's organization; but something still didn't feel right. Angel couldn't identify the cause of the uneasiness building inside her.

She got dressed in Olga's room and looked at herself in the full-length mirror. She had on black slacks that flared over her black three-inch heeled boots, a white collared blouse and a black fitted jacket that hung open. She pulled her hair back into a low ponytail and put a diamond stud earring in each ear. Taking in her reflection, she struggled to see beyond her own nerves.

Sophia tapped on the door and came in. She stood behind Angel and looked at her through the mirror. Then she reached over and pulled the ponytail holder, allowing Angel's hair to fall messily on her shoulders. "That's better," she smiled. "Just because you're in a man's world now doesn't mean you can't look like a lady."

Angel smiled and fluffed her hair with her fingers. "You're right, this does look better."

"Feminine always looks better," Sophia said and winked.

Olga poked her head in, "Am I missing a party in here?" She waddled in and plunked her wide hips down on the bed. "Let me see you," she said to Angel, "turn around and give your old aunt a look see." Angel spun to face her and Olga shook her head. "Merciful Heavens child, why are you wearing those lesbo earrings?"

Angel felt her ears. "They're diamond studs, Olga, and you can't say that word." Olga over-dramatically rolled her eyes. "I'm serious," Angle continued. "You can't use derogatory slang to describe people... any people."

"Pish-posh," Olga waved her arms in the air. "Elsa down at the hair salon says you'll never see a lesbian wearing anything but studs." Olga raised her eyebrows way into the top of her forehead. "And it's true. I've been keeping my eye out ever since."

"That's ridiculous," Angel argued, "lots of people wear studs."

"Lots of gay people," Olga blurted, "Elsa said so."

Angel rolled her eyes, "Well, if Elsa said it, it must be true."

"Ooh, you're just full of sass," Olga scooted off the bed and waddled out of the room, mumbling her way down the hall.

Sophia laughed. "Actually," she said, "and I'm not saying this because I think only lesbians wear studs, but a nice pair of silver hoops or something beaded might look better."

Angel looked at her reflection again. Now that her hair was down her earrings didn't even show, so maybe silver hoops would be better.

When she entered her bedroom to get her silver hoop earrings, Stefano and Kristen were talking in the bathroom. Their voices were raised and Angel couldn't help but overhear.

"Why do you have to go to this meeting?" Kristen asked. "I thought you weren't involved in this anymore."

"I'm not," Stefano said.

"You told me now that Frank was dead you were safe and we could go back home."

"I was wrong," Stefano hollered and Angel could hear the intensity of frustration in his voice.

"Why do you have to be at this meeting if you're not involved in this anymore?" Angel could tell by Kristen's tone that she didn't trust Stefano, not completely anyway.

Stefano was talking through what sounded like a tight jaw and gritted teeth. "Giovanni's people told me to be at this meeting. That's all I know."

"Can I leave?" Kristen started to cry. "Can I leave here and go home? I just want to go home."

"No, we've been through this a hundred times. You know too much, you've seen too much and if you try to leave they will kill you."

Angel grabbed her hoops and sneaked quietly out of the room. She wasn't sure what to think, other than Kristen was terrified and Stefano wasn't coming completely clean about something. She hoped Giovanni was right and that his real intentions would show through soon. She also hoped, for Stefano's sake, that he was telling the truth and his involvement was merely out of innocent stupidity.

At 6:00pm Angel walked into the penthouse floor lobby, where Giovanni, the square blonde man, Sophia, Andrew, Tony, Chase, Stefano and Dane had all gathered. Two of Giovanni's men escorted them to the elevator, where Giovanni punched in the code. The elevator went down and they exited into the special meeting room.

Giovanni directed them to a round mahogany table and stood with his hands behind his back until they were all seated. Angel noted in her mind how powerful he looked. He wore a black suit with a dark gray tie and there was an intensity in his expression that she was certain could not only be seen but also felt by everyone at the table.

"We are going to get started, as we have many items to discuss before Salvatore and the other invited Bosses arrive." He cleared his throat. "You are all aware of Moloney and his enactment of revenge against Salvatore Buscetta and myself. The good news is we have taken down two leaders in his administration, rescued those who were kidnapped and have found his base of operation. The bad news is that we have yet to identify the depth of his infiltration into our own families, and into organizations he can utilize to hurt us; like the FBI and the police. Traditori tra noi. There are traitors among us." Giovanni slammed his hands onto the tabletop. "We must find them NOW."

Giovanni looked to Andrew and nodded, which Andrew obviously took as his cue to stand up. He began to explain how the Shark fit into the picture, as one of Finnegan's sons, how he had shown up at Andrew's and how he had been sent into Moloney's operation as a mole.

Tony leaned back and crossed his arms over his chest. "That's not right," he said and all eyes stared at him.

"What do you mean? What's not right?" Andrew asked.

Tony shook his head. "The Shark was the one who shot me in the Penthouse that night."

Andrew wrinkled his brow. "That's not possible."

Tony glared at him. "Yeah, it is possible and it's what happened. You had to have seen him come in right after the blast. He filled up the whole doorway."

Andrew shook his head. "I didn't see anything after the explosion."

There was a split second of stunned silence and in that moment flashes of memories raced through Angel's mind. She remembered that night at the hospital when Tony said the word Shark and she didn't know what it meant. *He was trying to tell me that the Shark was the traitor.* If the Shark shot Tony then he had to have been there when the explosion blew the door open, which meant that he lied about killing the sniper. Did he also lie about his brother being the sniper? Was Gerald Finnegan, still alive?

Angel's pulse quickened. She remembered the duct tape on the stairway door and her mind raced to understand how that fit into the equation. *Why would someone need to tape the lock to keep the door open?* The emergency stairwell door on the penthouse level automatically locked. If you were on the penthouse level you could use the stairs to go down, but no one from below could access the penthouse through the stairwell door. *Unless the lock was duct taped open.* If someone knew there was going to be an explosion that would render the elevator inoperable, they could have taped the lock ahead of time to ensure that they could get back to the penthouse level after the explosion occurred. *Who would have known about the explosion ahead of time?*

Angel cleared her throat and stood up. She told them about the duct tape on the door.

"Who was there earlier in the day that could have taped the door?" Giovanni questioned.

"Olga and I were there all morning," Angel said, "and then Andrew came by to bring me the letters he found in Venito's office."

"We don't know what time the Shark really arrived in town," Andrew piped in, "so it's conceivable that he could have been the one who taped it earlier in the day, ensuring he could access the apartment after the explosion, shoot Tony and myself and rescue Angel."

"Why save Angel?" Chase asked, and then darted his eyes to her. "No offense."

"Like he told us," Andrew nodded toward Angel, "keeping her alive was helping to prove his loyalty to Giovanni."

"Like he's working both sides?" Chase narrowed his eyes. "I don't see him as a work-both-sides type of guy."

"Tony," Andrew blurted as if the idea just jumped into his head, "maybe the Shark did shoot you and that's why you're not dead." Angel could see Andrew getting excited. "Maybe the Shark was onto something, maybe he even knew something was going to go down, which is why he arrived early and taped the door so he could get to Angel if necessary. Then he deliberately shot me and Tony so that no one else would, knowing anyone else would shoot to kill."

"I don't know, man," Tony shook his head.

Andrew directed his attention to Giovanni. "I've looked in the man's eyes. I've read his face and his body language. I heard his story and I'm telling you, he's not a traitor. We may not understand everything he's done, but everything has been done to protect your people."

Chase jumped up and threw his hand in the air. "I second that."

"Sit down hot-shot, we're not taking a vote," Tony slurred.

"You said the Shark has provided photographs of Moloney's organization. Do we know if these photographs are indeed accurate?" Giovanni asked.

Andrew sighed. "If you would have asked me that question before this meeting, I'd have sworn to their accuracy. Now, my gut says yes, but I won't have proof until we compare them to the images from the chopper Chase flew over."

Giovanni nodded. "Let's look at them anyway."

The square blonde man hit the switch that lowered a projector screen from the ceiling and then he turned out the lights. Chase worked the slides and Andrew pointed out details of what little they knew.

It looked like Moloney's operation was headquartered in a giant barn in the middle of a large corn field. There was nothing fancy or impressive about it. In fact, you could easily pass by it without taking notice. There were two wooden sheds that sat fifty yards from the barn and faced the giant barn door.

"Chase," Andrew asked, "is this the picture you saw when flying overhead?"

"Yep, except it all looks a lot bigger in person."

"Can you show us where you landed the chopper?" Tony asked.

Chase got up and walked to the projector screen. "Over here," he said, pointing to a section of field just behind the two wooden sheds. "There's barbed wire, electrical fencing that you can't really see in these pictures, but it stands about two feet high and pretty much circles the entire area. My guess is it's set beyond the stun level."

"So where were you able to drop the bugs?" Andrew asked.

"Unfortunately, they're probably not close enough to pick up anything going on in the big barn, but we might hear stuff around the shed areas."

Giovanni folded his hands on the table. "When do you expect the Shark to make contact?"

Andrew shrugged. "Our bugs in that field are the only contact we have and it's one way. He talks to us if and when he can but we have no way to communicate with him."

Tony sat with his arms folded over his chest and a look of skepticism on his face. He glared at Chase. "They just let you land and take off, no problems, no questions asked?"

"They searched me and the chopper but Andrew had it all covered. He told me to tell them that I was working for Selovich, that the chopper was Selovich's and all the weapons were his, so it was smooth-sailing."

"Huh," Tony exhaled. "Andrew set all that up for you?"

"Yeah," Chase nodded his head up and down, "and it worked like a snap."

Tony licked his lips and cocked his head, then glared at Andrew. "I bet it did."

"Do you have a problem?" Andrew stared back at Tony.

"Yeah, man, I have a couple problems. First, you were at the penthouse that morning and could have easily taped the door. Second, you were wearing a vest that night almost as if you were anticipating taking a bullet. Third, you disappeared at the hospital right before we encountered Frank Vilachi. Fourth, the Shark magically appears at your house while Angel is with you, seemingly so she can vouch for both of you if needed. Fifth, sending hot-shot here in to drop off the Shark seems a little too convenient and easy, like maybe you arranged the whole thing with someone on the inside." Tony was on his feet and breathing heavy.

Andrew stared at him. "Have you lost your mind?"

"Sixth, I think things would be a lot easier for you if I was out of the way." Tony's voice escalated.

"I don't even know what the hell you're talking about!" Andrew hollered back.

Giovanni rose and slammed both hands onto the table. "Sit down, both of you. This is neither the time nor the place. We have greater matters at hand. Everyone's actions will be accounted for."

Giovanni ordered a thirty-minute break, during which time he took Andrew and Tony to the apartment where Manzini had been held. Angel crept down to see if she could speak to them but was told by the square blonde that access was forbidden.

"Giovanni's orders," the square blonde said, "I'm sorry Ms. Maratinzano."

"Angel," she said. "Just call me Angel."

He nodded.

"Do you have a name or should I keep referring to you as the big blonde guy with the square shoulders?" She asked and saw him fight back a smile.

"Thomas."

"Thomas," she repeated, "nice to finally, officially, meet you."

Angel went back to the Penthouse and paced around the family room. What was Giovanni talking to Tony and Andrew about? It was driving her crazy. Why did Tony all of a sudden doubt Andrew? *Was it all of a sudden or had he doubted him all along?* She wondered and then the worst feeling of all encompassed her. *Am I doubting Andrew? Did he sleep with me intentionally to cloud my judgment?* Angel needed fresh hair to clear her mind and walked onto the patio where Chase and Dane were having a smoke.

She bent down to give Mo a scratch behind the ears. "That was uncomfortable," Chase commented, obviously referring to the meeting.

"Yeah," Angel sighed.

"I was in there thinking, man, I wish I had just stayed at the pub and never got involved in this wild-ass shit," Chase said, taking a hit of his cigarette and exhaling.

"You have that luxury," Angel mumbled. "By the way, did you remember to put a sign on the door that says we're closed for renovations?"

"Sure did."

"Thanks." Angel walked back inside, feeling exhausted. She sat down at the dining room table, slumped her shoulders and stared.

"Merciful Heavens, child, look at your posture," Olga said, walking in from the kitchen and pushing Angel's shoulders back. She let them slump forward again. "What's the matter with you?" Olga asked.

Angel looked up. "I don't know who to believe."

Olga set her dishtowel on the table, pulled out the chair next to Angel and sat down. "Tell your old aunt what's happening and I'll help you sort through it."

There wasn't time to tell her everything. Salvatore and the other invited Bosses would be arriving soon. Angel sighed. "Do you think Andrew is a good man?"

Olga narrowed her brow. "You've never doubted him before and he's always been there to help you."

"There's just something that feels so wrong about this whole thing, but I can't put my finger on it." Angel let her head fall against the table. "It's making me nuts."

"Merciful Heavens, child, you were already nuts, this is just making you feel uncomfortable," Olga teased and it made Angel grin.

Thomas came through the front door and announced that Giovanni would like everyone

back in the meeting room immediately. Angel told
Chase and Dane, who quickly put out their
cigarettes and headed down, while Olga informed
Sophia and Stefano, who were in the bedroom
talking with Kristen. When they had all
reassembled at the round table, Andrew projected
the pictures they received from the hidden camera
installed on the chopper.

"We installed ten cameras, so we'll have to
weed through to find the best images," he
explained. "They're uploading them to my
computer now."

The pictures looked similar to the ones the
Shark had given them, which lent credence to his
story. The majority of the pictures were taken from
the air, with the exception of a couple on the
ground. There was a picture of a man patting
down Chase, though they were standing too close
to the chopper so both their heads were cut off the
picture. Another picture showed the Shark from
behind, walking toward the big barn. The barn
door was opened slightly and a man was standing
in the doorway. If you looked closely you could
barely see his face. The next picture was of the
Shark walking through the barn door, which was
opened wider and two men were visible inside the
barn.

"Can we zoom in and see the faces of those
men?" Giovanni asked.

Chase jumped up. "I can do it. I'm real
good with graphics." Andrew shrugged and
scooted out of his way.

Chase worked his magic and the first
picture came up on the screen. The man standing

in the doorway of the barn was holding what looked like a machine gun. His hair was light brown and he was wearing a tan jacket. "He's holding an AK-47," Chase excitedly pointed out. "That's a sweet-ass piece of equipment right there," he said.

He clicked around and brought up the second picture with a close-up image of the two men standing inside the barn. A shadow covered the face of the man on the right, so only his dark hair was visible. Both men stood about the same height and were armed. The man on the left had blonde hair, wore blue jeans with a brown leather jacket and had a rifle slung over his back. "Can we get the image any clearer?" Andrew asked.

"Working on it," Chase quipped.

When the picture appeared back on the screen, Sophia gasped and leapt to her feet, covering her mouth with both hands.

"Is there a problem Sophia?" Giovanni asked, but Sophia didn't respond. She stood stone still, her eyes bulging, as if she was in shock.

"Mom," Angel said. "What is it?"

Sophia blinked back tears. "Non può essere," she whispered. She lowered her hands from her mouth and slowly moved toward the projector screen. "Non può essere." Tears streamed down her cheeks as she stood face to face with the image of the man on the screen. "Non può essere."

"What does that mean?" Angel asked.

"It cannot be," Andrew answered.

"What can't be?"

"No, she's saying 'it cannot be,'" Tony clarified.

Angel walked to her mother and took her hand. "What cannot be? Do you know him?"

Sophia fell against Angel and wept. "Quello è il mio marito." She repeated it over and over, sobbing. "Quello è il mio marito. Quello è il mio marito."

"What is she saying?" Chase whispered to Andrew.

"She says that's her husband," Andrew said softly.

"What!" Angel blurted.

"Whoa, I did NOT see that coming," Chase's eye bulged.

"Il mio Denny," Sophia cried, "Il mio Denny Moon."

Giovanni cleared his throat. "Michelangela, take Sophia upstairs to Olga and return immediately."

The room was eerily silent as Angel walked Sophia out and took her upstairs. Angel didn't know what to say to console her. Nothing seemed appropriate. She couldn't imagine how shocked and betrayed Sophia must have been feeling. Thomas opened the penthouse door and the moment Olga heard sobbing, she dashed out from the kitchen.

"Merciful Heavens," she exclaimed. "What did Giovanni do now?"

"It isn't Giovanni," Angel said, "it's…" All of sudden Angel wasn't sure how to explain it and she feared the very utterance of an explanation would wound Sophia's heart even more.

Olga draped her arms around Sophia, "it's what, child?"

Before Angel could form the words, Sophia burst into a tearful explanation in Italian. Olga moaned aloud and embraced her, moving her to the couch. Angel backed out of the room, leaving Sophia and Olga sobbing and speaking in Italian, in low, mournful tones. Angel stepped into the elevator, heading back down to the meeting, her eyes glassed over with sympathy for her mother.

"Are you okay Ms. Maratinzano?" Thomas asked.

She swallowed hard and fought the emotion rising within. It was important to appear strong. "Yes, Thomas," she said. "Thank you."

When she returned to her spot at the table, Andrew was standing by the far windows, talking on his cell, Chase was working on the computer, trying to clarify pictures, Tony and Dane were talking about weapons and Giovanni was speaking with Stefano.

"Michelangela," Giovanni spoke loudly, "you are back. Let us all take our seats and resume the meeting." Stefano looked uncomfortable and was avoiding eye contact with anyone else at the table. Chase announced that he was putting up more images on the screen and Andrew lowered his phone and slid into his seat.

"That was my contact at the FBI," Andrew said to Giovanni. "They are running the name Denny or Dennis Moon and cross-referencing him with Moloney, Finnegan, Selovich and Carlachi."

"Very good," Giovanni nodded. "We need to know under what circumstances this Denny is with them."

Giovanni motioned toward Stefano, "Stefano has worked closely with Frank Vilachi and has agreed to identify any men he has come in contact with."

The first image went up. There were three men in the picture. Sophia's husband, Denny, was standing to the left of the other two. He was holding a .38 and still had the rifle over his shoulder. "Other than Sophia's husband, Denny, do you recognize either of these men," Giovanni asked Stefano.

"No, I don't know those men," he said.

Chase brought up the next picture and Angel studied Stefano's face. He swallowed and blinked slowly and Angel could see his breathing quicken. "Do you know this man?" Giovanni asked.

Stefano looked like he was going to burst into tears. His hands started to tremble and he gripped the back of his head with both hands and buried his face between his elbows. He sounded like he was hyperventilating as he rocked back and forth.

"I'm gonna take that as a yes," Tony quipped.

"A big frickin' fat-ass yes," said Chase.

Angel frowned at them and slid over into the chair next to Stefano. She felt sorry for him because he was obviously freaking out. "Stefano," she whispered, "you need to calm down and breathe."

"I'm in so much trouble. I'm in so much trouble," he chanted, rocking back and forth faster and faster.

"You're safe here," Angel touched his shoulder.

"They're gonna kill me." He lifted his head and terror flashed in his eyes. "They're gonna kill me."

"Who's going to kill you?" Angel tried to keep her hand on his shoulder but he was rocking too quickly.

"Them," he pointed to the screen, "all of them."

"Them, who? Who is the man in the picture?" Angel tried to keep her voice calm and quiet; but she knew if Stefano didn't provide the information Giovanni wanted he would join Manzini.

Stefano's eyes were glassy and he grabbed his knees with both hands, rocking violently back and forth. "That's my uncle," his voice shook, "Vincent Carlachi." He ranted quickly, "My dad told me never to get involved with Uncle Vince but I didn't listen this time. Vince offered me $25,000 dollars for just a couple weeks of work. Twenty-five thousand dollars is more than I make in a year. He told me all I had to do was make sure some lady didn't escape. I didn't know anyone was gonna die. I swear." Stefano was full-out crying now.

Angel took his hand and felt his fingers trembling in hers. "It's okay," she tried to console him, "everything will be okay. No one's going to kill you." Angel gazed around the room and it became clear that she was the only person feeling sympathetic toward Stefano. All of them sat expressionless except for Chase who looked shocked.

"Is your father in any of these pictures?" Giovanni asked.

"No, my dad would never work with my uncle. He hates him." Stefano was trembling. "I swear to God, I didn't know about all this."

"Why does your father hate your uncle?" Giovanni questioned.

"Because he says Uncle Vince is shady and doesn't obey the law and hangs out with bad people."

"Have you worked for your uncle previously?" Giovanni rested his forearms on the table and folded his fingers together in front of him.

Stefano shook his head. "No, no sir, never. This was the first time and I only did it because I needed the money to buy Kristen a ring and make a good start for us."

"Have you ever seen Sophia's husband, Denny, before?" Andrew asked him.

Stefano shook his head. "No, I never even saw Sophia until after she was tied up in the basement." His eyes darted around the table. "I swear I was only brought in to guard her."

Giovanni said to Chase, "Let me see the closeup image of Sophia's Denny." Chase put it on the screen. "I would like to hear your thoughts on whether you believe this man is operating under duress or if he is a voluntary participant."

They all stared at the picture. In her mind, Angel kept hearing her mother's voice tenderly calling him, "My sweet Denny."

"Mom said she saw a picture of him bound and gagged and beaten up," Angel said. "Maybe, once she escaped, they decided to force him to help them lure her back?"

Chase glanced up, "Don't look like he's been beaten up to me."

Andrew sighed, "I don't know, sweetheart, he looks mighty comfortable with that .38."

"He can't be involved voluntarily," Angel argued, "he doesn't even know my mom's real identity. She said he doesn't know anything about her real life."

Stefano tentatively lifted his eyes to meet Angels. "If he's working with my uncle then he knows exactly who she is."

"When you were assigned to guard her, who were you told she was?" Tony asked.

"They said she was the daughter of the man who killed Moloney's father, and brutally murdered Finnegan's father, Selovich's father and put my family out of business. They said we were holding her for ransom."

"I'd say that's pretty exact." Tony crossed his arms over his chest and leaned back in the chair.

Giovanni called Thomas over and instructed him to escort Stefano back to the Penthouse. "Have a man keep an eye on him," Giovanni instructed, "and inform me the moment Salvatore arrives."

CHAPTER TWENTY-FIVE

Salvatore Buscetta arrived at the Towers with an entourage of security. Even after he entered the building, his men stood guard at the front entrance, at the elevator and at the emergency stairway. When he entered the special meeting room, his men stood near to him at all times.

He looked nothing like Angel had imagined. He was shorter than Giovanni and much thinner. He had high cheekbones, naturally red toned lips and white gray bushy eyebrows. His hair was thinning silver and slicked back from his face. He wore a black silk suit with a silver collared shirt and a black silk tie, covered by a long black trench coat. A black fedora sat atop his head and black, shiny wing-tipped shoes on his feet. A thick silver bracelet hung from his left wrist and he was adorned with silver rings on each hand. Upon entering, he removed his coat and hat and handed them to one of his men.

Giovanni rose from the table, meeting him near the entrance and the two men greeted one another with a light kiss on each cheek. Giovanni then turned to face the table. "May I present to you, Salvatore Buscetta, Head of the Cosa Nostra." Angel and the others stood as a gesture of respect.

Salvatore tipped his head slightly downward in acknowledgment of their presence. As they neared the table, Angel realized how nervous she had become. She felt her face flush with warmth and her stomach dance with butterflies as Salvatore neared. After all, this was the first time she had ever seen her grandfather from her mother's side, and she suddenly felt curious, like she couldn't take her eyes off him.

Giovanni introduced Salvatore to everyone individually, saving Angel for last. "Last, but far from least," he said and smiled. "This is Michelangela."

Salvatore eyed her momentarily, then stretched out his hand, took hers and kissed the top of it. "We do not have women in our administration in Sicily," he spoke with a heavy accent, "perhaps we can learn something from your ways after all."

When Salvatore's men pulled out his chair and he sat, Angel realized he had no idea she was his granddaughter. A twinge of sadness swept over her, followed by indignation and then anger. *You don't know me because you disowned your own daughter!* She screamed in her mind while sinking into her seat.

"Giovanni, I would like to see Sophia," Salvatore said.

Giovanni opened his mouth to speak, but Angel jumped in. "She is resting upstairs in the penthouse. She requested to visit with you privately at the conclusion of the meeting."

"Very well," he nodded.

Giovanni briefed Salvatore on Moloney's operation, what men were already taken down, and how the Shark had been planted as a mole. He did not disclose the fact that Sophia's husband was involved.

Salvatore snapped his fingers and one of his men immediately handed him a folder. "We have been keeping tabs on Moloney's people for many years."

"Good foresight," Andrew said.

"In Sicily we have a motto: 'un nemico è lungamente cento generazioni.'"

"One enemy is one hundred generations long," Andrew translated.

So much for forgiveness, Angel silently quipped.

The folder was passed to Giovanni, who handed it off to Chase and asked him to spread the pictures across the empty table next to the windows. "We can all look together that way," Giovanni explained.

Salvatore's people had done their homework. The pictures looked like actor headshots, each labeled with the person's name and last known location, whether they were alive or deceased and approximate age. Angel gawked at the table and sarcastic thoughts ran through her mind. *Oh, sure, he can find out about all these strangers, but he doesn't even recognize his own granddaughter!* She folded her arms as she stood in front of the table.

"What's your problem?" Tony mumbled under his breath.

"Nothing," she scowled.

"I know that pouty face means something, babe. What's up?"

"Nothing." Angel shrugged and began scanning the pictures on the table. She stopped in the middle, picked up a picture and stared at it

more closely.   The name across the top read:
Moloney. "Is this the original Moloney?" Angel
asked.

"Si, that is the Moloney who embezzled
from us in the late 1960's and met with an
untimely death," Salvatore explained.

Angel scanned the table. "Do you have any
pictures of his son?"

"No. His son's name is Sean Michael
Denarius Moloney, but we have been unable to get
close. He is known to be a recluse."

"Chase," Angel said, "can you pull up the
image we looked at earlier. The close up of the
man holding the .38, with the rifle over his
shoulder."

"Sure thing."

Chase went to the computer and clicked
around until the image appeared on the projector
screen. Angel carried Moloney's picture over and
held it up next to the screen. The likeness was
uncanny.

"Where did you find this man?" Salvatore
asked. "It is undoubtedly Moloney's son."

Chase slapped his palm down on the table,
"now THAT I really didn't see coming! That's what
you call freaky-ass irony."

Everyone gathered around for a closer look.
Angel raised her eyebrows and sighed,   "Sean
Michael Denarius Moloney."

"A.k.a. Denny," Chase added.

"He must have pulled Denny from
Denarius," Angel surmised.

Salvatore narrowed his bushy brows. "How is it that all of you have come to know this man as Denny?"

His question met with silence and blank stares. Angel imagined everyone was thinking the same thing. No one wanted to be the person to tell Salvatore that his daughter is married to Denny. Angel shuddered. *He thought her being with my dad was bad. Ha! This makes my dad look like a prince.*

"Let us take a short break," Giovanni announced. "Thomas will bring in food and drink for everyone. We will begin again upon the arrival of Don Andriachini and Don Venturini, who will be joining us shortly." He walked toward the elevator. "Michelangela, please accompany me to see if Sophia is rested and ready to join us."

When they entered the penthouse, Sophia and Olga were on the couch in the family room, sipping coffee and talking. Sophia had calmed down, but her eyes were still red and glassy from sobbing. Giovanni sat in his armchair and Angel paced by the fireplace.

"What's the matter with you two?" Olga belted out. "She's the one whose husband is being forced to help criminals."

Sophia jumped in, "I know they're probably using Denny to get to me, knowing I'll go back to save him. I understand it is dangerous, but I have to go back for him." Her eyes were pleading. "Please, Giovanni, there is no sweeter, more innocent man on the Earth. He would never join these men voluntarily, and if I don't go, you know as well as I that they will no longer have use for him."

Giovanni and Angel shot each other a glance indicating that this was going to be a lot more difficult than either of them presumed. Angel slid onto the couch next to Sophia and took her hand. "Mom," she spoke softly, "you know how earlier today you told us that Denny doesn't know who you really are?"

"He doesn't." Sophia wiped the tears from her face. "He doesn't know anything about my past at all."

Angel took a deep breath. "Well," she exhaled slowly, "he wasn't exactly honest with you about who he is or his past either."

Olga sat up straighter and looked into Angel's eyes so deeply it felt as if she were reading everything before the words came out. "I don't understand," Sophia said.

"His name isn't Denny," Angel began and Sophia interrupted.

"It's Dennis Moon, but I called him Denny."

Angel shook her head, "No, mom. His real name is Sean Michael Denarius Moloney."

Olga's mouth fell open and Sophia's eyes grew wider as the reality of the name sank in. Sophia grinned nervously and her eyes darted back and forth between Angel and Giovanni. "That's not possible," she said, "you're wrong."

Giovanni blinked slowly and shook his head.

"Merciful Heavens," Olga gasped. "They followed her to Iowa?"

"They must have been watching the whole time," Angel guessed, "or maybe Frank Vilachi was working with Venito and he knew from your letters that you were in Iowa."

"So this Denny knew exactly who she was the whole time?" Olga's eyes were flaring with anger.

Angel nodded and Sophia buried her face in Olga's shoulder and cried. "I'm so sorry, mom," Angel said.

Giovanni rose from the chair. "Michelangela, bring Stefano and Sophia down to the meeting in twenty minutes. Olga, please remain here with a watchful eye on Kristen. I will go down now and inform Salvatore of all that has transpired."

By the time Angel, Stefano and Sophia ventured down to the meeting room, the other Bosses had arrived and Andrew had already received information from the FBI to support the notion that Sean Michael Denarius Moloney and Dennis Moon were one in the same. There was enough evidence to render deniability void.

Sophia stared at the FBI photographs on Andrew's laptop, as if she were searching for a way to disprove the evidence.

As requested, Stefano looked at the table of pictures Salvatore provided and pulled out the only two he recognized; one was his uncle Vincent and the other, his grandfather, Joseph Carlachi. Salvatore approached Stefano and asked, "How do you know these men?"

Stefano told him and at the snap of his fingers, two men drew their guns on Stefano, and he threw his hands up and yelped.

"Giovanni!" Salvatore seethed, "You bring me to meet with traitors and thieves? This is a Carlachi."

Sophia leapt to her feet and wedged herself in front of Stefano. "Have your men stand down," she said through gritted teeth. "This man saved my life."

Salvatore waved and his men lowered their guns. Stefano looked at Sophia and breathlessly uttered, "Thank you."

"Why have you allowed a Carlachi among us?" Salvatore confronted Giovanni.

"He lives because he saved Sophia."

Salvatore made a spitting motion toward Giovanni. "You were weak with his people once and they have come back. Now, you are weak again."

Angel could see the anger building in Giovanni's face. Salvatore snapped his fingers and everything happened in slow motion. Angel could hear her heart pounding loudly in her ears as she watched Salvatore's men draw their guns on Stefano.

Sophia screamed, "No!" and dove across the table toward him.

Andrew, Tony and Dane were on their feet with guns drawn. Andrew and Tony blocked Stefano and took aim at Salvatore's armed men, while Dane held a .45 to Salvatore's forehead.

Giovanni rose slowly and calmly from his seat and walked toward Salvatore. "Abbassi la

vostra arma e sieda," he spoke loud and deliberate.
Angel guessed what he said must have meant put
away your guns and take a seat because that's
exactly what Andrew, Tony and Dane did.

Sophia slid back across the table and into
her chair.

Giovanni stood face-to-face with Salvatore,
and Angel knew in an instant Andrew had been
right. They were like two rabid pit bulls ready to
tear each other limb to limb. Giovanni gritted his
teeth, "We have a motto in our country as well: il
figlio più non paga i peccati del padre."

Angel looked to Andrew for translation.
"The son no longer pays for the sins of the father,"
Andrew said softly.

A smile filled Angel's heart. Her message
was getting through Giovanni's crusty exterior and
she couldn't have been more proud of him than at
that very moment.

"You are a fool," Salvatore spat and
something inside Angel snapped.

She leapt to her feet with such force the
chair tipped over behind her and slammed against
the tile floor. "You are the fool!" she hollered at
Salvatore and the room was stunned into silence.
"You are so rooted in your tradition that you cast
aside your own daughter. You clutch onto your
anger and revenge with pride, stating one enemy
lasts one hundred generations; but that notion is
wrong." She walked briskly to the other side of the
table and put both hands on Stefano's shoulders.
"Should he be forced to pay with his life for his
grandfather's mistakes? Don Andriachini, would
you ask Tony to pay with his life for your errors?

Don Venturini, would you ask Andrew to pay with
his life for your mistakes?" Neither man answered,
but Angel didn't stop and wait for an answer. She
walked over and stood in front of Salvatore.
"Would you ask your granddaughter to pay for
your mistakes with her life?" Angel leaned down
and looked Salvatore in the eyes. "Would you?"
She lifted herself from his stare and walked back
toward her chair. The room was silent as she bent
down and returned her chair to an upright
position. Before she sat down, Angel scanned the
table with her eyes, and then fixed her stare on
Salvatore. "My name is Michelangela. I am half
Buscetta and half Maratinzano. I am the
granddaughter of the Cappo di Tutti Capi and of
the Head of the Cosa Nostra, and I will NOT pay for
either of your mistakes." Salvatore's eyes bulged
from his head and Giovanni's sparkled with pride.
Angel cleared her throat and lowered her voice.
"Gentlemen, this is a new generation and we will
be held accountable for our own choices; not those
of our forefathers." She slowly lowered herself into
her chair. "Stefano lives because of the choice he
made to save my mother. Period."

Giovanni rose from his chair. "Let us take a
ten-minute break. Thomas will show you to the
wine and bread in the bar area."

Thomas directed Salvatore, Andriachini,
Venturini and their men to the bar and served
them, while Angel bolted upstairs. She was sweaty
and shaking as she entered the penthouse and
stepped onto the balcony for some fresh air.
Chase pranced onto the balcony, lit up a cigarette
and beamed at her. "That was the hottest thing

I've ever seen," he took a hit and exhaled smoke. "You could line up ten naked women and it would be no contest to how hot you were down there." Angel couldn't help but laugh at him. "Damn girl!" he said and grinned, "that was some hot-ass, powerful speech."

"I wasn't trying to be hot," Angel smiled.

"Girl, you don't have to try."

~

When they had all returned to the meeting room, Salvatore sat staunchly at the end of the rectangular table, staring at Sophia and Angel. Angel wasn't sure if it was disappointment, anger or regret in his eyes.

"Gentlemen and ladies," Giovanni spoke loudly, "please sit down so we may discuss the next course of action." Once everyone was seated, Giovanni lowered himself into his chair and folded his hands atop the table. "We now know who we are up against, the motive behind his attacks and the length to which he is willing to go to take us down." Giovanni's jaw tightened. "Until his operation is dismantled, our families are not secure."

The Andriachini Boss spoke up. "What do you need from us?"

"Manpower," Giovanni said. "We need every inside connection we have in every agency on alert to flush out Moloney's people."

"Why are the Galantes and Cullatos excluded from this meeting?" the Venturini Boss questioned.

Giovanni didn't miss a beat. "I do not trust them."

"And yet you have a Carlachi present?" Salvatore quipped.

"That matter is closed," Giovanni said with a piercing stare. "I need input Gentlemen," Giovanni said and leaned back in his chair. "How do we get rid of this Moloney problem once and for all?"

There were rumblings up and down the table as people discussed ideas, determining feasible options. Sophia stood slowly, brushing her fingertips against the mahogany tabletop. "I have an idea," she said softly. You could hear a pin drop as Sophia licked her lips and began to speak. "The only men who know you have found me are dead. That means, as far as Denny knows, I am still running and hiding." She took a deep breath. "Let me contact him, and play the role of the fearful, fragile wife who needs him to save me. I know he will come for me."

"No!" Salvatore stood and pounded his fist against the tabletop. "My daughter will not be used as bait."

"How can you be sure he won't just send some men to pick you up?" Andrew posed.

"Because he doesn't know that I know who he really is, and after I've been kidnapped and hunted he knows I will not get in a car with men I don't know. He will have to come alone and play the role of worried husband."

Salvatore leaned forward, "I do not like this plan."

Giovanni rubbed his hand over his jowls. "Andrew, what do you think of the idea?"

"I think it's risky, but it could work. We'll have to choose a location that gives us the upper hand because I guarantee he won't be coming alone even if it looks like he's alone."

"What if I go with her?" Angel interjected.

"No!" Giovanni, Sophia, Andrew and Tony blurted in unison.

Angel rolled her eyes. "She has to have been hiding out somewhere in the city where his men couldn't find her, right? So, it's conceivable that she went to the one person she could trust; the daughter she never told him about."

"That's too muddled, babe, we got to keep it simple," Tony shook his head.

"Well, she can't go alone," Angel argued, "what if he shoves her in a car or helicopter and takes off with her?"

"He won't get that chance," Sophia uttered under her breath. They all stared, one to the other. "Please," Sophia pleaded, "I know I can do this. We were married for ten years and I know he will come for me if you let me call him."

"What if we hit the barn location at the same time, like a sneak attack," Chase said excitedly. "I could fly us over it and BAM, we could blow the roof right off that barn. They'd never expect it."

"Calm down hot-shot." Tony smirked, "one devious plan at a time."

CHAPTER TWENTY-SIX

They all slept on the idea and reconvened at 9:00am in the meeting room. Andrew set up a recorder and tracer on the call and a headset to listen in. "Remember to keep him on the line as long as possible," he told Sophia.

"Why are you tracing it if we already know his location?" Angel asked.

"First, we don't know if he's still in Iowa at the barn. Secondly, if he is anxious to get off the phone then we can assume he probably knows Sophia is with us and we're tracing the call. If he talks to her like a normal husband would talk to a wife who has been kidnapped and escaped, then we'll proceed with the plan," Andrew explained.

Angel looked at Sophia. "Are you okay? Are you nervous?"

"No, I'm ready," she said.

Chase worked the computer, with instructions to signal Andrew when the trace was complete. "Will he be able to see the number she's calling from?" Angel asked.

"No, we've blocked this number in the system and re-entered it to look like a generic city number that doesn't even really exist," Chase explained.

"What if he calls it right back?" Angel raised her eyebrows.

"Why would he do that?" Andrew asked.

"To make sure she's really calling from where she says she's calling from." Angel threw her hands up as if to say duh. "It might just be me but I'm guessing Denny might have some deep-rooted trust issues."

Andrew stared at Angel, his mind calculating the odds of that happening. "Damnit," he blurted and grabbed his cell. When the person on the other end answered, he said, "It's Officer Venturini, I'm going to need an untraceable cell phone number that appears on the grid to be a landline number. It can't be tracked by satellite. I need to be able to make a call and receive a call leaving absolutely no tracks other than the data I've already requested." He hung up the phone and looked at Angel, "You think too much."

Angel grinned.

When the number was set up and Chase was ready on the computer, Sophia made the call. "Denny?" Her voice shook when she spoke. "Denny, is that you?"

Andrew and Angel wore an earpiece so they could hear his responses.

Denny erupted into what sounded like tears. "Oh, my sweet Sylvia, where are you? Are you okay? Are you hurt? I've been so worried. "

Sylvia must have been her made-up name, Angel surmised. Sylvia and Sophia weren't all that far apart and Angel thought perhaps her mom should have been more creative when selecting an alias.

"I got away but there are men after me. I was stabbed and I need help but I don't have any money," Sophia started to cry, "and the man who helped me escape is dead."

Brilliant! Angel thought. Sophia just took Stefano out of the equation and thus, off the hunted list.

"Where are you? I'll come get you right now. I've got every policeman in every town looking for you. Can you get to a police station?"

"Sixty more seconds," Andrew mouthed to Sophia, indicating how much longer she needed to keep him on the line to get a trace.

"I'm in Chicago and I'm scared. I don't now who I can trust, not even the police. Please come get me."

"Chicago?" He sounded almost genuinely shocked. "How did you get all the way to Chicago?"

"I told you, a man helped me escape but they killed him and now they're after me." There was a second of dead air. "Denny?" Sophia cried.

"Why would someone want to kill you Sylvia?" His tone changed and Sophia looked at Andrew, who motioned for her to keep talking.

She took a deep breath, "Because of my past that I've never told you about."

"Go on."

"My family is Mafia and it's a long story. I promise I'll tell you everything in person. Please just come get me before they find me."

"I don't know the city very well. The only place I've been is Union Station. Are you near Union Station?"

Andrew gave Sophia a thumbs up. "Yes," Sophia answered, "I can get to Union Station."

"Meet me at the Madison Street entrance. I'm leaving now. It will take me six hours to get there. Do you know anyone in the city that can help you until I get there?"

"No, I don't trust anyone else."

"Do you have a place to hide for that long?"

"Yes, but please hurry."

"I'm coming Sylvia. I love you."

It looked like the words caught in Sophia's throat and she forced them out, "I love you too."

They disconnected and Chase said, "The trace shows he's in Clearfield, Iowa."

"Good job, Sophia," Andrew grinned. "You did great."

Chase nudged Andrew. "For not knowing the city very well, he sure spit out the name Madison Street entrance pretty quick."

"Yeah, I caught that too," Andrew bit his lower lip.

Angel studied Andrew's face. "You think he knows she's with us, don't you?"

Andrew didn't speak, just gave a nod.

"Is the plan still on?" Angel asked.

"That depends on Sophia."

Angel turned to her mom. "You don't have to do this. We can find another way."

"I want to," Sophia said with tears forming in her eyes.

Angel hugged her. "Are you okay?"

Sophia nodded her head yes, despite the fact that her eyes said no. "I loved him," she whispered. "I really loved him."

Sophia returned to the penthouse to lie down, while everyone else devised the plan. Angel's heart ached for her mom and, though she tried not to let it show, her eyes got watery. Tony draped his arm around her shoulder. "Are those tears, babe?"

"No."

He squeezed her shoulders and kissed the top of her head. "Your mom's a strong lady. She's gonna come through this."

"I know. I just wish her heart didn't have to be broken in the process."

"How about when all this is over, you and me take a little road trip?"

"Where to?"

"I've been craving Shakespeares." He winked at her as he walked away to join the Andriachini Boss, and she felt a rush of warmth. She glanced to the left and saw Andrew hovering over Chase's shoulder at the computer. Andrew caught her eye and smiled and she smiled back and felt her face flush. How was it possible to feel so much for both of them at the same time? How could one heart care equally and differently for both?

Five hours passed and Angel felt they were ready. They had studied the lay out of Union Station and had men assigned to every entrance. The majority of their men were to be stationed along the outside streets on Madison, Jackson and Adams, monitoring every vehicle that came near those entrances. They assumed Denny would attempt to get Sophia into a vehicle as quickly as possible and everyone knew if that happened she was as good as dead.

Angel felt confident with the combined efforts of Salvatore's, Giovanni's, Andriachini's and

Venturini's men, that they had ample manpower to give Sophia full protective coverage.

Angel helped Andrew wire Sophia so it could not be easily detected. "What if he searches her and finds the wire?" Angel asked.

"Sweetheart, he already knows who she is. If he finds the wire then all that does is confirm we're watching, which he probably already knows."

"Then why wear the wire at all?"

"Because he might say something that will help us take his organization down," Sophia answered and Angel let out a loud sigh. She didn't like having her mom be the bait. Sophia gently patted Angel's cheek. "Don't be afraid. I'm not going down today."

When the wire was in place and had been thoroughly tested, Andrew looked at Sophia. "Are you ready?" he asked and she nodded. "Remember, we will be lining the streets so if he tries to get you in a car, run. We'll have men in either direction to intervene; but do not get in any vehicle with him."

"I won't."

He handed her a .22 which she slid into her right coat pocket. "It's ready to go so don't pull it out unless you're going to use it."

"I know," Sophia exhaled.

At 5:00pm they left the apartment in separate groups and headed for Union Station, each man with his assignment. Sophia, Angel, Andrew and Chase were the last group to leave the Towers. Angel, Andrew, Chase and Stefano were by the elevator talking with Giovanni when Sophia came out of the penthouse. "Has anyone seen Kristen?" she asked, "I can't find her."

"What do you mean you can't find her?" Stefano huffed.

"I went into Angel's room to say goodbye and she wasn't there. Olga is sleeping in her room, but I couldn't find Kristen anywhere."

"Did you check the bathrooms?" Angel asked and Sophia nodded.

"Yesterday morning she was asking to leave, saying she wanted to go back home," Angel said.

"But I told her it wasn't safe to leave," Stefano argued.

"I know," Angel nodded, "I heard you tell her."

Giovanni put his hand on Stefano's shoulder. "Let us not panic or jump to conclusions. She could not have left the building. I will send my men to find her and bring her back safely."

"If anything happens to her I'll never forgive myself," Stefano wailed.

"Giovanni will find her," Sophia rubbed his shoulder.

By 5:45pm every man was in position and Angel was watching Sophia from inside the station. She could see Sophia standing right outside the glass doors of the Madison Street entrance. From where Angel stood she would have a clear view of Denny's face whenever he approached. There were only a few passengers inside the station and most were exiting. Angel was too focused on Sophia to give the emptiness of the station much thought.

She kept her eyes on her mother every second silently praying for her protection. *God, please let my mom come through this alive. I just got her back and I don't want to lose her again.*

Angel slid to the side wall and behind a pole when she saw someone approaching the Madison Street entrance. She watched closely as a woman, wearing a tan trench coat, sunglasses and a scarf on her head, passed slowly by, momentarily turning her head toward Sophia.

Sophia reached out and grabbed her arm and the woman pulled away from her. Sophia reached again but the women dodged her grasp and ran inside. Sophia ran after her, neither of them noticing Angel hiding behind the pole. *What is she doing?* Angel's heart sped up. *Why is she following that woman? What if Denny shows up and she's not there?* Angel pulled her cell phone and dialed Andrew but the call wouldn't go through. There was no signal. She couldn't tell if Sophia and the woman had exchanged words, but she knew whatever her mom was doing there had to be a good reason. Angel took off down the hall to follow them.

The halls were long and once Angel had a visual of Sophia, she kept a distance and crept quietly behind. Angel followed her mom down a set of stairs and into the boarding area, all the while wondering who this woman was and why Sophia was so intent on catching her. Angel slowed her pace and pulled out her cell to try Andrew again. Still no signal. She peered around the station, realizing for the first time how eerily empty it was. Even though Chase had announced the train schedules in their meeting and they anticipated foot traffic in the station would be low, Angel felt something was terribly wrong. *Where are the ticketing people?* She wondered. *Where are all the passengers?* Angel felt panic starting to creep up her spine.

Stay calm, she told herself and focused on the fact that Sophia was wearing a wire which meant Andrew had to be picking up on what was happening. There had to be men on their way to Sophia's location.

As they entered the boarding platform which sat between two trains, Sophia yelled, "Please wait," and the woman stopped. Sophia was out of breath and limping on her wounded leg as she slowly approached the woman.

Angel crawled behind the train to her right so she couldn't be seen and crept toward them. The woman turned around, removing the glasses and pulling the scarf from her head and Angel silently gasped. It was Kristen. That explained why Sophia was chasing her. *She's probably telling her how worried Stefano is, how unsafe it is to be in the city alone and trying to talk her into coming back with us.* Angel felt a little better, although she was still concerned about Sophia getting back to the Madison Street entrance before they missed their opportunity to get Denny.

Angel inched her way closer and contemplated stepping out and helping her mom convince Kristen to come back with them. Just as she started to step out a man's voice came from the platform entrance and startled her.

"Sylvia?" he hollered and ran toward her like someone runs to meet a lover.

Omigod! Angel gasped and quietly slid back behind the train.

Sophia embraced him and they lingered in each other's arms. Angel quietly inched closer so she could hear what they were saying.

"I was worried sick," Denny said, pulling Sophia back so he could look into her eyes. *Lying scum,* Angel responded in her mind.

He wrapped his arms around her again and kissed her lips, her cheek and her forehead. *He's really pouring it on thick,* Angel thought.

"Let's go home," he said and he took her arm and started walking slowly back the way they'd come. "We have a lot to talk about."

All of a sudden an alarm went off in Angel's head. This was all wrong. What was Kristen doing walking behind them, as if she belonged there? How did Denny know to find Sophia way down here in the loading area? How did Kristen get out of the Penthouse in the first place? How did she get passed all Giovanni and Salvatore's men at the front doors? *Unless one of them escorted her out.*

"How did you find me all the way down here?" Sophia asked.

Denny stopped and reached in his pocket. "You left clues behind, dear." He pulled out two rings, "Here's your wedding band back." He handed it to her and then stretched out his arm and handed the other ring to Kristen, "And here's your grandmother's ring back. I stopped at the pawn shop and retrieved them for you."

Sophia's eyes widened. "Now," Denny grinned, "would you like me to call you Sylvia or Sophia?" Sophia stood speechless and Angel wasn't sure by the look on her face what she was contemplating. Maybe she was trying to figure out a way to get Kristen to safety before anything bad happened. Maybe her mind was desperately trying to figure a way out of this. Maybe she was getting ready to kill him. Angel felt helpless as she stared at her mother.

"It seems we both have a past we didn't want to share," Denny chuckled and moved toward Kristen, draping his arm around her shoulder. "Kristen is my daughter." Sophia looked at Kristen and even from across the room Angel could see the hurt and shock in her mother's eyes.

Denny and Kristen started to walk forward but Sophia's legs didn't move. "The wire you're wearing won't transmit with the electromagnetic interference down here, at least not clearly," Denny said, "so don't waste what little breath you have left, trying to signal for help."

Kristen crossed her arms. "My dad's taken care of everything."

"Besides," Denny added, "none of your people are listening. My men are keeping them busy fighting for their own lives. Even if someone survives they won't give you a second thought."

Angel's head ached from worry. *What does he mean our men are busy fighting for their lives?*

"Why?" Sophia asked, a single tear running down her cheek.

"Let's not pretend. We both know why," Denny said with an eerie grin as he wiped the tear from her face with his thumb. "If I didn't know better, I'd say that was a real tear; but that can't be right because Buscetta's don't have feelings."

Sophia looked like she could barely move, like the weight of the world was pressing her into the platform. Her head drooped, her shoulders slumped and her arms hung lifelessly at her sides. She lifted her head and stared into his eyes. "I know why you want revenge. My question is why did you marry me?"

Denny put his hands on her shoulders and grinned, "Look at you, my beautiful Sophia, why not marry you? I had the best of both worlds. I could easily keep tabs on you and I could have you at the same time."

"Why didn't you just kill me?"

Denny raised his eyebrows and chuckled. "Because I'm sure finding out his little girl is married to a Moloney is slowly killing Salvatore."

Sophia raised her voice. "My father disowned me years ago. He doesn't care if I live or die so you have failed to enact your revenge on him." Angel could see the anger building in her mother now. Her chin was lifted high and her shoulders were back.

Denny shook his head. "You are ancillary. My revenge will come when we hit both Salvatore and Giovanni where it hurts the most. When we take the one and only grandchild from both bloodlines and we sacrifice her for their sins on an alter of sweet justice."

Sophia spit in his face. "Salvatore doesn't even know he has a grandchild, so you will still have failed."

Denny wiped his face and laughed. "There's that wretched Italian temper. I'm going to miss that." He put his arm on Kristen's shoulder. "Kristen, sweetie, is it true that Salvatore doesn't know he has a granddaughter?"

Kristen grinned, "Nope. Your plan worked perfect. Salvatore came to the States, just as you predicted and he most definitely knows about Angel."

Sophia narrowed her eyes at Kristen. "You and Stefano really had me fooled."

"Stefano's the fool," Kristen flipped her blonde hair over her shoulder. "He doesn't even know we used him. We set him up a long time ago because he's weak."

Sophia shook her head at Denny, "So that's how you knew our rings were at the pawn shop."

Kristen smiled. "Why do you think I got on the bus in Sterling and stayed on it for so long? It was the only chance I had alone to call my dad and fill him in on everything."

Sophia glared at Denny, "And you, putting me in the hands of Frank Vilachi." She slapped Denny across the face and he grabbed her by her throat.

"Vilachi was as ancillary as you are. When he heard about the assignment, he begged me to be in charge of you." Denny released her throat and smirked at her with a slanted grin. "I thought you would like it. You and Frank, just like old times."

"You son of a bitch!" Sophia took another swing at him, but he grabbed her wrist and twisted it until she hit the floor. Angel pulled the 9mm from her waistband, but she couldn't take a shot. She couldn't risk hitting her mom or missing Denny altogether. If she was going to be the one to take him down, she had to get closer.

"You just don't get it. I orchestrated all of this. I hired Vilachi to kidnap you and hold you prisoner and I placed Stefano to guard you because I knew he would let you escape. Once you escaped Vilachi was going to be killed whether he retrieved you or not." He pulled Sophia to her feet. "Kristen here was my ace in the hole. Nobody knew she was my daughter, not Stefano, not his uncle, not even Vilachi. I knew once Kristen was in the picture that you wouldn't be able to resist protecting an innocent young girl. It's what you've done your whole life."

Kristen smiled, "I actually started to like you. It was Stefano I wanted to see dead." She flipped her hair out of her face. "You try spending six months playing lovely dovey to someone as weak and pathetic as him."

"He loved you," Sophia murmured and Kristen rolled her eyes.

"Time to go," Denny said, glancing down at his watch. "The doors should have been re-opened exactly three minutes ago and passengers and employees will be entering this area again right… about…now." Almost instantly Angel could hear voices and footsteps nearing. "Like clockwork," Denny said, pulling Sophia by the arm, and reaching in her jacket pocket to retrieve the .22. "You won't need this."

"How did you know she had a gun in her pocket?" Kristen asked.

"Why do you think I hugged her for such a long time?" Denny answered, "You didn't think I was feeling sentimental did you?"

Kristen shrugged, "Ten years is a long time."

"You don't have to tell me," Denny quipped, "soon I will be tragically widowed and wonderfully free."

Angel felt anger rising up from her toes. *Someone's going to be widowed, but it isn't going to be you!*

Sophia walked between Kristen and Denny, with Denny's arm wrapped tightly around her waist. Passengers and train personnel began to fill in the space around them and Angel started to panic. The volume of noise increased to a level that she could no longer hear anything they said and they were moving quickly through the crowd. Angel shoved the gun back in her jeans, crept out from the other side of the train and into the flow of people, scanning the area for one of their men, anyone she could flag for help; but there was no one in sight.

She followed them down the corridor, up the stairs and toward the Great Hall. Angel's heart was racing as she grabbed her 9mm and held it low against her leg. She knew she couldn't let them leave the building and risk Sophia being shoved in a car and whisked away. With her breathing growing more rapid and louder in her ears, she drew closer to Denny. She knew what she had to do. She needed to take him down before they reached the Great Hall, where the crowd would dissipate.

Angel quickly scanned the area one last time. She had to time it perfectly. Hit Denny, grab Sophia and get them out of there. She didn't know if Kristen had a gun, but she knew from the incident on the roof that Kristen was not afraid to use one. *I'll shoot Kristen too, if I have to,* she concluded in her mind.

Fear wanted to immobilize her but she refused to let it. This was her mother and she wasn't losing her again. She knew once she raised the gun toward Denny she had to pull trigger fast before anyone saw her. Andrew's voice played in her head, "If you hesitate you die."

The Great Hall was in sight up ahead and Angel quickened her pace. Everything moved slowly as she looked to the left, blinked and then looked to the right. She drew in a deep breath, raised the gun toward Denny's back and pulled the trigger. The shot was louder than she expected and the screaming of people around her felt numbing.

Denny fell forward, knocking over a lady in front of him. Kristen screamed and took off running into the crowd. Angel reached for Sophia's hand when someone in the crowd yelled, "He's okay! He's wearing a vest!" Angel glanced over her shoulder as Denny slowly rolled to his side. Without a thought, she released Sophia's hand, raised the 9mm and shot Denny in the head. Blood splattered on the floor and all over the people standing nearby. People screamed and gasped, but the only sound Angel heard was the pounding of her heart and her own rapid breathing. As soon as she pulled Sophia through the exit, Tony and Dane rushed toward them, hurrying them toward a black SUV. Tony jumped in the driver's seat, Angel jumped in the back behind Tony and Dane helped Sophia into the back next to Angel. Dane told Tony he was going to stay behind to help, to which Tony gave a nod and sped off.

Angel looked back through the tinted windows and for the first time, noticed all the police cars and ambulances lining the streets. There were bodies lying on the sidewalks, and EMT's rushing to cover them.

"What happened?" Angel gasped.

"The second Sophia walked inside the station they opened fire on our men. Somehow they locked every entrance so we couldn't get in." Tony was breathing heavy. "They had snipers from every angle trying to pick us off. We couldn't move."

"How many men did we lose?"

"I don't know," Tony sounded both deflated and enraged, "but we should have seen it coming." He tightened his grip on the steering wheel.

"Where's Andrew?" Angel asked.

"I don't know, babe. He was on Madison Street and we were on Jackson." Tony looked at Sophia, "Are you still wired?"

She had completely forgotten. "Yes." Angel helped her work the wire out from beneath her shirt and they handed it up to Tony, who held it to his mouth like a microphone.

"This is Tony confirming I have Angel and Sophia. They are unharmed and we are heading to the Towers." Tony threw the wire on top the dashboard. "This isn't a mob fight, this is a war."

"What's that noise?" Angel blurted. "Ssshh, do you hear that sound?"

"Like a really high pitch clicking?" Sophia asked. "Yeah, I hear it too."

"It sounds like its right in the seat with us." Angel scooted around, feeling the seat and the floor.

"Angel," Sophia's eyes grew bigger as she reached into her right coat pocket and pulled out a small square device. It was making the high-pitched sound.

"What is it?" Tony hollered.

Angel held it up so he could see it in the rearview mirror. "I don't know, maybe a recording device?"

"Give me that," Tony reached back and snatched it from her hand. "Holy Shit!" he yelled, swerving the SUV as he rolled down the window and chucked it out. He hit the gas so hard and fast that Angel and Sophia slammed backwards against the backseat. They all instinctively ducked and then turned their heads at the sound of the explosion behind them.

Tony and Angel locked eyes in the rearview mirror and Angel grabbed Sophia's hand and squeezed it.

CHAPTER TWENTY-SEVEN

Salvatore stood in the Penthouse doorway and embraced Sophia the moment she stepped off the elevator. Angel couldn't understand what they were saying because it was in Italian, but she could see from their body language as they walked arm and arm to the penthouse patio that they were on the path of reconciliation.

Angel walked inside and made a beeline for Giovanni. "Traditori tra noi," she said and explained that someone helped Kristen leave the building. "Are all of your men accounted for?"

"No, and the surveillance cameras have revealed her escort."

"Who?" Angel asked.

"Thomas."

Angel sank down into the couch. *The big square blonde.* It made sense. Thomas was the only one inside the meeting room with them. He would have known the exact plans for the placement of their men around the train station. He had been the one to coordinate food, medicine and whatever they needed, so he would not be questioned coming and going from the building. If anyone could escort Kristen out without raising suspicion, Thomas was the one.

"It is my error," Giovanni shook his head. "I was hasty in his placement because I was shorthanded."

"They made you shorthanded so that you'd have to be hasty in your decision making," Angel reminded him. "They set us up from the beginning."

"Si."

"Grandfather," Angel moved from the couch and knelt in front of him, "how do we stop these attacks? If the Moloney clan has been infiltrating our organizations for years, how do we find the traitors among us?"

Salvatore's thick accented voice came from behind them, "By working together." He walked to the coffee table and lowered himself onto it. Then he looked down at Angel kneeling between them. "You are right, Michelangela. Your generation should not pay for the mis-dealings of our generation." He pointed his finger to Giovanni and himself. "We must clean up this mess from the past so that you can have a future." He folded his hands beneath his chin and exhaled. "Our traditions may seem violent and unnecessary to you now, but it was the assurance of loyalty that mattered most to us. It is the protection of that loyalty that matters most to us now."

Giovanni gave a nod in agreement.

Salvatore continued, looking down at Angel. "You are both Buscetta and Maratinzano and you have the backing of the Cappo di Tutti Capi and Head of the Cosa Nostra." He took her hand in his and Giovanni held her other hand. "There is no attack that we cannot stop together and there is nothing that can break this bond between us. We are blood." He squeezed her fingers. "Our organizations in Sicily and here in the States have thrived much longer than Moloney's group. Our ways may seem out-dated and weak, but our roots run deep and strong."

Sophia crept in and stood between Salvatore and Giovanni, sliding her hand in each of theirs. Salvatore looked up at her and smiled, and then raised up his hands with theirs. "Our circle is complete." He released Sophia's hand and touched Angel's cheek. "Michelangela, siete la mia famiglia. L'anima in mie vene è l'anima in il vostro."

Angel looked at Sophia who translated. "You are my family. The blood in my veins is the same blood in yours."

Angel wrapped her arms around his neck and hugged him. His eyes didn't sparkle like Giovanni's and he wasn't as warm, but he was her grandfather nonetheless; and she felt the strength of that bond.

Olga waddled in from the kitchen. "Merciful Heavens, if you all aren't a sight for sore eyes." She wedged her hips onto the coffee table next to Salvatore and Angel. "Why, Salvatore, you're looking good for an old coot," she patted his knee and winked. Salvatore's eyes bulged and he made a frightened face.

"You should be very afraid of this one," Giovanni smirked, pointing at Olga.

"Pish-posh," Olga stood up and waved her hand in the air, "I have some freshly baked Cannoli in the kitchen." She took Salvatore's arm and led him to the kitchen.

Angel looked at Sophia with surprise, "Was she actually flirting with him?"

Sophia laughed, "I think so."

"At least he's her age," Angel said. "She usually likes them a lot younger."

Giovanni made the sign of the cross over his body. "May God help him."

~

When the men who survived the station attack had returned, they all gathered in the meeting room to debrief Giovanni and Salvatore on what took place. Giovanni sat at one end of the long mahogany table and Salvatore sat at the other. Angel sat in the middle on one side, with Tony and Dane to her right and Stefano to her left.

Giovanni began, "I have asked the Bosses from the Andriachini and Venturini families to join us again this evening." They sat next to Salvatore, across the table from Tony and Dane.

The meeting had just started when Andrew entered and apologized for his tardiness. "I have been sorting through bodies and surveillance video," he said, taking a seat across from Angel. "I can confirm we lost six men today." There were rumblings around the table. "But we also managed to identify a few of their people on the surveillance video. The names may surprise you." Andrew cleared his throat and read the first name from the list. "Thomas Boglevich."

"Bah," Giovanni waved his arm angrily, "that was my foolish error."

"Gerald Finnegan." Andrew said.

"So, the Shark did lie about killing his brother?" Angel asked.

"It looks that way. Gerald Finnegan was definitely on the video which means, for now; I think we have to assume the Shark is one of them."

Giovanni's scowl grew deeper.

"I told you, man," Tony shook his head.

"If he's one of them than why did he save my life two times?" Angel asked.

"I don't know. It's something we're going to have to analyze further," Andrew said and then glanced back at his list. "Kristen Warren Moloney," Andrew read and looked at Stefano.

Stefano jumped to his feet, "What?! If this is a joke it isn't funny!

"It's not a joke," Angel said softly. "Kristen is Moloney's daughter and she was a part of this plan from the beginning."

"That's not possible. How could they have known I would help Sophia escape?"

"They used you," Angel said and felt sorry for him. "They put you there to guard Sophia knowing she would be able to convince you to help her."

Stefano shook his head, "That's a lie."

Andrew interjected, "We have the whole conversation on tape. You can listen to it when Chase gets here. He was able to weed out a lot of the interference and, well, Kristen's role and your role are pretty clear."

"You're lying!" Stefano yelled and Giovanni rose to his feet.

"Stefano, sit down," Giovanni's voice was stern and Stefano sank angrily into the chair. "We have all been deceived, tricked, and made to be fools." Giovanni's face turned red. "We have allowed compassion to cloud our instincts and because of this compassion WE have let them infiltrate our organizations. From this point forward, ALL traitors will be eliminated and excuses will not be tolerated." Giovanni lowered himself into his chair and motioned for Andrew to proceed.

Andrew stared at the piece of paper. "Dane Kelinski."

The Andriachini Boss rose to his feet. "Traditori," he spat at Dane. Dane reached for his gun when a bullet smashed into his forehead, knocking him and his chair over backwards. Stefano leapt from his seat, turning his back to the body and covering his mouth as if he might vomit, while Tony angled his body to block Angel from the splattering blood.

Angel looked down at the blood pooling out the back of Dane's head, then turned her gaze back to Andrew who stood staunch, with his .45 still outstretched.

"What did he do?" Angel asked.

"We have video of him slipping the explosive device into Sophia's pocket when he helped her into the SUV."

"That explains why he didn't get in the car with us," Tony quipped, shaking his head.

Chase arrived and was escorted inside, stopping abruptly when he saw Dane's body. "Damn," he blurted, "what'd I miss?"

"We were crossing names off our list," spoke Salvatore.

"Glad I'm not on your list," Chase said and walked around the table toward Andrew.

"Do you have the recording and the surveillance video?" Andrew asked him.

Chase patted the black bag that was slung over his shoulder. "I've got the recording right here and as soon as I can set up, we can upload the rest of the surveillance feed."

Angel tilted her head, "How do you know how to do all this stuff?"

Chase shrugged, "What stuff?"

She narrowed her eyes, "For starters, you're a chef and you know all about weapons, you can fly a military helicopter, and appear to be computer savvy."

"I sound like a real talented guy when you list everything together like that," Chase gloated. "I told you, I was in the military for a while and I picked up a few things."

Giovanni leaned forward and placed his forearms on the table. "Chase is being modest about his training. His scores were so high he was considered for Special Ops and even approached by the CIA."

"Okay, the truth's out, below this manly exterior I'm a tech geek," Chase joked.

"Why did you not become Special Ops or go with the CIA?" Salvatore questioned.

Chase swayed back and forth, like he was uncomfortable. "I was discharged and it wasn't the honorable kind."

"I see," Salvatore nodded.

"Gentlemen," Giovanni rose, "we will reconvene tomorrow to discuss our tactics for the attack on Moloney's Iowa group."

The meeting room emptied and Giovanni sent two men to clean up Dane's body.

Once in the penthouse, Chase played the recording for Stefano, who broke down and openly wept. Sophia sat next to him and rubbed his back while Olga tried to comfort him with homemade cheesecake. An hour later the front door opened and Tony paraded in with three extra-large pizzas.

"Merciful Heavens, does that smell good," Olga gasped, following Tony to the kitchen to help serve it up. Angel had just gotten out of the shower and slipped into her cream, satin robe when she heard a knock on her bedroom door.

"Babe, can I come in?" Tony asked through the door.

Angel opened it and immediately recognized the smell. She looked down at the plate in his hand and gasped, "Is that Shakespeare's pizza?" Tony grinned from ear to ear. "How did you get it?"

"Babe, you know I'm magic," he teased.

He picked up the slice and held it to her lips so she could take a bite. The moment she tasted the crust, the sauce, the pepperoni and the spice her mind exploded with memories of being at Mizzou with Tony. Flashes of them sitting together on the Columns, strolling through Jesse Hall and the countless nights gorging on Shakespeare's, lit her eyes. It was a time when life was simple.

Angel turned and sat down on the side of her bed and Tony followed, closing the door behind him. "Everything used to be so easy," she sighed.

Tony laughed out loud as he sat down next to her, "You didn't think it was so easy back then."

"That's true," she rolled her eyes. "Sometimes I wish we could go back."

He held the plate in his left hand and draped his right arm over Angel's shoulders. "It's all gonna turn out okay, babe," he leaned his forehead against hers. "Everything's gonna be okay."

Angel turned and buried her face in his chest. All of a sudden she couldn't hold back the emotion. She wasn't even sure why she was crying, other than from sheer stress and exhaustion. Tony set the plate on the end of the bed and wrapped his arms around her. "Let it out, babe," he said, "get all that shit out."

When her sobbing finally ceased, he wiped her face with the edge of his sleeve and she apologized for breaking down. "You didn't break down," he nudged her playfully, "you just exhaled." He leaned in close to her face. "I know what would make you feel better." She looked deeply in his eyes. "I know what you need," he whispered.

She envisioned his lips on hers and flushed with the warmth of wanting. Her breathing quickened as she leaned ever-so-slightly into him. "Shakespeare's," he said, grabbing the plate and holding it under her nose.

"Right. Shakespeare's." She sighed and tried not to let her disappointment show.

"Remember at the hospital, you told me you wanted to go back to Shakespeare's and have me tell you everything was gonna be okay." He tucked a piece of hair behind her ear. "With everything going on right now, we can't go back there, so I brought a piece of there, here." He handed her the plate.

"Thank you."

Tony stood up and moved toward the door. "You know they ship the pizza's here unbaked, in dry ice. My freezer is packed full of them now, so we can have Shakespeare's any time you want."

"Okay," she nodded and lowered her eyes, not wanting him to see how conflicted her feelings for him were. .

"Oh, and, babe," Tony paused and Angel looked up. "I wanted that kiss too, but not with all these people around and not while everything's so…complicated."

He left the room and Angel set the plate down and flopped backwards on her bed. If ever there was a word in the English language she hated, it was the word, complicated. Not only was her identity, her family and her life complicated, but so was her heart.

After everyone had eaten pizza, Angel sneaked onto the balcony and stood staring up at the moon. It was full and bright and the night air gave her a sense of calm amid the chaos. There was no question her life had radically changed in the last several weeks. No longer was she Angel May Martin, owner of a small pub; she was Michelangela Maratinzano, the only granddaughter of both the Cappo di Tutti Capi and Head of the Cosa Nostra, and now head of the Chicago Maratinzano Bogata.

She sighed, soaking in the peace and quiet. Yes, there were still major issues to be resolved…

the Moloney family and their encampment in Iowa, locating the moles in the police department, the FBI and within their own families, reuniting the bogatas, and her own personal questions of the heart. But for now, in this moment, staring up at the moon she was at peace.

The door opened and Andrew stepped next to her.

"Beautiful," he said.

"I know, I love the moon," she gazed upward at the sky, unaware he had moved closer.

"I wasn't talking about the moon."

She lowered her eyes from the sky to his and felt herself blush. He moved behind and wrapped his arms around her, and she leaned her head back against his chest.

"You were the star in one of the surveillance videos," he said, and her breath caught in her chest. "I got rid of it after I watched it."

"Thank you," she murmured.

"You know, sweetheart, killing someone is never easy to deal with..."

Angel cut him off. "He was going to kill my mother and I couldn't let that happen. I didn't kill someone today. I protected someone. I protected my family."

A moment of silence fell between them and then Andrew slowly kissed the top of her head. "That you did, sweetheart. That you did."

ABOUT THE AUTHOR

S.R.Claridge, nominated for the 2010 Molly Award, 2013 Pushcart Prize and awarded the 2011 Rocky Mountain Fiction Writers Pen Award, writes full-time and lives in Colorado. She loves autumn, moonlight and Grey Goose martinis with bleu cheese or jalapeno stuffed olives. She believes Friday nights are for indulging in Mexican food and margaritas and Sunday mornings warrant an extra-spicy Bloody Mary. Growing up in St. Louis, Missouri and earning her BA in Psychology from the University of Missouri, Columbia, S.R.Claridge is a mixture of mid-western family values and western wild nights. She loves Jesus, believes in the power of prayer, in the freedom of forgiveness and that life is a gift that should be enjoyed to the fullest. With a background in theatre, S.R.Claridge creates characters with dramatic flair and is known for her intense plot twists and engaging humor. S.R.Claridge would rather walk dangerously where there's a view than sit in idle safety and let life pass her by. Her spirited outlook comes shining through in her novels, as she takes readers to the edge of their seats with bone-chilling suspense.

BOOKS BY S.R.CLARIDGE

Tetterbaum's Truth *(book 1 in the Just Call Me Angel series)*

Traitors Among Us *(book 2 in the Just Call Me Angel series)*

Russian Uprising *(book 3 in the Just Call Me Angel series)*

Death Trap *(book 4 in the Just Call Me Angel series)*

Loose Ends (*book 5 in the Just Call Me Angel series)*

Divine Intervention *(book 6 in the Just Call Me Angel series)*

Petals of Blood *(short story; Pushcart Prize Nomination 2013)*

House of Lies (*Political cult suspense)*

No Easy Way *(debut novel; nominated for The Molly Award from the HODRW 2010)*

The Candy Shop *(Suspense Thriller)*

Men Take Pause (Non-Fiction)

'Twas the Night Before COVID (Short-story/Poetry)

** S.R.Claridge has also ghostwritten ten additional novels.

AUTHOR ACCLAIM

"The Just Call Me Angel series is suspense at its best."
- RipeReviews

"A unique series from a one-of-a-kind author."
- APEX Reviews

"Riveting!"
- TrueBlueEbookReview

"One thrilling moment after another!"
- CanadaReviews

"A best-seller candidate indeed."
 - BookWatchMagazine